The Circuitry We Share

A Novel

MOLLY DUNN

The Circuitry We Share

MOLLY DUNN

The Troy Book Makers
Schodack Landing, NY
2026

CONTENTS

Karolina | 1 • Big Sur | 10 • Alessandra | 25 • Moffett Field | 32 • Family Ties | 45 • Sasha | 53 • Brothers | 63 • The Speckled Boar | 69 • Sketching | 79 • The Salenan Institute | 88 • Lillian | 100 • Bloodlines | 106 • A Different Frequency | 110 • The Diagnosis | 115 • Ambrosia | 122 • Pulled | 131 • An Enigma | 135 • Profiling | 142 • Synthetic Consciousness | 152 • Signals and Stories | 166 • The Bond of Betrayal | 175 • Unmasking Mimicry | 181 • Erased | 191 • A Call | 198 • Salinas Valley | 204 • The Meridian Works | 212 • A Strange Stillness | 220 • Rewired | 225 • Singularity | 236 • Lionesses Hunt in Groups | 243

"Truth is a Matter of the Imagination"
– Ursula K. Le Guin, *The Left Hand of Darkness*

"One does not become enlightened
by imagining figures of light, but by
making the darkness conscious."
– Carl Jung, *Alchemical Studies*

CHAPTER ONE

Karolina

"It's him." The detective confirms what Karolina already knows. She takes a deep breath. The police station in North Hollywood smells of burnt coffee and something cloyingly sweet, out of place. A wave of nausea crawls up her throat. Her right leg tingles, it's numb. She shifts her weight in the metal chair, trying to regain the feeling she lost.

The detective motions for her to follow him. Karolina jumps up, palms sweating. As they walk down a long hallway together, he continues: "The DNA matches. Our officers have taken him into custody."

Karolina's heart pounds in her throat as the detective opens the door to a stark white room. A uniformed officer sits at a metal table, his bald head glowing beneath the harsh glare of fluorescent lights. The scent of cinnamon clings to her nostrils from a box of buns left open in the middle of the table. She hesitates before stepping inside.

The uniformed detective rises and drags out a chair for her. As Karolina lowers herself onto the seat, her fingers brush the cold metal surface. She straightens her spine, lowers her shoulders, lifts her chest, and stares at the blank white concrete wall. The weight of the detectives' eyes fall on her, heavy, expectant: it's a silent interrogation. Karolina casts her gaze downward, presses her lips together, and allows their gaze to go uninterrupted as the fluorescent lights hum above. Her subtle act of submission lets the detectives think they are in control, making it easier for them to believe her.

As a child, Karolina was always performing. She was sensitive, complex, and deeply emotional. She felt everything with an intensity that would often overwhelm her. Back then, she didn't know that not everything she felt belonged to her. So, acting became her refuge, a way to hide, to escape from a world that often felt too chaotic and consuming. As she grew up, disappearing into roles became second nature. It is still easy for Karolina to lose herself.

One of the detectives clears his throat.

"Thanks for coming in. I'm Detective Alvarez, and this is Detective Grey," he says, pointing toward his partner. "Do you mind if we ask you a few questions?" His tone is clipped, but his accent carries a warmth Karolina finds familiar. He reaches for one of the buns and takes a bite, licking the icing from his fingers.

Karolina's throat tightens as she glances up. "Could I have some water first, please?" Her tongue scrapes against the roof of her mouth. It feels like sandpaper.

Detective Grey pops up out of the chair and leaves the room. Detective Alvarez stays, sitting across from her in silence. Karolina guesses he's in his forties though he looks older. His face is weathered and haunted, the crease between his brows frozen in a deep furrow. He offers a tight-lipped smile and watches her with a quiet curiosity, something she is used to.

"My grandmother is a big fan of yours," he says, breaking the silence. "She watches all of your telenovelas." Karolina feels the heat rise in her cheeks as his face flushes pink.

Karolina's doe eyes, framed in thick lashes, make direct contact with the detective. She forces a small smile, tilting her head just so, an expression that makes people believe she sees something in them that others don't. She switches to Spanish, asking for his abuela's name. Karolina is sweet and humble, lending to others an unrequited sense of familiarity. She knows the role well, the girl next door who's been inside everyone's home.

Growing up in Madrid, Karolina chose a career in acting as an escape, a way to slip into an imaginary world. But fame found her. Everywhere Karolina turned, there she was: on billboards, bus stop signs, and the flickering screens of TVs. She had become the main character in the lives of Spaniards, showing up in their living rooms, bedrooms, and most often, their kitchens. Karolina's image would hover over a counter or refrigerator, keeping them company as they cooked away. Strangers gazed deeply into Karolina's dark brown eyes while they relaxed on couches, smoking cigarettes, mesmerized by her. At night, in their bedrooms, couples would make love to the sound of her voice, each one picturing her olive skin, chestnut hair, and full cherry lips. Politicians, teachers, doctors, lawyers—an entire nation had become spellbound by her. They believed they knew her, or at least, they convinced themselves they did. But for Karolina, the weight of their expectations became suffocating. She felt consumed by their unrequited knowing.

After fame found her, Madrid became too small. Once so vast, her native city shrank before her: familiar sidewalks narrowed into a catwalk, and buildings loomed above as hungry fans searched for Karolina, eyes peering out every window. Her anxiety, which had once seemed manageable, began to metastasize into agoraphobia. She knew she needed to leave Madrid, and the idea of moving to Los Angeles, once an intoxicating notion, quickly became a reality. Such a sprawling city held the promise of a different life. There, she could be just another actor pretending to be someone they weren't, someone no one would recognize.

The door swings open. Grey returns with a paper cup dotted with daisies, places it gently in front of Karolina, and glances at her wedding band.

"Do you want us to call your husband to let him know you are here?" His voice cracks with concern.

"No, that's alright," Karolina replies firmly. "He's on a business trip, and the cell service is pretty spotty."

Despite being newlyweds, Karolina and Max spent more time apart than together, thanks to his career. She had met Max at a film screening one month after she arrived in Los Angeles. He was one of the panelists, a documentary filmmaker who was sharp and charismatic. He instantly recognized her as he had spent a gap year in Spain. The familiar dread of an unrequited knowing gripped her at first: was Max captivated not by who Karolina was, by the projection of a person she played on screen? But Karolina sensed something different about Max, he exuded a sense of calmness and electrifying charm, a disarming and intoxicating combination that put Karolina at ease while simultaneously thrilling her. There was an electricity between them. He spoke of his work with Oneness University, a Silicon Valley tech incubator. Max had recently been hired to direct the University's latest film, *Architects of the Mind*, which aimed to recruit students, visionaries willing to reshape the world using technology. His calling it a film seemed a stretch in Karolina's mind. The project felt more like a two-hour-long sales pitch promoting the University, a typical Silicon Valley hype piece. Of course, she didn't share her feelings about the project with Max. He didn't need to know. And the events of today would be another thing to keep from him. Besides, it would be useless to worry Max now, he was impossible to reach. She had already tried.

Karolina lifts the cup to her lips and takes a slow sip, aware of the detective's stare.

Grey leans forward. "So, Karolina, let's get straight to the point. How did you figure out it was him?"

She shrugs, hesitating, and glances down at the paper cup, her gaze lingering on a daisy. "I'm not sure how. I just... knew." A partial truth, but not the whole story.

As Detective Alvarez furrows his brows, Grey begins rubbing his eyes, frustration rising from his tense shoulders. "What do you mean you 'just knew'?"

Karolina stares blankly ahead. After a long moment, Grey exhales sharply, dropping his hands from his face before clasping them together on the table. She sits in silence, unsure if she can explain herself in a way the detectives will understand, or better yet, believe.

Grey leans forward, breathing heavily. "My wife likes to say she 'just knows things.' Like when I stay for an extra drink after work. Nine times out of ten, she's right." Karolina catches the trace of last night's argument on his breath, a yeasty scent of stale beer turned sour overnight. Grey continues, "But I'm not sure she could solve a crime with a feeling. So, can you help us understand how exactly you 'just knew' it was him?"

A vein in Karolina's neck throbs as a familiar surge of electricity courses through her body. The intensity of the sensation threatens to push her to say or do something they could later use as evidence of her perceived emotional instability. She grips the table and begins counting silently in her mind. Her strength is in her silence, at least for now.

Karolina's grandmother was the first to tell her she was different. Sadness seemed to attach itself to Karolina as a child, following her around like a shadow. She worried about things well beyond her years: nuclear war, death, and her parents' impending divorce, which would follow a decade later. She often felt ill, plagued by mysterious stomachaches, headaches, and a racing heart. "*She's just an old soul,*" teachers would say, or worse, "*She's just too sensitive.*" But sadness wasn't the only emotion she felt intensely. Waves of rage would take over her, seemingly out of nowhere.

One day on the playground, she watched as a boy kicked her younger brother, making him wail in pain. Fury surged through Karolina. Eyes wide, her tiny fist clenched, she sprinted toward the boy and punched him in the face, knocking him to the ground. It didn't take long for her to realize that girls weren't supposed to throw punches, especially not good girls like her. So, she learned to swallow her anger, to stuff it down deep inside. She came to recognize when a wave of rage was about to take over. Her body would instantly send certain signals: a throbbing in her neck, a rush of blood through her veins, a quickening in her chest. Then, instead of releasing her anger, she would let it surge through her, pulsating beneath her skin. To calm herself, Karolina learned to count in her mind, saying each number slowly and deliberately, a measured attempt to regain control.

At the age of seven, Karolina learned the truth from her grandmother, who told her she wasn't just a sensitive child. She had inherited a rare gift, an ability to feel other people's emotions in her body as if they were her own, a powerful intuition passed down through the women in her family for generations. Over time, Karolina grew to know things, unspoken, unseen truths that others either failed to notice or didn't want to know. But her gift came with a warning: "*You must be careful, mija. There are people in this world who will fear you. And others who will try to use you.*" Karolina had stared back at her grandmother that day, her large chestnut eyes taking in her abeula's words yet not fully understanding their meaning or how they would play out. That is, until now.

"Perhaps we can start by describing his physical characteristics?" Alvarez chimes in, trying a different approach. "Was there anything that stood out to you about his appearance?"

Karolina closes her eyes, replaying the moment the photographer had first walked up to her to shake her hand. She had looked away, only to find, when she glanced back, that he was still staring at her. "His eyes. They were... strange."

The room suddenly feels cold, and Karolina folds her arms. "I don't know if it was the way he looked at me or just his eyes, but something seemed... off."

Detective Grey shifts forward, perched on the edge of his seat. His gaze sharpens. "How so?"

Karolina takes a deep breath, searching for the right words to describe the unsettling, empty look behind the photographer's gaze.

"He had a piercing stare," she says slowly, as if testing the words. "But his eyes seemed... flat. Empty."

Alvarez's pen moves swiftly across his notepad, the faint scratch of ink filling the silence. His brow furrows deeper with each stroke. Then he pauses, pen in hand, and looks up at her, his eyebrows lifting. More lines crease his forehead.

"What color were they?"

"Dark. A very dark brown."

Alvarez nods, making another quick note before glancing back up. His expression is unreadable. "And this was the first time you met him?"

Karolina takes a sip of water, finishing what little is left. She sets the cup down but doesn't let it go. "Yes," she admits, voice quieter now. "He was recommended to me by a friend, another actress. He did her headshots."

Despite her success in Spain, Karolina was having a difficult time finding work in LA. She needed new headshots and had to pay for them herself, which led her to this particular photographer. He wasn't as expensive as some of the others.

"Is there anything else you noticed about him?" Alvarez watches her closely, his pen tapping lightly against the page.

Karolina grips the cup, which lets out a crackle as one of the daisies tears in two. She pictures the silver chain around his neck, the pendant shiny, dangling at the end. A sharp pain jabs behind her left eye. She blinks, wiping the image from her mind, and looks back at the detective.

"He was nervous. Sweating. Shaking." She swallows hard. "I found it bizarre. If anything, I should have been the one who was nervous."

The detectives exchange glances before turning their attention back to Karolina. Alvarez smiles, but his eyes narrow, studying her. "Maybe he recognized you?" Alvarez suggests.

A wave of nausea creeps up Karolina's throat. She shakes her head. She knows the kind of nerves she inspires in her fans, at least in Spain. They emanate a very particular energy, a mix of starstruck awe and admiration. This was different.

"No. He wasn't nervous because of me. It was like he was afraid of himself. Like he was worried he couldn't control something."

She hesitates. Or maybe... maybe it *was* because of her. Not for the reason the detectives thought—not her beauty. Something else. Something the photographer *sensed*.

The detectives share a look.

"After you met him, what happened?"

"He asked me to follow him into another room. Then, he touched my lower back." A cold shudder runs up her spine, remembering the moment. "The second his hand landed on me, I knew. My back stiffened. My stomach tensed. Everything in me screamed—something was *wrong*."

Both detectives look confused.

"So, you just... had a feeling?"

Karolina exhales sharply. A *feeling*? The word barely scratches the surface.

Before she can answer, Detective Grey leans forward. His voice drops to a low whisper. "And then that was it? You just *knew* it was him?"

Karolina takes a deep breath, scanning her body with her mind's eye to see what emotions, if any, she could pick up from the detectives. Her breath moves smoothly through her ribs, her muscles loose. No tightness, no prickling at the back of her neck. Just stillness, her pulse steady, her skin cool. The detectives' faces remain neutral, their bodies still. They are well-trained, contained, not unlike her. Nothing suggests she should hold back. If there was venom behind their eyes, she would be able to taste it.

She lifts her chin and continues. "No. There's more." Her voice is now firm, controlled. "When he touched my lower back, a chill shot through me. And then..." she pauses, choosing her words carefully, "something flashed before my eyes."

Detective Grey stiffens. "A flash? Like from a camera?"

Karolina sighs, shaking her head. Her long chestnut hair sways, casting a shadow over her face. She releases her grip from the crinkled paper cup, her fingers settling in her lap. Purple ink from one of the daisies had bled onto her palm. She tucks her hair behind her ear and meets Grey's eyes. "No, no one took my picture." She sits taller. "I saw something flash before me in my mind. An image."

Alvarez leans in. "An image?" he parrots.

She lets the silence stretch, forcing the two men to feel the weight of it. "Yes, a newspaper headline." The air in the room thickens.

"You saw this... in your mind?"

Karolina doesn't flinch. Detective Grey leans back, lacing his hands behind his head, elbows raised, suspended in disbelief. His gaze sharpens.

"And what did it say?"

Karolina can feel his impatience growing. She takes a deep breath and leans back into the cold metal chair. "Woman Disappears in Big Sur." A surge of energy runs up her spine as the words leave her lips. She exhales, steady now.

The detectives snap their heads toward each other. Grey's pen freezes mid-stroke. Alvarez narrows his eyes, the crease in his brow deepens with confusion. They haven't released any information to the media. No one, except the two detectives, knows the details of the case.

The headline Karolina saw has yet to be written.

CHAPTER TWO

Big Sur

"You wanna play a game?" Zoe asks, sliding her hand across the car's console, touching Max's thigh. The top is down on his convertible, and the wind snaps between them, whipping her long, strawberry-blonde hair.

Their third date is Max's idea: a ten-hour road trip to the Oneness University campus on Moffett Field near San Francisco. Driving for hours, winding along the jagged edge of the California coast, is thrilling. The road twists and turns like a ribbon curling along the cliffs. As they enter Big Sur, the Pacific stretches wide beneath them. Waves crash against the cliffs with a force Zoe feels vibrate through her body.

Max grins. "What kind of game?" He reaches over and places his hand on her knee, sending a surge of electricity through her.

Zoe's ever-reeling mind, usually a carousel of second guesses and instinctive alerts, goes still. She feels different around Max, a strange stillness settles inside her whenever he's near. Being in his orbit feels calming, peaceful even.

She glances at him, and Max squeezes her knee with a smile that suggests he assumes the game is of a sexual nature.

"Not that kind of game," Zoe says with a playful glint in her large, brown eyes. "Alright, I'm going to ask you a bunch of questions, and then you'll ask me." There's a quiet intensity behind her eyes, a depth that reveals her emotions before she even speaks. She pulls out a torn page from a magazine; it's the Proust Questionnaire. Originally a parlor game, it's a list of introspective questions designed to reveal a person's true nature: their favorite quality, greatest fear, idea of perfect happiness. It had been around since the Victorian era and was later made famous by *Vanity Fair* interviews. Zoe frames it as a game, but in truth it is something much deeper. She naturally picks up on the subtext behind people's answers, and this questionnaire gives her a structured way to understand Max's mind, a safe and quick roadmap to intimacy. A way of gathering intel without making her intentions obvious.

Max's phone buzzes. With one hand on the steering wheel, he picks it up and turns it off without looking at the screen. Zoe glances at him as her hair dances in the wind.

"Someone looking for you?" she teases, tucking her hair into a low bun behind her ear.

Max shrugs. "Just work, my dear." Zoe studies him closely, unsure if she believes him. His hands rest casually on the wheel, his posture straight and composed. He's linear and contained. His dark curls catch the light, coiled just enough to appear unruly. Zoe glances down at her phone. No service. Even if there were, there's no need to check in with work since she's between assignments, floating for the moment.

She had told Max exactly this on the first night they met on the rooftop at Casa del Sol. It had been sunset, the sky a deep shade of warm copper. He stood in the doorway, tall, with a mess of brown curls and a half-smile that seemed both rehearsed and utterly spontaneous.

"Excuse me," he said in a velvet British accent, "I don't mean to be rude, but I recognize you from that news show. And I read your piece on Ryan Sowell in *The Daily Quest*. It was brutal, but I must say, it was also brilliant."

Zoe blinked in surprise. It wasn't just that he knew her article. He quoted parts of it back to her. It was the first time anyone had seen her beyond just the byline.

At the age of forty-five, Silicon Valley billionaire Ryan Sowell had wanted the body of an eighteen-year-old and poured an average of $5 million a year attempting to reverse the natural aging process. A team of researchers and scientists monitored him daily and performed experiments on him. Zoe had to admit he looked at least ten years younger than when he began his age-defying project. His skin was poreless, as if it was made of silicon, and the whites of his eyes were so bright they seemed to glow. Still, it was difficult to determine whether the transformation was due to some yet to be divulged anti-aging, pseudo-scientific hack or his endless disposable income. Zoe guessed it was most likely the latter.

The article she'd written about Sowell had gotten far more traction than she or her editor had expected. Originally, she had set out to cover Sowell's latest start up, UpRoot, which developed self-sustaining regenerative farms housed within old shipping containers, where the produce, air, and soil would not be exposed to elements of the outside world. Zoe was fascinated by Sowell's confidence in what seemed an apocalyptic future for the global food supply chain. She'd intended for the piece to be a slightly absurd profile of yet another Silicon Valley founder pushing boundaries and profiting from society's demise. Yet when Zoe dug deeper, she uncovered something much darker. The story shifted into an exposé of Sowell's repeated abuse against women in both his personal and professional life. After it ran in *The Daily Quest,* word spread quickly. Sowell became a lightning rod for scrutiny, and his company lost millions. Zoe still couldn't decide which cut deeper: the blow to his ego or the hit to his bank account.

"I'm Max, by the way," he'd said that night, extending his hand. His left eye twinkled when he grinned. She took it.

"Zoe."

He walked beside her through the hotel lobby, their steps in sync, as if they already knew each other, and he took her to the rooftop. Music flowed from a hidden speaker as David Byrne's high, melodic voice drifted through the rooftop and echoed softly in the air. Max glanced toward the bar and asked Zoe something she couldn't quite make out. The ocean rumbled in the distance, waves lightly crashing against the shore. His voice was low and soft, the words catching in his mouth, struggling to escape. He looked at her, waiting, half-curious and half-shy.

Zoe felt her cheeks burn. She wasn't sure if she hadn't heard him or simply didn't understand. Was it the accent, the way he mumbled, the music? She guessed his question and replied, "I'll have a mint julep."

Max raised an eyebrow. Zoe realized she hadn't even thought about what she wanted, her mind too busy decoding him to check in with her own thoughts. She didn't even like bourbon. She watched as he strolled to the bar, moving slowly and deliberately, as if he'd been there a million times before. When he returned, he handed her a frosted silver cup, sprigs of mint bursting from the top. She took it, and a jolt ran through her fingers, sharp and electric, sparking something in her chest. Then, just as quickly, a stillness settled over her body. She felt like she was in a trance.

"Here's your mint julep," Max said with a smirk. His eyes traveled down her body with purpose. "So," he continued, his gaze returning to her face, "how long have you been in LA?"

She took a sip of the drink. It clung to her throat, and she swallowed hard. "Just a few weeks," she said, setting the cup down. "I moved from New York. I needed a reset. The news cycle is overwhelming, and I was on the verge of burning out."

Max raised an eyebrow, intrigued. "A reset, huh? But why did you decide to leave the network to move to print?" He gazed down into his bourbon, the block of ice inside resembling an iceberg, barely melting and unmovable.

Zoe felt her throat tighten and her stomach churn. Her eyes drifted over the railing toward the ocean, sensing a pull. Pressing herself back from the edge, she gripped the railing with her palm to steady herself. "I'd rather not get into it," she said, as a wave of nausea washed over her.

Max cocked his head and turned his body toward her. "That juicy, huh?" He flashed a boyish grin. "Well then, how lucky am I that you decided to move to LA?"

Zoe locked eyes with him and returned the smile, relieved he hadn't pressed her to share more. His gaze caught hers before traveling down to her mouth. His pupils danced mischievously upon her lips, while her mind went blank.

Max came off the railing and walked toward a couch, with Zoe following silently. As they sat down across from each other, she asked what he studied in school. While Max spoke, she leaned in to take him in, her gaze drifting to his mouth, noting his overlapping front teeth. At Oxford, he studied neuroscience, fascinated with how the brain creates meaning. He then won a scholarship to Yale, earning a PhD in memory studies.

He leaned in closer and lightly touched her knee with his finger. A wave of electricity coursed up her leg. He asked about her studies as she took another sip of the julep she hadn't really intended to order. When she mentioned her majors in psychology and journalism, something in him shifted. The sparkle in his eyes faded. They sat in silence for a moment.

"How did you end up becoming a documentary director?" Zoe asked, redirecting the conversation back to him.

Max's lips curved into a half-smile, the sparkle in his eyes flickering back to life. "Ah, well... that's a story for another night." He paused, then added, "Right now, I'm focused on a film about a university based in Silicon Valley called Oneness University."

"What's the documentary about?" Zoe had never heard of Oneness University.

His gaze drifted toward the ocean as he hunched slightly, his shoulders drawing in. After taking a long breath, he said slowly, "Oh, you know. The Singularity. It's quite boring," his voice lowered, hurried.

Zoe had nearly choked on her drink. "The Singularity?! You're working on a documentary about artificial intelligence taking over humanity, and you think that's boring?!"

He sat up straighter. "You know about the Singularity?"

"Of course I do," she said excitedly, as if it were obvious. "It's one of the handful of things we constantly debated in the newsroom. That, climate change, quantum entanglement, whether we're living in a simulation... pick your philosophical poison."

Max smiled, intrigued. "Well, I wouldn't define the Singularity the way you do. To me, it's about using advanced technology to help solve problems humanity has created."

"Like?"

"You know, things like climate destruction, contaminated water, food insecurity...war."

Zoe tilted her head back and laughed. "War! Technology has caused some of these problems, and now you think it will save us? With what? Smarter drones? More nuclear weapons? More pesticides?"

Max faced her squarely, "How else would we solve these problems? With our minds? Using prayer? Religion? Hope?"

"No, of course not," she'd said, her tone softening. "Listen, I'm not anti-tech. But we're creating Godlike technology faster than we can understand it. That kind of unchecked power... it's terrifying." She stared down at her hands, suddenly aware of how tightly they were clenched in her lap.

Max swirled the bourbon in his glass. "My documentary is all about reframing how we see things. It isn't about replacing humanity. It's about upgrading it."

Zoe nodded slowly, but a part of her recoiled. His words were clean, polished, factual, but something in his tone didn't sit right. They felt practiced, like lines from a script he'd rehearsed too many times. Upgrading humanity sounded robotic, inhuman, to her.

She looked toward the horizon, but the ocean no longer soothed her. Something about Max's calm had unnerved her, like still water on the surface, but with a riptide underneath capable of pulling you under.

She needed to know more.

Zoe squinted. "What exactly is Oneness University?"

Max hesitated, then met her eyes. "It's... not what it seems. They call it a university, but it's more like a tech incubator. It's invitation-only and very under the radar. Funded by people who don't want their names in press releases. Their mission is to create the minds of tomorrow."

"So, it's not just another Silicon Valley startup hub?" she asked.

"Not even close," Max said.

Zoe was skeptical and intrigued. "What's your documentary called?"

He smiled faintly, as if it were a secret, "*Architects of the Mind.*"

The words landed heavy, sending a prickle up the back of Zoe's neck, which seemed to buzz into her skull. It struck her like a wrong note, sharp and dissonant: *Architects of the Mind.* Something twisted in her gut. She managed a smile, but her body betrayed her. Her shoulders tensed as she held her breath. It wasn't just the name of the documentary; it was the way Max had said it. There was something in his tone again.

Her intuition stirred.

Zoe's intuition was difficult to explain, even to herself. She had always had a strange sense for things, long before she became a journalist. As a child, she'd blurt out truths no one had spoken aloud. She could feel tension brewing in a room and sense when someone was lying, when something unspoken hung thick in the air. Her mother called it her super sensitivity. Her teachers termed it her wild imagination. But Zoe knew she carried something more than that, something deeper, stranger, and harder to name. It lived in her body like a second nervous system.

It also made her life complicated.

Her intuition and imagination had always been on a collision course with one another. One gave her insight, while the other told stories. But because the two overlapped so often, she had trouble separating them. Was her intuition sensing something real? Or was her imagination just spinning possibilities out of fear? This collision followed her into adulthood, into journalism, and into every big moment of her life when she needed clarity the most.

Her intuition made her a gifted reporter, sure, but also someone who second-guessed herself constantly. She could read people and predict outcomes with unnerving precision, but she could also convince herself of threats that weren't there. Time seemed to shift, the timeline between what she could sense, and the timing of actual events often reversed. And when it did, she'd learned to stay quiet. People didn't like being seen too clearly, or knowing what their future may bring before the present showed itself. It made them feel uncomfortable, and that was the polite word for it. In truth, her sense of knowing terrified others, and sometimes, it terrified her too.

Zoe had studied journalism at Columbia. She was used to being too much, too driven, too curious, too sharp-edged for the men she dated. They either faltered under the weight of her ambition or mistook her intelligence as something to compete with or contain. But Max seemed different. Max was smart and charming in a low-key, under-the-radar way that didn't announce itself. He was articulate, self-assured, albeit at times a bit arrogant, but it was well-earned. And he'd done something rare: he had actually read her work, quoting it back to her in a way that felt less like flattery and more like recognition. This novelty disarmed her. When they spoke, something sparked in Zoe's brain, sharp and electric. He met her curiosity with curiosity, matched her thoughts beat for beat. That was the first pull: although it was not attraction in the usual sense, it was the rare thrill of being mentally met. Of not having to shrink.

So, when *Architects of the Mind* set off a flicker of warning with a familiar intuitive tug in her gut that night at Casa del Sol, Zoe decided to bury it. She told herself she didn't have enough information yet. That her imagination could be doing *that thing* again, putting her on a collision course with a dystopian destiny of her own design.

"Is your family back in the UK? Are you close to them?" she'd asked, switching topics, letting her discomfort fade into the background, where it could quietly wait its turn.

Max leaned toward his drink, staring into the ice cube. "They are back in England. And we're not particularly close. They're very religious. I have a twin, but we rarely speak." His face seemed to morph into a boy's, childlike, innocent.

Before Zoe could ask more, he'd turned to her with an urgent look in his eyes. "I'm heading up to Oneness University next weekend. I usually drive through Big Sur. It's a beautiful drive. Any interest in joining me?"

"I'd love to," she'd said.

Her friends would later say it was bizarre to go on a road trip with a man she had just met. But Zoe was rebellious, and her curiosity often got the best of her. That edge, the part that should've made her pull back, had always drawn her closer. There was a thrill in the unknown she didn't like admitting, a low hum beneath her skin that made everything feel heightened. It made her feel alive. Desire and danger were woven together so tightly inside her that she couldn't always tell them apart. Her defiant side always promised to inch her toward an imaginary danger that never actually materialized.

This trip, she'd thought, would be no different.

Max's phone buzzes again, bringing Zoe's mind back into the passenger seat with the cliffs of Big Sur unfolding beside them. Zoe blinks and lets the memory of the first night they met fade. The wind tousles her hair, the salt air brushing her cheeks.

"I'm ready for the first question," Max says.

She clears her throat. "OK. What is your idea of perfect happiness? Also, only one-word answers, please." She's shouting the question at him over the whirling wind.

He swerves his face toward her. "My idea of happiness? What does that even mean? Oh, my dear, I despise this game already. Can I skip questions?"

"Absolutely not. Back to the question, what is your idea of happiness?"

"Hem. Happiness to me means freedom."

She watches him. "Freedom from what?"

"Plans. Routine. Expectations. Institutions." He waves vaguely at the road, then taps his buzzing phone on the console with two fingers. "Freedom from this."

"This?" Zoe echoes, watching him. The phone vibrates again.

Something inside her tightens. That low internal frequency, the flicker of knowing.

"Are you single?" The words leave her mouth before she grasps the absurdity of them. They'd been on a handful of dates, and they're here on a road trip together for the weekend. Someone in a relationship wouldn't extend an invitation like this, but she needed to test his reaction to sense the true answer.

Max bursts out laughing and then shoots her a look of concern. "Darling, of course I'm single. I'm here with you now, aren't I? Please tell me you're not the jealous type, because…" It's a vague threat that silences Zoe's doubts. He doesn't elaborate, and she doesn't press for more. She reminds herself how her intuition has a way of blurring the line between fact and fiction. Especially when it comes to men like Max.

"Forget I even asked," she says, poking him gently in the leg. "OK. Next question. What is your greatest fear?"

"Death."

Zoe glances sideways. "Really? Just… death?"

He smirks. "Isn't that everyone's?"

The wind lifts strands of her hair, tangling them in her lashes. They're deep into Big Sur now, the cliffs sheer and sun-blasted, the Pacific glittering below. "I'm more afraid of losing myself than death," Zoe announces. Max casts her a look of confusion. Zoe continues, voice low, almost lost beneath the rush of wind. "I'm afraid of forgetting who I am. Becoming unrecognizable to myself."

Max grips the wheel tighter and keeps his eyes on the road. He's silent. Zoe leans back against the seat, taking in the warmth of the sun on her face. Freckles dust her ivory skin, having faded with age.

Then something catches Zoe's eye, perched high above the Pacific, half-shrouded in marine mist. A structure, sleek and angular, is tucked into the cliffside, barely visible from the road. Yet it has a quiet intensity that draws her in. "What's that?" she asks, pointing toward the building, now coming into focus. Made of redwood and glass, the structure is so seamlessly layered into the landscape, as if it were vanishing into the cliff itself.

Max doesn't even look. "Salenan, an exclusive wellness retreat. Guests must be invited to stay there." The car whips past, and Zoe twists in her seat, watching Salenan vanish behind a bend. Something about it sticks; it feels both raw and restrained to Zoe. Not just the architecture, but the stillness. She feels a pull. Max says something, but she barely hears him. Her mind's already wandering inside the halls of Salenan. *Who gets invited? What happens there? What are they retreating from?* Zoe inhales deeply. The air is thick with salt and eucalyptus, briny and sharp, cutting through her thoughts. Max taps her knee, pulling her mind back from Salenan. She glances down at the list of questions.

"Oh, this is a good one. What trait do you most deplore in yourself?" she asks.

Max drums his fingers on the steering wheel, considering. "Hedonism," he says finally, with a faint, unapologetic smile. "Though I'm not sure I dislike that side of myself as much as I should. I've grown rather fond of it."

Zoe raises an eyebrow.

He shrugs and continues. "Life is short, darling. Why not do whatever pleases you in the moment? I like to live in the now."

She studies him, silently wondering how far he lets his pursuit of pleasures take him before reaching for the brakes. "And in others? What trait do you despise?"

"Being too emotional," he replies quicker this time. The car crests a tight curve. The wind shifts, carrying a new scent—ocean mist, wild sage, the faint char of firewood from hidden cliffside cabins.

Zoe rolls her eyes and laughs, sharp and sudden, "That's ironic."

"I'm British, darling." He tugs at her sleeve and smiles. "We're constitutionally allergic to feelings. They can be messy."

"Yes, but you're making a film about the mind, aren't you?"

"Yes," he says, unfazed. "But it's not about feelings. It's about structure, patterns, upgrades."

Zoe turns her gaze to the right. Golden hills are studded with cypress and bent pine, their roots clutching at the crumbling coastline. Max is all logic and precision, his mind so linear it moves like clockwork. Zoe is the opposite: where he is exacting, she is more abstract, feeling her way through the world, letting her instincts guide her. No wonder they are drawn to each other.

"Next question. Which living person do you most admire?" she asks.

Max mumbles something. Zoe can't hear him.

"Who did you say?" The wind dies down.

"Ryan Sowell." He smirks.

"You can't be serious." Zoe shakes her head.

Max's head swivels toward her, a wide grin crawling across his face. "I'm joking, clearly, darling. I loved the piece you wrote on him; you know that."

Zoe rolls her eyes. He was only trying to rile her up. "Let's try this again. Which living person do you admire?"

"Fine, John Wilder."

Zoe tilts her head and squints. "The Tex Chemical guy?"

John Wilder was recently named CEO of Tex Chemical, the largest pesticide company in the world, long plagued by scandal. The company had been blamed for tainting crops, poisoning water supplies, and causing illness in vulnerable communities for decades. It was the kind of name that came up in exposés and lawsuits, not admiration lists. Zoe watches him, eyes wide, unsure if he's joking again.

He continues. "He rebuilt a sinking empire. Gave it a mission." Max is serious.

"Which is?"

He hesitates. "Something like... 'Feed the world.'"

Zoe can sense him retreating on his words. His phone starts buzzing again. She thought he had turned it off. Zoe narrows her eyes. "With what? Engineered wheat? Designer pesticides?"

He glances at her from the corner of his eye. "You're quite cynical, aren't you, my dear?"

She doesn't answer, letting her instincts hum quietly. She can't tell if she's being too skeptical, or not skeptical enough. With Max, everything is beginning to feel like a test she isn't prepared for.

"What is your current state of mind?" She asks.

"Hungry."

Zoe wonders if he's deflecting, not wanting to share his inner thoughts, or is simply a man ruled by his appetite. Perhaps both. It's clear from his answer that Zoe will have to delve deeper to inch closer to Max; she scans the list of questions to find what she's looking for.

"What do you regard as the lowest depth of misery?" she asks.

"Boredom."

The word lands like a stone. Zoe looks at Max. His sunglasses are on now, hiding his expression. He drives with the same ease and confidence with which he likely does everything else, measured and controlled, one hand on the wheel as if he doesn't need the other. Like the road might bend for him if he asks it to.

"Boredom?" she echoes.

Max nods. "People think pain is the worst, but boredom is what destroys you. It makes you do strange things just to feel something again." His voice stays even, but Zoe senses something cold beneath it. She turns her gaze toward the trees blurring past the car window, then back out to the sea. The cliffs drop suddenly and violently in places, as if the earth has been bitten away.

Strange things.

Zoe places a palm over her stomach. That subtle churning again, a slow crawl of unease takes over her body. She sets her eyes forward on the road now, worried that motion sickness is coming over her.

"OK, now it's my turn. What do you want to know?" Zoe had already rehearsed some answers to the questionnaire in her head.

"Not now, my dear, maybe later. I'm hungry. Let's stop for food," he says. "I know a place up ahead." He grabs her thigh; her mind feels oozy. They drive for ten minutes in silence, winding through Big Sur, golden light flickering through redwoods.

Zoe sees her first, just a flicker. A figure steps out from the trees and onto the road without warning, slipping through the mist. The air freezes in Zoe's lungs as her body jerks forward. She digs her nails into Max's thigh and lunges for the wheel.

"Watch out!" She yanks it hard. The car veers toward the mountainside, tires shrieking. For a second, the sky tilts, and then the car straightens.

Silence.

Zoe's heart hammers against her ribcage. Her palms are slick with sweat. She twists in her seat, craning her neck to see behind them. The woman is already across the road, disappearing into the brush. She's not running, instead she is walking, slowly and calmly, as if nothing happened.

"Holy shit, Max. Where did that woman come from? Should we stop to see if she's okay?"

Max glances at her, then smiles, eyes twinkling with delight. He reaches over and grabs her hand, giving it a squeeze. Zoe's body goes still, her breathing becomes shallow. Instead of slowing down, he presses on the gas. "Oh darling, don't be such a stiff. Honestly. Isn't this exhausting for you?"

Zoe snaps her neck toward him. "What do you mean?"

"How do you enjoy anything if you're constantly bracing for disaster?" He waves a hand casually toward the road. "We weren't even close to hitting her. She's fine." His voice is smooth. Steady. Like nothing happened at all.

Zoe's legs begin to shake. She silently wills the quiet tremor, now stronger, to stop, but her legs keep pulsating, her body defying the commands of her mind. How is Max so calm? Too calm. A memory surfaces: a quote from her Ryan Sowell exposé. Her source describing Sowell's eerie stillness after an assistant fell from a company balcony. "He looked at her like she was part of the furniture. There was no sense of panic, no remorse. He just tilted his head and said, 'Accidents happen.'"

Max's voice cuts back in, velvet and unbothered. "You really should just try to relax and enjoy this drive."

A flicker of doubt creeps in. Zoe's brain scrambles to replay what just happened, but the moment's already dissolving. Maybe he's right. Maybe she did overreact. Sometimes her body responds before her mind has time to make sense of it, distorting everything. Her nervous system is always on alert, overfiring, exaggerating any perceived threat into an immense sense of danger, whether it's real or imagined. Zoe says nothing as she stares out the window, legs twitching. The cliffs blur past. She turns backward searching for the spot where the woman had been, but the road behind them is empty now. All she sees are trees and golden light.

The woman vanished.

Max turns up the stereo. Annie Lennox's voice floods the car.

Zoe leans closer to the dashboard, listening.

And I warned you, I warned you.

The chorus lands in her gut.

Max cocks his head toward Zoe. "Do you know the song?"

Zoe slowly shakes her head, listening as the chorus drifts in again, low and distorted.

And I warned you, I warned you, I warned you, it's suspicious.

"I warned you?" she echoes, glancing at Max, uncertain she's heard right.

Max throws his head back into a low laugh. "No, darling, that's not it at all," a grin unfurls on his face, slow and sharp, like he's just won a prize. The chorus bellows again, and he hums the lyrics under his breath, the words slipping just out of Zoe's reach.

CHAPTER THREE

Alessandra

Alessandra sits on the edge of her bed in her private cottage at the Salenan Institute, her hands resting loosely on her thighs. Her breathing is steady, and her body is still, yet something inside her buzzes faintly with electric energy. She closes her eyes, and fragments of a memory flash before her like a warped slideshow. The sequence is scrambled; her memories shuffled like a deck of cards. The roar of an engine and a black convertible speeding away. A woman with blonde hair whipping wildly in the wind sits in the passenger seat. The car accelerates and then vanishes around a bend in the cliff. Just before the car disappears, the woman turns, their eyes locking in a split second of recognition, as if she had been searching for Alessandra.

And then, the car disappears.

Alone on a cliff in Big Sur, is where Alessandra feels most like herself, or at least closest to whatever version of her that still lingers. Every morning, she takes one step closer to the edge. It wasn't a death wish, exactly. It was the opposite, a craving for intensity. A deep desire for danger, proof that she can still feel things. That she is alive.

That morning, Alessandra had been on her usual morning hike, following the trail bringing her to the cliff's edge. When she reached the edge of Highway 1, she didn't pause. Instead, she stepped onto the road slowly and deliberately without checking for oncoming traffic. The wind moved gently against her skin. Alessandra has always respected the danger of Highway 1, that narrow stretch of pavement carved into the cliffs two hundred feet above the Pacific Ocean, with only a thin guardrail preventing drivers from tumbling into the ocean's fatal grasp. She knows the terrain well; it is carved out like a map in her mind. This trail is part of her daily ritual, taking her to the cliff's edge where the wind cuts sharply, stirring something within her.

But that morning, her mind was elsewhere. She was preoccupied with the email she had sent, having finally decided to reach out to the journalist. Though her body moved on autopilot, she heard the screech of tires and the whirl of a car speeding around the bend somewhere between her footsteps. Or maybe it was the other way around; she can't quite place the moment in its proper order. But then, something strange happened: Alessandra didn't flinch. Her body didn't tense or scream for safety. Instead, as she continued to stroll across the road, a jolt surged through her, not of panic, but of thrill. It felt sharp, hot, and exhilarating. It caught her off guard. She hadn't felt anything that intensely in a long time.

She supposed she had become bored. Not in the restless, fidgeting way, but in a way that felt like a weight, a gravity deepening, threatening to take her down. The days blurred into night, sleep became elusive. She moved through her daily routine feeling like she was outside of her body, like she no longer belonged to herself, or even to humanity. Her emotions didn't quite catch, she felt neither up nor down, just flatlined. But at that precise moment, when the car nearly hit her, something pierced the numbness inside of her. Being on the edge of danger sparked the electric awareness of her own body.

She opens her eyes, jolted by a sound, it's the subtle groan of wood as her cottage settles. The air is colder now, and her back aches from sitting in one position for so long. Blinking in disorientation, she realizes she is no longer on the cliff; she is back in her room at Salenan. The light is different; it's muted and subdued. Gripping the edge of the bed, she braces for the boredom to return. She exhales slowly, reaching for the nightstand drawer.

The invitation is still there, staring up at her like an artifact. She lifts it and feels its substantial weight, heavy cardstock with gold-etched letters gleaming against a maroon background: *You've Been Selected to Join Us for The Mind Reclaimed.* She flips it over. *Welcome to the Age of Synthetic Consciousness. By invitation only. Discretion and security will be provided for all attendees.*

The workshop promises a convergence of spiritual guides and elite technologists. Alessandra suspects the Institute is looking for another donation from her father. Still, something about the phrasing resonates with her. *The Mind Reclaimed* is what she has been searching for, and Salenan seems to be the ideal location.

Dangling high above the Pacific Ocean, the Salenan Institute has been called the birthplace of humanist psychology. Founded in the 1960s by four MIT students, it drew seekers in pursuit of spiritual awakening. Abraham Maslow, often credited as one of the founders of humanistic psychology, is rumored to have drafted his hierarchy of needs here, a model suggesting that humans must first secure and satisfy basic needs like food, safety, and belonging before reaching "self-actualization," or their fullest human potential. Maslow's presence, whether lore or not, gave the Institute an aura of legitimacy as a frontier for exploring human consciousness outside the bounds of traditional academia.

Hot springs rise from the ground in colors that defy logic, shimmering grays, coppers, and milky blues. Salenan has long welcomed nudity, eccentricity, and seekers of all kinds. A famous novelist once wandered the halls naked with a shotgun, humming lullabies. For decades, psychologists, mystics, and wanderers came here seeking self-actualization. Now, Salenan is filled with tech CEOs and startup founders looking for a "spiritual upgrade", mimicking the language of enlightenment and the posture of awakening.

Alessandra's phone buzzes. She checks it and sees a text from Susan, a woman she met when she first checked into Salenan a few days prior. Susan and her husband Jack own Ambrosia, the restaurant just down the road.

"Would you like to join Jack and me for dinner tonight?"

She replies with an immediate "yes." She could use the distraction.

At Ambrosia, the scent of burning wood wraps around her. She walks onto the terrace, where fire pits glow and built-in benches overlook the cliff's edge. She ties her sandy, wavy hair into a messy bun and spots Jack, then Susan, waving from their neighboring cabin. Alessandra has the kind of face people remembered without knowing why. Her golden blonde hair catches the light as if it belongs to another time, and her skin, scattered with freckles, makes her seem younger than she was.

In their cabin, Jack and Susan serve octopus salad with red onion, lemon, parsley, and olive oil from their grove in the north, and pour Los Olivos wine. They talk about Susan's art show, which Jack is helping curate. The conversation drifts to Susan's grandmother, who first owned the restaurant.

"How did your grandmother come up with the name *Ambrosia*?" Alessandra asks.

"Well, it's an old word," Susan says. "In Greek mythology it is known as 'food of the gods.' It was believed if you consumed this special food, you would become immortal. My grandmother liked the idea of the afterlife and of playing with the notion of eternity. It was reality, the here and now, that she struggled with."

"Was she suffering from something?"

Susan nods. "Later in life, she was diagnosed with Alzheimer's. But I remember as a child my grandmother would tell me about the strange dreams she had at night. Night terrors. She knew this land did not belong to us." Susan and her family had inherited the property from her grandmother, who had bought it from a white settler. "Her disease led to a forgetfulness, or perhaps even a hope for forgiveness for what had happened on this land."

A silence falls over the table.

"Did something happen here?" Alessandra asks softly.

Jack takes a sip of wine. "A few years ago, we were looking to build an addition and had to go through the state's historical office before we could begin excavating."

"And?" Alessandra prompts.

Susan lowers her head. Her voice is barely audible. "They found fifty human remains."

Jack continues, "Buried here on the property. They were all in the fetal position, facing the sea."

Alessandra lowers her head, like Susan, and stares down at the wooden floor. "Do you think it was a ritual, perhaps?"

"I assumed they died in battle," Jack says unflinchingly.

"Or maybe the land was poisoned," Alessandra's voice drops. The story feels familiar, like a memory she doesn't want to own.

Susan shrugs. "We don't know for sure, all we know is that the remains are of one of the local tribes. They were most likely protecting their land. Their relationship to the land and nature is spiritual, unlike ours. They saw the hot springs here and the cliffs as sacred. And we took not only their land but their lives."

Jack cuts in. "Not 'we'—it wasn't us, Susan."

She doesn't look at him. "Well, it was white people."

Alessandra asks, "Is there anything that can be done?"

Susan exhales. "Our family decided not to abandon the land but to respect it as best we can. Keep it fertile, grow food, and share it with the community. But the land remembers," she says, staring at the sea.

Jack changes the subject. "Let's move closer to the fire."

As they settle in, they ask about Alessandra's background. When she mentions her last name, Jack and Susan exchange a glance but say nothing about her father's company. Alessandra is grateful for that. More wine flows, and the conversation lightens. Jack plays music from his vinyl collection, and they dance late into the night. Alessandra moves easily, her body picking up the rhythm of Susan's, a subtle imitation.

Back at her cottage, Alessandra reads a few pages of a book before sleep pulls her under. A harsh knock wakes her. She bolts upright. The book falls to the floor. She leans for it and slips it into the drawer, rises, and peers through the peephole. No one is there. But there's something beneath the door.

A yellow post-it note. She picks it up and reads: "The car is waiting."

Her pulse quickens, and the electric hum under her skin returns. She grabs her bag, skips checkout, and slips out the side entrance. In the lot, a black Suburban idles. Two men in suits step out. One greets her by name. The other glances at her, and Alessandra notices an earpiece dangling in his left ear, about to come lose. Neither speaks. She nods at them, making deliberate eye contact. Her eyes are large, wide set, a deep and watchful brown that gives the impression she is always one step ahead, even when she remains silent. There is something open and yet unreadable about her, and she realizes the power this holds over people. She shares just enough personal details to feel known by others, but not enough to be truly seen; she excels at being a mirror surface that allows people project their own stories onto her without their realizing they are doing so. One of the men opens the door to the backseat. She smiles faintly at him, gets in, and falls asleep.

When Alessandra wakes, the car is pulling up to a gate. The driver pulls down his window.

"Here for the project?" a guard asks.

The driver nods, and the guard ushers the car ahead. They drive by abandoned buildings and decaying structures. A row of colorful buildings appears in the fog, and Alessandra perks up. The driver puts the car in park, gets out, and opens her door.

"You're here," he says, grabbing her hand and slipping a business card into her palm.

"Thank you," she murmurs, still a bit woozy from the drive. A fog swirls over a row of colorful buildings in the distance. The driver points toward a tree-lined path, and she begins walking. She hears a click as a streetlamp flickers above her. She glances up to see cameras camouflaged along the entire walkway, watching. An iron gate looms ahead. As she nears it, she turns around to see the black suburban is no longer there. The men are gone. She pushes on the gate, but it is locked.

She turns once more to see if anyone is around. She is alone. Yet somewhere just beneath the surface of her skin, she wishes, not for the first time, that someone else might follow her. Someone who is drawn by the same current and already knows the way. She recalls the woman's face in the car, recalling a sense of familiarity, as if looking into a slightly altered version of herself. And for a split second, she wonders: what if they mistook one of us for the other?

She presses her palm against the sensor on the keycode. A light blinks on. The gate creaks open, and Alessandra walks into Oneness University.

CHAPTER FOUR

Moffett Field

Zoe and Max arrive at Moffett Field a little before midnight. As they reach a gate, a security light flashes, and a guard appears from a vestibule. The area is surrounded by barbed wire where a fence would have done justice enough. Zoe's stomach tightens. Max makes eye contact with the guard in the floodlit booth, flashes his badge, and the steel gate lifts with no words exchanged between the men.

Moffett Field is the US headquarters of NASA's Ames Research Center and is now, somehow, home to Oneness University. Zoe tracks the terrain with her eyes. The old military base stretches before them: it is eerie and low-tech with rows of cracked asphalt, shuttered barracks, and sagging warehouses. She notices a maintenance facility shed, a warehouse labeled Building 6 and a water tower labeled Building 5, which seem no longer in use. Rows and rows of desolate barracks tower in the four corners, which are guard-less, at least for now. Several satellite dishes tilt toward the sky, like sunflowers turning toward the sun.

A tingle runs through Zoe's body as she sees the barbed wire fencing. The area feels suspended in time, like it's been deserted in another era. The grounds go on for miles, consisting mostly of what look like abandoned army barracks. Moffett Field feels low-tech, run-down, and borderline non-functional, not at all what Zoe has imagined.

Then, Zoe spots a sign of life in the distance: an enormous metal dome of interlocking scaffolding, its beams crisscrossing like a web stretching into the clouds. It reminds her of a brain stripped bare, with its synapses exposed. She stares, mesmerized, imagining the structure as a network of neurons surging with energy, pulsing in unison. For a moment, she sees it humming with electricity, alive.

The barracks at Moffett Field loom ahead, dull and blocky against the darkening sky. Max parks the car, and they head inside a small lobby with fluorescent lights buzzing overhead. Zoe stops at a wall of framed photographs, portraits of astronauts frozen in mid-history. One photo catches her eye.

Without thinking, she gestures. "You know when Ronald McNair was just a kid, he was banned from his town library for being Black? He was nine. He tried to check out a book on physics, and the librarian called the cops on him." She looks at Max. "He went on to get a PhD from MIT and later died in the Challenger disaster. He was only thirty-five."

Max glances at the photo, then at her. "You know a lot about astronauts," he says, absent of emotion.

"I do." Zoe smiles faintly, picturing her childhood bedroom, its walls plastered with NASA posters, and quietly recalls the way she'd whisper to herself that outer space was the only place big enough to feel free.

Max studies her a beat longer. "I bet you didn't know astronauts ended the Cold War."

Zoe snorts, surprised. "Seriously?" She laughs, not because she believes him, but because Max seems to always try to control their conversations with a hint competition and a dash of absurdity.

"I'm serious." He doesn't back down, "It happened in the hot springs at Salenan."

Zoe shoots him a look, unsure if he's joking. She files it away in her mind to confirm the truth later.

They step toward the front desk. Behind it, a woman with tired eyes and a stained yellow rotary phone resting beside her watches them approach.

Max checks them in. The woman behind the desk hands over the key without looking directly at him, a plastic chain with their room number scrawled in fading marker. Zoe can sense the woman's disdain in the handoff. What a strange irony, to work at a place like NASA, the frontier of the future, and end up behind a desk tethered to a rotary phone.

Max opens the door to their room, and her eyes scan the low Styrofoam ceiling, landing on a small blinking light that flashes green, then red, and back to green. The smoke detector appears barely attached to the ceiling, with wires exposed. Two twin beds, covered in yellowed bedspreads, are separated by a wooden nightstand topped with a lamp that has a crooked shade. The walls are made of white concrete blocks, giving the room a stark, jail-like appearance. The windows are framed in aluminum and fitted with plastic shades that have yellowed over time. The carpet on the floor is a harsh gray, stiff, and commercial grade: arguably, it is the only thing in the room that looks like it's been replaced in the last twenty years.

She examines Max as he unpacks his bag, seemingly unphased by their surroundings. Zoe sets her luggage on one of the twin beds. Suddenly, she notices something on the carpet near the bed. She steps back and then leans in to take a closer look. It's an open candy bar wrapper, suspiciously clean, with no traces of the candy inside.

Zoe leans down closer to read the label that says "PAYDAY." Her throat tightens. How could the cleaning staff at NASA have missed such an obvious item? Zoe stands there, staring at the candy wrapper, unsure what to do.

"Max," she calls out to him. "What's this?"

He looks down and laughs. "Do you mind picking it up?"

Zoe gives him a look.

"I'm highly allergic to peanuts," he says casually. "I shouldn't touch it."

Her imagination snaps into gear. Zoe blinks at the wrapper, still pinched between her fingers. PAYDAY. She holds it a second longer than necessary. The absurdity of it, the lethal threat wrapped in something so ordinary, sends a ripple through her. It is the first vulnerability Max has shared with her.

He could die from contact with a candy bar wrapper. This strikes Zoe not with concern but with something quieter, stranger. The thought of Max, so composed, always so sure of himself, being killed by something so stupid and ordinary... it lodges in her chest. Not from a gun, or a car, or some enemy in the shadows. Just a trace of peanut. She turns to him. He's searching something in his phone. Zoe looks back at the wrapper, at the crumpled plastic edges. It feels like something that's been placed between them on purpose. Not by destiny, but by design. She carries it to the trash and drops it in. Her face stays neutral. But something inside her twists.

Zoe glances out the window of their room into the empty lot, filled with burnt grass and bleached gravel. *Why did Max bring her here?* The longer she stares, the more certain she is of something she doesn't want to name.

She shakes it off. *You're tired. You're overthinking. Don't let you imagination ruin this.* She turns to Max and watches him casually scroll through his phone. She tells herself everything is fine.

They leave Moffett Field, find a restaurant for dinner and drink too much wine. When they return to their room at the barracks, Max pushes the twin beds together. He locks his eyes on hers, unblinking, like he is studying her, memorizing her responses in real time. There is no fumbling, no hesitation. Every movement is precise. His intensity is total, all-consuming. As if he already knows what her body wants before she does. Max possesses a kind of control in bed that makes her feel both safe and dangerously exposed. It isn't a tenderness between them that draws her in but something more animalistic, a sensation she can't reason with. Their chemistry feels primal, instinctive, and beyond language.

Max drapes a leg around her and pulls her close, his fingers tracing the length of her arm. "You know I don't normally like being attached to anyone," he whispers, his breath moist against her ear, "but there is something about you." Zoe understands. She often feels trapped by relationships, but Max could be the exception.

The yellow glow of the lamp throws long shadows against the concrete walls, softening nothing in the room. Zoe's phone pings on the nightstand, she reaches for it and checks her email; a new message sits in her encrypted tip line with the subject line *Tex Chemical files*. She clicks and sees there are no attachments. She tries to reply, but the address bounces back. The tingle at the base of her neck sharpens. She gets plenty of anonymous tips, usually of the conspiratorial sort, but this feels different. The timing seems odd, since she and Max had just talked about Tex Chemical on the drive earlier that afternoon. She tells herself not to go down the rabbit hole, at least not yet.

Max's voice cuts through the silence, and it takes her a moment to realize he's speaking to her. He's leaned back against the headboard, long legs stretched out, a wine glass balanced loosely in his hand. "I didn't really have hobbies," he says. "Not like normal kids. School took up most of my life. It was... competitive, really intense, there wasn't much room for anything else." She nods automatically, but her thoughts keep circling the empty email and the unreachable sender.

She turns her focus back to Max; something about how he says the word "competitive" makes her skin prickle. Not self-pitying. Not nostalgic. Just... clinical. Her mind wanders. Without meaning to, she pictures a long, dark dining hall, boys in tuxedos with stiff collars, sitting rigidly at a narrow table carved from old oak. In her mind's eye, they're reciting Latin under their breath like a spell. She hears the words, *Scimus. Imitemur. Vincamus.* And then, for no explainable reason, loneliness rises in her chest; it's sudden and overwhelming. It grips her.

"Did your brothers go to the same school as you?" Zoe asks softly, genuinely curious now.

Max glances over, puzzled, like the question itself is odd. "No," he says simply. "It was just me. I was picked to go because I was the smartest." The way he says it, so flat, absolute, lands like a stone dropped into still water.

Zoe hesitates. "That must have been difficult, though. Being separated from them like that." She's imagining it, four brothers in a house, rough and loud, until one is pulled out like a rotten tooth. Max shrugs, utterly unmoved. "Not really. It made it easier to focus. They weren't around to distract me."

Zoe blinks. *Distract me.* As if love, or kinship, was just an interference.

Max adds casually, "I have ADHD. I found studying difficult because I get bored a lot."

There it is again, boredom, a constant undercurrent for him. "Your job doesn't seem boring now," Zoe offers, gently steering the conversation back to safer territory.

Max huffs a small laugh. "You have no idea." He looks down at his hands.

She wants to ask more, but something in his body language walls her off. The precision of it. The glow of the barracks lamp softens him slightly, the yellow light flattening the hard lines of his face. Max turns his head toward her. Something catches the dim amber light on his chest, a flicker of metal. A small, flat pendant. Simple, but deliberate. She hadn't noticed it before. Without thinking, she reaches toward it, her fingertips grazing its cool edge.

"What's this?" she asks.

Max hesitates just slightly. "A gift from a friend," he says, almost too quickly, too casually. He turns away from her.

His answer feels strange to Zoe. She looks over at him, his eyes are peeled open, staring at the ceiling. "Do you have trouble sleeping?" she asks, her voice quieter now, more careful.

He exhales, rolling onto his back, the pendant disappearing beneath his shirt like a secret swallowed whole. "I usually fall asleep around 7 a.m."

"That late?"

"I'm a night owl," he says. "Apparently it's a sign of intelligence."

Zoe forces a small smile, but her thoughts are already moving. "What do you do all night?"

"Work," Max says, his voice flat again. "Sleeping is boring."

Zoe turns toward the window; heart ticking faster than it should. "But what about dreaming? I love it," she says. "It's like traveling into a whole different dimension, a new world."

Max is quiet for a beat too long. Then, "I don't really dream."

"Everyone dreams," Zoe replies.

"Maybe. But I don't remember my dreams. Or maybe I just don't have them at all."

She studies him. Something about that strikes her as sadder than anything he's admitted so far. "Want me to teach you how?" she offers, lighthearted but sincere.

He laughs under his breath. "Teach me to dream?"

She leans over him, places two fingers gently on his eyelids like closing a book. "Close your eyes," she says. "Picture your favorite place. Somewhere you love."

Max hesitates. But he humors her. "The Sahara," he says.

"You've been?"

"Yes, on a mini-motorbike trip," he says flatly, like it's the most normal thing in the world.

"Perfect. Picture it. Smell it. Feel it. Let it surround you. That's how dreams come."

Max opens his eyes and slowly sits up. "That won't work," he says. "I can't picture things in my mind."

Zoe frowns. "What do you mean?"

"I have aphantasia," Max says, like he's diagnosing bad weather. "I can't form mental images. At all."

She stares. "You can't picture anything?"

He shakes his head. "No. Not faces. Not memories. Not places. Nothing. It affects how I remember people. How I dream. Maybe even how I feel."

Zoe's mind reels. Her inner world is so visual, so vivid, it feels impossible to imagine his. *His mind is a void, dark.* Like standing on the edge of a black hole. But what really unsettles her isn't the absence of images. It's the casualness with which he says it. Like it's just another fact about him.

Max settles back into the sheets, pulling away like a tide receding. "Time for sleep," he says. And just like that, the realm between them shuts down.

Zoe watches him for a long time. Eventually, his breath evens. His hand loosens, and his body stills. She props herself up and looks at the pendant, it's slipped out of his shirt and is resting on his chest. It is small, elliptical, mirror-like. Polished to a sheen so clear she can see her own reflection in it, warped slightly by its curve. Her face stares back at her from his body. It doesn't look like a family heirloom or a token of love. It looks engineered.

Zoe's eyes catch something along the rim of the pendant, a faint inscription. The words are in Latin. She leans closer. *Scimus. Imitemur. Vincamus.* Her stomach tightens. The words ripple through her like déjà vu. The phrase that had echoed across her imagination when Max talked about school, she'd heard the boys high pitched voices in chorus chanting: *Scimus. Imitemur. Vincamus.* And now... here it is, etched into the metal pressed against Max's chest. But why? She doesn't know what it means, but every part of her recognizes that it *means something.*

Her fingers hover above the pendant. It feels almost warm. She noticed earlier that Max touches it in moments of tension, his thumb grazing it like a worry stone. Now, as he sleeps, it lies still, like a machine gone idle. The idea comes suddenly and unwanted: what if it isn't symbolic at all? What if it does something? The pendant glints again. Her reflection stares back at her.

Zoe is suddenly reminded of being a little girl, standing at the edge of the subway platform, refusing to move onto the train as the doors opened. She shook her head, tears building, unable to explain why. Zoe had developed a fear of public transportation, a phobia that frustrated her mother, and also made her furious.

What Zoe's mother had chalked up to motion sickness, was something different, something beyond her grasp. It wasn't the motion that affected Zoe, nor the bus or the subway train. It was the people. She couldn't separate herself from feeling the sadness of a slumped man on the bus or the jittery panic of a woman gripping her purse. Her sensitivity became overwhelming, especially in small spaces, where other people's emotions seemed to soak right into her skin.

As she grew older, Zoe learned to push her sensitivity down and disguise it as anxiety. But she never stopped feeling it. And now, here is Max. Sleeping beside her, wearing a pendant like a second skin. An object, she imagines, that might help him access what she has too much of. She eases back onto the pillow, watching the pendant rise and fall with Max's breath.

The sun creeps into the room through the yellowed shade on the window. Zoe hasn't slept, consumed with a restlessness she's not sure is hers. She needs to leave the room and get some fresh air.

Outside, the air is unnervingly still, like the world is paused mid-thought. She moves quickly, cutting across the base toward the great wire dome that looms over Moffett Field like a rusted cathedral. It rises in her mind without warning, as if summoned from outside her own thoughts, that strange, skeletal dome she glimpsed earlier, half-swallowed by fog and distance.

Up close, it unsettles her. It isn't just the scale of it, though the scale is disorienting; it's the feeling that clings to it. The metal lattice seems to pulse faintly in her imagination like steel synapses firing overhead. Criss-crossing beams resemble the tangled circuits of a neural network, a giant, skeletal brain suspended in the sky. It looks alive.

"Hi there," a woman calls out lightly, almost cheerfully. Zoe flinches, her attention snapping back like a rubber band.

The woman is already approaching from the edge of the hangar, hands loose at her sides, a NASA badge catching the thin morning light. She's in her mid-thirties with a sharp ponytail, and perfectly neutral athletic wear. Zoe clocks the earpiece immediately, a faint coil of wire visible at her collar.

"Forgot your ID?" the woman asks, voice easy, casual in a way that feels practiced. Everything about her smile is tight and professional.

Zoe shrugs half-apologetically. "It's back in the barracks," she lies.

"This campus is a secure federal facility. It's not open to the public," the woman says, stepping a little closer. Her tone is pleasant, conversational, but it lands like a warning. "Visitors need an escort." Useful information Max had not shared with her.

"My guide's meeting me soon," Zoe lies again, keeping her voice neutral, unbothered.

The woman doesn't press. They both glance upward toward the impossible sweep of the hangar overhead.

"Pretty incredible, isn't it?" the woman says casually. "It's big enough to have its own weather system." Zoe throws her head back to see the clouds forming at the top of the hangar. "That's probably my favorite fact to tell people, also, if you remove the Statue of Liberty from her pedestal, she can stand upright right here in the center of dome."

"Incredible. How long has it been here?" Zoe asks.

"It was built in the 1950s to store airships," the woman says.

"Surely not uncovered like this?" Zoe gazes at the patches of sky exposed through the rusted steel framework, watching as the cloud cuts through the metal beams.

"No, the skin had to be removed because PCBs were found. Polychlorinated biphenyls were commonly used to protect electrical devices from fire. And now, of course, we know how harmful PCBs are," the woman explains. "There's a laundry list of health issues that arise from exposure to PCBs, from skin disorders to birth defects, low IQ, and neurological disorders. So, they had to skin the Hangar, leaving the metal skeleton exposed. The poison was trapped under the skin, protecting the structure."

Zoe's stomach tightens. *Skeleton.* The word hangs there between them, heavy. "Has NASA been working on reconstructing it?"

"Oh no, we don't have enough funding to take on something this massive." The woman's eyes flick over Zoe like she is cataloging her question. "Oneness University signed a sixty-year lease," she adds, her voice dipping. "Nobody really knows what they're planning to do with it." Another pause. "They don't share much." Zoe waits long enough to signal disinterest, but the woman doesn't move. Instead, she gives the faintest tilt of her head. "But they say the collaboration will be... synergistic." Zoe feels her mind split, the way it sometimes does, one part of her cataloging every detail, every choice of language, and the other part quietly, instinctively unsettled.

Before Zoe can ask anything else, the woman's phone buzzes. She glances down at it, already stepping back. Zoe forces a polite nod and turns to leave when something catches her eye: a shimmer of color. A cluster of candy-colored buildings peeks from behind a high fence, like a rainbow. It almost looks like a mirage. A village painted in dollhouse pastels dropped in the middle of all that rust and gravel. Which means, of course, that she is already walking faster. Past the barbed wire and concrete bones of Moffett Field, drawn toward the sudden pop of color.

The closer she gets, the stranger it feels. It's not just surreal but deliberate. As if the color itself is causing her to soften her instincts, catching her in a daze. That is when she notices the entrance. There isn't a gate exactly, nothing so obvious as that. Just a narrowing in the path. Two minimalist pillars on either side, unmarked except for a subtle glint of embedded sensors. No guards in sight, but she doesn't doubt for a second that she has already been clocked. It reminds her of something hidden, half-buried, the way museum exhibits or theme park rides gently usher you forward. A subtle, subconscious architecture of control.

Beyond the threshold, she spies a clean, curated street lined with storefronts like pieces of a movie set. Hand-painted signs announce a coffee shop, a Mexican restaurant, a barbershop, a flower stall, a bike rental shop, all lined up like facades waiting to be filled with extras. There is even a gleaming jumbotron overhead, looping soft-focus footage: sunsets, forests, slow-motion laughter.

Oneness University. It feels less like a campus and more like a simulation of a city.

Zoe thinks of Ryan Sowell, the way he used to talk about Sympara at every tech conference she covered. *Sympara.* The name alone makes something low in her stomach tighten. Sowell had been one of its earliest evangelists. Sympara is the experimental city he and a team of investors were building off the coast of Honduras. He insisted it would be the first city where people regularly lived past a hundred. Zoe remembers how his eyes lit up when he talked about the privatization of the city, the promise of biomedical advances and biometric surveillance.

Sowell has no idea what Zoe is working on now. Certainly not after her exposé, the one that blew up his carefully curated reputation, exposing his harassment and his manipulation of women in the industry. After understanding the machinations of his mind, and the absence of his moral compass, Zoe finds the idea of Sowell creating an entire city of his own design to be repulsive. She reminds herself that as a journalist, her job is to stay neutral, to keep the story clean from emotion. But this one has gotten under her skin. Sympara has become an obsession.

Her apartment in LA is littered with evidence: printouts, whistleblower emails, and internal decks pulled off dark corners of the web. Stories about locals being displaced, contracts impossible to escape, and biometric systems tracking not just movement but mood. "Behavioral harmonization" was the phrase they used. Sympara is a city where dissent isn't punished; instead, it is designed out. But the thing that lives in her body, which sticks behind her ribs, is something Sowell once said years ago at some rooftop bar in San Francisco, back when he still thought Zoe might be someone he could manipulate.

"Empathy," he told her, swirling the ice in his glass, "is just another form of infrastructure. Most people don't have enough of it to function at their full human potential, at peak scale. Imagine being able to use your empathy to read people's minds, to predict what's happening in a room, just by walking into it, just by knowing? The majority of humans don't have that ability, but that's a structural problem, not a moral one. We can build around that." He said it as if it is already happening.

Now standing on the edge of Oneness University, staring at this pastel-perfect town with its curated storefronts and frictionless calm, Zoe feels the same way about the campus as she does about Sympara. It's too clean, too controlled.

She steps onto the pristine courtyard. An alarm sounds; it's sharp, clinical, not loud, but designed to get inside of you. A guard appears almost instantly, as if he's materialized out of the air.

"Badge?" he asks.

Zoe freezes. Her mind scrambles for footing.

"Agency ID?" he clarifies.

"I'm just here for breakfast," she tries, keeping her voice steady.

"Escort?"

"Max Furtherlore," she says, maybe too quickly, without thinking. But it does something. The guard glances down at his phone. A flicker of activity there, something registering or maybe recalibrating. When he looks back up, his tone has shifted.

"You're part of the program, then?"

Zoe's stomach gives a cold little twist. She hesitates. "What program?" But the guard doesn't answer. His silence feels deliberate. Zoe glances back, over her shoulder, toward the hangar.

Then, out of nowhere, three Latin words flare hot in her mind: *Scimus. Imitemur. Vincamus.* The same words etched into Max's pendant.

She grabs her phone, types the words into the search bar and hits translate. As she waits for it to load, she can hear her pulse pounding in her ears.

Her phone buzzes in her hand. She jumps. A news alert appears across the top of the screen:

WOMAN DISAPPEARS IN BIG SUR.

Her thumb hovers over it, but another text cuts in, this one from Max. "Where are you?"

Her stomach turns, and she types quickly: "Gone for a walk, be back soon."

But Zoe doesn't move. Not yet. She stares at her phone, waiting. When the translation results finally pop up on the screen, Zoe stares at the words: "We observe. We imitate. We conquer."

She looks back toward the pastel campus. Then it hits her, low and certain: *I need to get out of here.*

CHAPTER FIVE

Family Ties

Max's mother stands in the doorway, beaming. Her soft, reddish hair is pulled back into a loose twist, and her warm, expressive eyes immediately put Karolina at ease. The first night she met Max, they'd spoken for hours about their mothers. She had opened up to him about how her mother had Alzheimer's, something she rarely talked about, and as if fate had taken hold, he admitted that his mother also suffered from the disease. This commonality between them had unlocked something within Karolina, a deeply buried pain she rarely shared, and somehow, he'd found it instantly. They'd bonded in that dimly lit bar, their hands brushing over each other's on the table as they swapped stories of loss, of forgetting, and of remembering. She had felt seen; he understood her grief, because he was experiencing it too. Now, seeing Mary in the doorway, there's a brightness in her gaze that Karolina hasn't seen in her own mother's eyes in years. It takes her by surprise. Mary seems present and aware, not the shadow of a person Max has spoken about. She hugs Karolina and Max, wrapping her slender arms around both of them, squeezing them close.

"It's been too long! My dears, how was your trip over here? Come in, please." She releases her grip and waves them inside. Karolina walks in, and the smell of rosemary and roast chicken greets her.

"So nice to see you, Mary," Karolina says.

"You must be so tired from the flight. Are you hungry? Care for some snacks, sweetheart? Perhaps some tea?" Mary calls after Max. He mumbles something. Still beaming, Mary turns to Karolina. "Why don't you head to the sitting room while I fix something."

As Mary leads them inside, Max leans close to Karolina, his voice low. "Remember, don't mention her diagnosis. It confuses her." Her stomach tightens. Karolina drops her luggage in the foyer and steps inside. Max had suggested the trip to Europe to reconnect with their families. They hadn't spent much time together as a couple recently, and she'd hoped the change of scenery might bring them closer. Something had shifted in her. Lately, her dreams had stopped. And her days were filled with a dullness from deep inside, a quiet detachment she couldn't quite explain. She felt like her body no longer belonged to her.

She hasn't told Max about how numb she feels. About the heaviness in her chest each morning. Or about the secret she is carrying that wakes her at night in a cold sweat, making her unsure of who she is anymore.

Karolina takes a deep breath, and her eyes scan the living room. It's neatly arranged with two navy couches facing each other, a wooden coffee table, and two navy and white-striped wing-backed chairs. The bookshelf is massive and draws Karolina in, an entire wall lined with leather-bound scripture books arranged meticulously. She steps toward it, compelled. A wave of lightheadedness washes over her, and she steadies herself against the edge of the shelf. Her body had been doing that lately, reeling for no reason. Vertigo hits her suddenly and sharply. The floor beneath her feels uncertain of its own weight. It passes quickly but leaves behind a throb of unease. Earlier, on the plane, Max had asked if she was coming down with something. He'd placed the back of his hand on her forehead, checking for fever. "Maybe it's the altitude," he'd said. She'd nodded, letting him believe it. Better that than the truth.

She inches closer to the shelf. Her fingers brush over a row of spines, identical in size and texture, the titles gilded in faint, fading gold. *Reasoning from the Scriptures. Let God Be True. Keep Yourselves in God's Love.* The sight of so many volumes of faith with so many rules, codified and bound, sends a familiar chill through her. Max had warned her not to bring up religion. His parents are devout Jehovah's Witnesses. Max, however, believes in little beyond logic and control. That part of him always intrigued her, the gulf between his upbringing and who he has become.

Raised Catholic, Karolina had long since distanced herself from religion. She knew the rhythm of ritual, the weight of guilt that clung like the smell of incense to her hair. Recovery from Catholicism hadn't been dramatic, just gradual, like unlearning a language she'd once spoken fluently. Now, she held a quiet suspicion for organized belief. Especially ones cloaked in secrecy.

Her eyes scan the books and one title makes her pause: *Knowledge that Leads to Everlasting Life.*

Her fingertips rest for a beat too long. Something about the phrasing unsettles her. She slowly slides the book free from the shelf. It's heavier than she expected. The leather binding is stiff with age. She opens it, the pages thin and tissue-soft beneath her fingers. Her heart beats in her chest. The inside cover bears the faint impression of an inscription, neat, deliberate handwriting in black ink, now faded to a soft brown.

> *Dearest Max and Arthur—*
> *The world does not reward goodness.*
> *It rewards discipline, observation, control.*
> *Learn to master yourselves first.*
> *Then everything else will follow.*
> *— Love, Dad*

Karolina stares at the words, her pulse dull in her throat. What bizarre life advice to give your young sons. And why is this cloaked in any form of Christianity? *Master yourselves first.*

She closes the book gently and slides it back into its place on the shelf. Her hand lingers there for a moment longer than necessary, committing the inscription to memory.

She's still standing near the bookshelf when Max's father walks in.

"There you are!"

Karolina jumps and turns. "Frank! So nice to see you."

He nods, settling heavily into an armchair. Frank's posture is military-stiff, as if the years never quite took the soldier out of him. As he smiles, Karolina feels a pulse of heat travel down the back of her neck. Frank's tall, looming frame hasn't softened much with age.

"Are you still acting?" her father-in-law asks flatly. Under a full head of neatly combed gray hair and behind his charm, there is something unreadable about Frank, much like Max.

"Yes, but I've been diving into some criminal psychology lately," she says lightly. After her initial meeting with the LAPD, they'd asked her to consider helping detectives review cold cases. It was just informal at first. But what she picked up during the meeting startled the detectives. Her instincts had been sharp, her words eerily precise. They'd urged her to take her skills further. Now she is quietly pursuing coursework in criminal psychology, less for the degree and more for the curiosity it satisfied.

Frank's brow lifts slightly, his voice dry but controlled. "Psychology, is it? Hmm. A curious field. Funny how some people are always trying to make sense of the worst parts they see in others, yet they rarely take a look at themselves." His eyes never meet Karolina's. He turns to Max instead, as if Karolina has simply vanished. "You don't get involved with all that mind stuff, do you, chap?"

A chill runs along Karolina's spine. There is something unnerving in Frank's composure, like a room with all the furniture arranged just so, with her being the only thing out of place. She cuts in before Max can answer. "Don't you know about the documentary he's working on?" she says coolly, her eyes on Frank.

Max shifts in his seat, his shoulders tensing. "Dad, how's the restoration on the boat coming along?" he says abruptly, his voice louder than before. He's used to redirecting his father, clean and rehearsed.

A grandfather clock dings. One sharp note after another, echoing through the house like a warning. It's noon.

The sound draws a silence over the room. Before anyone can speak again, Mary reappears, gliding in with a tray balanced neatly in her hands. She sets it down on Frank's lap, filled with coffee, toast, jam, butter, and orange juice, and then carefully unfolds a napkin and hands it to him, her smile looking worn out from a lifetime of pleasantries.

"A late breakfast. Frank's always been a night owl. He never really sleeps at night. Usually has breakfast in his room, but we're being polite for company today, aren't we, sweetheart?" She pats his shoulder.

Karolina forces a smile. "Max never sleeps at night either. His day begins around midnight."

Frank looks up, pleased. "It's a sign of extreme intelligence, you know." He takes a bite of toast.

"Being nocturnal?" Karolina asks, masking her skepticism as her gaze lingers on a crumb dangling from the corner of Frank's mouth.

"Did you hear that, Max? I passed along my intelligence and my night owl habits to you." He beams, once again ignoring Karolina's question.

Karolina glances at Max, sitting beside her. He's hunched forward, eyes on his feet. Usually so puffed with confidence, now he looks small, like a boy again. His father's words land on him like an anchor dropped in dark water.

Her eyes drift back to the bookshelf. A framed photo catches her attention. She leans toward it; it's Max's family in front of a Jehovah's Witness temple. The four boys wear matching oversized black suits, lined up by height. Her eyes settle on the twins at the end. One of them is unmistakably Max, who is staring at the camera with a look she knows well: the flat boredom. His twin, smiling, has his arm around his shoulders.

"Max, how old are you in this photo?" she asks.

"Oh, he and Arthur were probably around five then," Mary answers from behind.

Karolina picks up the photo. Max's mother's eyes radiate warmth. His father's gaze seems to narrowly miss the camera as if he is looking elsewhere. But it's the twin boys, Max and Arthur, that hold her attention. They are identical in every visible way, down to the posture and the tilt of the chin. Even their suits seem to blur into one. Karolina could imagine someone, maybe even Mary, calling one by the other's name, not out of malice but confusion. She wondered what it would feel like to grow up mirrored by someone else. To see your face reflected back at you but animated by a different mind with different desires.

Suddenly, an image flashes before Karolina's mind. A teenage girl between Max and Arthur, the brothers circling one another like mirrors misaligned in a fun house. The girl's face is turned, unreadable, her body tense as though caught between the two. Karolina blinks. The image disappears as quickly as it came, like an overdeveloped photo, gone blank, blurred at the edges. Still, it leaves a residue behind in her mind.

A thought flickers through her. Arthur. She hasn't seen Max's twin since the wedding, where the two had barely spoken. They were awkward and distant, like they were strangers wearing matching skin. It had struck her as strange then. When she had asked Max, he brushed it off. But now it feels urgent. She needs to understand more about the space that has grown between the two brothers. Maybe it will help her make sense of how she's been feeling and what she should do next.

She turns back to the room. "How's Arthur doing?" she asks. Beneath her sweater, her hand presses her lower abdomen, protectively.

His parents exchange glances. Mary vanishes into the kitchen. Max says nothing.

Frank leans forward, elbows on knees. "When Max and Arthur were babies, we had to separate them in their cribs. Things got... complicated. Isn't that right, chap?"

Max hangs his head, he's folded into himself even more, as if the room had frozen him into the smaller, younger version of himself. And maybe that is part of what had drawn Karolina to him in the first place. That undercurrent of sadness he could never name. She felt it even when he smiled, sensed it tucked beneath his intellect and control. A boy left behind somewhere. Max's childhood held secrets she could feel, even if he never shared them aloud. Karolina wanted to protect him.

"Why is that? Did they keep each other up at night?" Karolina asks, her voice gentle.

Max's mom darts back into the living room. "Max had terrible ADHD, even as a baby." She grabs Karolina's hand, tugging her toward the hallway. "Come on, darling, let's go get some tea. We should leave the boys to catch up for a bit."

Karolina narrows her eyes. There was something strange in the way Frank had mentioned separating the twins and how Mary burst in, interrupting. This was not a fond memory of proud parents. It sounded more like an incident or an ongoing pattern between the boys. A sharp wave of nausea climbs up her throat, sudden and hot. A quiet confirmation ripples through her. It's not relief, exactly, but something close to it. She'd been right not to share what she was holding. At least not here, not now.

Karolina makes her way to the kitchen, and once she and Mary are alone, she says lightly, "Max told me how strong you've been through everything."

Mary tilts her head. "Through everything?"

"With your Alzheimer's..." Karolina begins carefully.

Mary's smile stills, her brow knitting ever so slightly. "Who told you I had Alzheimer's?" The question lands quickly, sharper than the warmth in her voice.

Karolina blinks, caught off guard. "Max mentioned it, the night we first met."

Mary's gaze flickers with confusion at first, then something else, a flash of recognition that seems to tighten the air between them. She lets out an airy laugh, just a tad too practiced. "Oh goodness, no. I'm forgetful sometimes, but that's just getting older." She waves a hand in the air, brushing the moment aside. "I'm sure Max just misunderstood something I said once. He worries too much about me."

Karolina feels a slow, cold thread slip down her spine. Did Max misunderstand or had he lied to her? A pit in her stomach twists, what if he made up this story of his mother's diagnosis to form an inseparable bond with her? It seems monstrous for Karolina to even imagine that he would lie about something so serious. What kind of person would do that? She replays the night she met Max, how he'd mirrored her grief about her own mother's decline, how it had bound them instantly. Back then it had felt like safety, but now it feels like a lure.

As Karolina stands frozen in the kitchen, her phone buzzes in her back pocket. She pulls it out and sees an unfamiliar number from Los Angeles. A tightness gathers in her chest. She lets it ring.

Mary is already halfway back to the living room, Karolina follows her, hesitating in the hallway, slipping the phone out of her pocket to check if someone left a voicemail. She raises the phone to her ear. It's Detective Alvarez, and he needs her help. His voice is urgent, but he leaves no details, just a request to call back as soon as she can. Karolina holds the phone to her ear a beat longer than necessary, her fingers gripping the case. A flutter, an unformed sensory impression passes through her: she can smell salt in the air, the feeling of wind off the cliffs, the sense of someone watching.

Karolina knows this isn't just any case. It's something larger. Something that has been waiting for her.

CHAPTER SIX

Sasha

Sasha knocks on the door of Max's apartment, the familiar metal echo dull against the noise of the street below. Her suitcase rests by her ankle. It is a sleek yet battered piece of luggage that has crossed more time zones in the past six months than she can count.

When the door swings open, Max grins that particular grin, bright, easy, the one that used to disarm her completely.

"Fräulein!" His voice lifts like an inside joke from another life.

She steps inside, and he pulls her close with a casual, practiced warmth. His kiss lands lightly at her temple before he's already turning, walking down the hallway toward the kitchen, calling over his shoulder, "How was the flight from New York?"

Sasha lingers in the doorway for half a second, letting the silence settle around her. The apartment smells faintly of espresso and soldered metal, the particular, sterile undertone of tech.

"Good," she calls after him, dragging her suitcase over the concrete floor. "Long."

Her voice catches the hollow acoustics of his place, echoing slightly. She rubs her eyes with the heel of her palm. Six hours on a plane to LA should not feel this brutal, but lately the travel has worn her thin in a way even her training as a pilot can't resolve. There's a difference between flying for yourself and flying to someone. The commitment was beginning to feel claustrophobic.

She trails him down the hall, her footsteps soft against the cool floor. Her words catch up to him.

"How was Big Sur?" she asks. Max had been in Big Sur for the weekend. A quick work trip, he'd said. The cell service would be spotty, he had added, impatiently.

There is a pause, barely perceptible, before his answer comes, tossed over his shoulder without turning.

"Quiet."

Sasha's pulse ticks a little faster. Quiet. It wasn't quiet for her. Somewhere over Arizona, cruising at 36,000 feet, she'd read the news alert flashing across her phone screen: *WOMAN MISSING FROM SALENAN RETREAT, BIG SUR.* Salenan. The same retreat Max took her to once, early in their relationship. Their third date. That detail clings to her now, prickling along the back of her neck. Her fingers tighten around the handle of her suitcase.

"Max," she says again, more carefully this time. "Did you hear about the woman who went missing?"

There's another pause. The clink of a wine bottle.

"Missing?" His voice is casual, too casual.

"Yeah," she says, frowning. "They found her car near the cliffs, but no sign of her."

Another beat of silence. He reappears with a wine bottle in hand.

"Probably a suicide," he says casually.

She freezes. "What?"

"Happens all the time up there," he adds.

"I just thought you might know more. She was staying at Salenan." Her voice lowers. "You took me there. On our third date."

"Of course, I remember," he says, voice bright again. "It was perfect."

She stares at him, searching for something beneath the charm. She wants to press further, but something holds her back. A small knot forms in her chest.

"I'm going to have a shower," she says, suddenly needing distance.

She starts toward the bathroom, dragging her suitcase. The hallway is cluttered. Cardboard boxes everywhere are uncharacteristic of Max, who is usually obsessively tidy. She nearly trips over one box, a flap hanging open. As she steadies herself, she glances down and stops.

Sasha crouches beside the open box, heart ticking hard against her ribs. Dozens of black-and-white grainy photos stare back at her. Women. Alone. Not filmed but documented. Their faces are strange, almost blurred at the edges. Like surveillance stills. She tells herself it's nothing, maybe leftover props, research materials, Max's chaotic way of working. But when her fingertips brush against the slick edge of one photograph, a cold shiver climbs up her arms.

She picks it up. It's pixelated, dreamlike, like the others, but the woman in this one is... different. Not just another blurred profile or distant silhouette. The background is murky and foggy. She could be on a cliff's edge or inside a studio designed to mimic it. It's impossible to tell. This woman is staring straight into the camera.

She's sitting cross-legged. Her posture is casual, but there's something electric beneath it, it's as if she's been caught mid-thought. Sasha pulls the photo closer, taking in the details. She looks like she's in her early thirties, maybe. Sandy-colored hair falls in loose waves over her shoulders, the kind of soft, sun-faded blonde that only comes from time spent outdoors. She has a scattering of freckles across her nose and cheeks and wide, watchful brown eyes.

But it's not her face that makes Sasha's breath catch. It's what the woman is holding.

A book: *The ESP Enigma.*

Sasha knows it instantly, the distinctive minimalist cover, the author's name printed cleanly along the spine: Dr. Diane Powell. She owns this same book. A copy of it is still in her apartment in New York, its pages dog-eared and soft from years of rereading. *The ESP Enigma*, part neuroscience, part case study, explores the scientific investigation of extra-sensory perception. Not magic or superstition, but real recorded phenomena. Children with telepathic abilities. Families who dream identical dreams. Twins separated by distance but connected by mind.

It was the first book that made Sasha feel less alone with the growing realization that she sometimes knew things without any explanation.

The woman in the photo cradles the book loosely in her lap. A sharp pulse of unease blooms in the back of Sasha's throat.

Sasha stares harder at the woman's face, the sharp cut of her jaw, the watchfulness in her dark brown eyes, the almost guarded curl of her mouth. She looks... familiar. But not someone Sasha can place.

She slides the photograph deeper into the stack, her heartbeat knocking hard beneath her ribs. Maybe it means nothing. Maybe it's a coincidence, but something inside her knows better.

Her voice cuts through the air. "Max. What is this?"

His footsteps approach, slow, deliberate. He wraps an arm around her waist.

"Oh, that?" he says lightly. "From the set. Just some test shots for the documentary."

She doesn't move.

"I told you; I'm filming gifted women. Future-makers. It's confidential."

He shuts the box almost too gently. "Please, no more snooping." He smiles and slides it into the closet.

Sasha knows Max is working on a film for Oneness University. *Architects of the Mind*, he calls it, a documentary about the pioneers shaping human consciousness. He says he's following the lives of several experts in various fields, neuroscientists, mystics, psychologists, futurists, people he describes, half-jokingly, as Future-makers. Individuals with rare cognitive abilities, people operating on the edges of thought itself.

Max is careful, a bit too careful, whenever the film's content comes up. He insists the identities of the Future-makers must remain confidential, even from her. Something about non-disclosure agreements, proprietary research, corporate paranoia. It's the only time Max ever sounds like just another Silicon Valley mouthpiece.

Sasha pressed him once, casually, asking why Oneness University would bankroll a film like this. What did they care about, empathy, intuition, or altered states of consciousness?

Max had smiled in response to her question, that thin, almost affectionate smile he used when closing a door without slamming it.

"It's boring, Fräulein," he'd said. "You wouldn't care."

But now, standing over this box, she isn't so sure.

Max pinches her waist, bringing her mind back into her body, and kisses her temple. "Shall I join you in the shower, Fräulein?"

She forces a smile. "No. I'm tired."

In the bedroom, she undresses slowly, her limbs heavier than usual. Sasha pulls her shirt over her head in a fluid motion, the fabric whispering as it leaves her skin. At nearly six feet tall, she is built like a figure from a drawing, long, lean, all lines and quiet strength. Her frame, though slim, carries presence. It is the kind of body made for runways, for stillness captured in flashbulbs, but she'd never quite seen herself that way.

She had moved to New York from Düsseldorf in her early twenties, chasing something she couldn't yet name. Modeling had been the gateway, not the goal. It was a means of entry into a life she hadn't been born into but one she learned to move through with a kind of detached grace.

She peels off her leggings, the second skin of her daily uniform, and bends to fold them neatly. Her golden-blonde hair spills over her shoulder as she reaches for her earring, a single gold hoop, laying it carefully on Max's dresser.

It lands beside a framed magazine cover in which her own face stares back at her. Younger. Slightly fuller cheeks. The same cool symmetry. Features neither sharp nor soft, just perfectly, unnervingly proportionate. Her most arresting feature, though, had always been her eyes, ice blue, almost translucent in a certain light, so light they could look like glass. In photographs, they stunned. In person, they unsettled. Sasha has a watchfulness that makes her seem otherworldly.

Sasha had never fully identified with being a model, and certainly not with the life people assumed came with it. She didn't move through the world the way other women in her industry did. No curated parties, no late-night scenes, no carefully staged glamour. Sasha preferred the quiet life: yoga in the early morning, a book cracked open late at night, the simple precision of cooking something slowly, methodically. She wore little makeup, her features striking enough without it.

But there was no denying her presence. Modeling had been a doorway for Sasha, but not her dream. It paid the bills while she chased the life she actually wanted. And that life, for Sasha, had always been in the sky.

She was a trained commercial pilot for Lufthansa and was now one of the youngest female pilots in her division. It all suited her well: the altitude, the solitude, the mathematical logic of flight paths and navigation. The way the noise of the world fell away at 38,000 feet and everything in the cockpit and sky narrowed to instinct and precision.

She could fly herself anywhere and often did.

It was in New York, years ago, that she'd met Max. One of those rare nights she'd been coaxed out by friends: she was standing at the bar, ordering a glass of wine, already debating whether to slip away early.

He approached her like someone who'd already decided he belonged there. He was charming and funny, a little too confident, but somehow, it worked. He had looked right at her, into her.

He insisted they meet for coffee the next day. She told herself it was ridiculous. She'd just ended a relationship. She wasn't looking for anything.

But Max was different. He had a hunger for life that rivaled her own. He had been all over the world and was incredibly smart.

Their first real date? It was a horse carriage ride through Central Park in the winter, romantic in a way that felt old-fashioned and oddly, deeply sincere.

Years later, despite the long-haul flights between New York and Los Angeles, despite the small moments of disquiet she sometimes caught in his gaze, they were still together and still in love.

Or at least, that's what she told herself.

Indeed, Max is planning to move to New York in the coming months. Finally, a life together, not lived in fragments or flight schedules. But tonight, standing in his apartment, this unusually cluttered, chaotic apartment, she can't shake the feeling that something essential about Max is drifting further and further from reach.

She steps into the bathroom and turns on the shower. The mirror fogs and steam rises. She steps under the hot water, hoping it will scrub the image of the box filled with hazy photos of women from her mind.

Then, a line of blood trickles down her thigh, her period arriving early. She watches as the blood swirls down the drain, deep maroon at first, then softening to pale pink as it mixes with water. And just like that, she is seven years old again, barefoot in her family kitchen in Düsseldorf. Her mother is making breakfast. A knife falls. Blood orange jam stains the tiles. The memory flashes bright, quick. Her mother's panic. The psychiatrist. The yellow couch. The realization that Sasha knew things she wasn't supposed to. Sasha's small voice breaks the air.

"Grandma has a son," Sasha blurts out.

A knife drops from her mother's hands and hits the floorboard with a thud, oozing purple and red, splatters of sticky maroon dot the white kitchen cabinets. Sasha's mother bends down and meets her ice-blue eyes with her daughter's.

"What did you say?"

"Grandma has a son named Thomas," Sasha stands tall as she repeats herself.

Sasha's mom stares at the knife she was using to spread blood orange jam on a piece of toast as it rests in a pool of maroon on the floor. She grabs Sasha's tiny hands.

"Sasha, how do you know this?"

Sasha looks directly into her mother's eyes. "Grandma told me last night in my dream."

Sasha's grandmother had passed away only a few months prior. In Sasha's dream, her grandmother appeared before her with a young boy around Sasha's age. Her grandmother bent down gently and introduced her son, Thomas, to Sasha. As an adult, she learned her dream had been real. Her grandmother had a child out of wedlock before marrying Sasha's grandfather. Sasha's grandmother had kept the secret from nearly everyone in her family except for Sasha's mother, who was the only one who knew of Thomas. Sasha's revelation scared her mother so much that she made an appointment for her daughter with a child psychiatrist.

"What brings us here today?" The psychologist asks Sasha's mom who sits next to Sasha on the yellow couch. Sasha looks up with giant crystal blue eyes at her mother, who is gripping her hand tightly, waiting for an answer.

"Well, you see, my daughter is having dreams of my mother, who recently passed away. And I'm concerned. I'm concerned perhaps she is... perhaps she is not grieving properly. Not able to accept the reality of her grandmother no longer being here with us." Sasha's mother holds back a tear.

The psychologist nods and writes down something. "And Sasha, why do you think we are here today?"

"Because I told my mother I met grandma's son Thomas, and it scared her."

The psychologist immediately looks at Sasha's mother. "Is this real, or is this imagined?"

Sasha's mother's face goes white. She can't seem to get the words out. She drops her head down and shakes it back and forth, overwhelmed by her daughter's ability to confront a truth no one had known for decades. "No, it's quite true. My mother did have a son named Thomas out of wedlock, but she never shared this information with anyone. Anyone except me."

"And Sasha." The psychologist smiles at young Sasha. Her ears perk up. She sits taller.

"No, you must be confused. My mother never told Sasha. I am the only one who knew," Sasha's mom says.

"Perhaps your mother communicated this to Sasha in a way we have yet to fully understand?" The psychologist continues. "There are still many phenomena in this world that medical professionals have yet to uncover, including communication from the other side."

Sasha's mom raises her head and swivels it to face her young daughter. The psychologist smiles and looks directly at Sasha while addressing her mother. "Children have active imaginations, yes, but they also have the openness and ability to see and absorb things in the world that we adults are closed off to."

Sasha's mom nods, reluctantly. "So, I shouldn't be concerned about her mental state?"

The psychologist folds both hands in his lap. "Not in the least. It seems Sasha may have a super sensing ability to pick up on things others don't. This is unique and something she should guard to protect herself from those who may not understand."

Sasha stares at her feet with a bent neck. A nervous smile escapes her mouth. The doctor continues.

"Now, let's talk about why we are really here. How are you processing the grief of your mother's death?" Sasha's mother breaks down and sobs.

Sasha quickly understood she had a powerful ability to know things no one else knew and the havoc it could bring. From that moment on, sitting next to her mother on the couch crying, Sasha made a promise to herself to never share what she learned in her dreams.

Sasha snaps back to the present, heart thudding. She shuts off the water, wraps herself in a towel, and walks back into the bedroom. Max is waiting with two glasses of red wine. His eyes lock on her the moment she enters, unblinking. That stare of his is so intense, yet also still. It thrills and unsettles her in equal measure, like the final second before turbulence hits at thirty thousand feet.

She takes the wine glass. "Danke, sweetheart."

He's in his usual uniform: a fitted white V-neck, the fabric clinging to his frame in a way that feels intentional. His beard is fuller and slightly unkempt, giving him a roughened edge that doesn't match the memory of the man she first met.

Resting just below the dip of his collarbone, Max's pendant catches the light with a faint, mirror-like sheen, flat and polished, like glass over an instrument panel, almost like a device masquerading as jewelry. That's what it reminded her of, suddenly, in a way she couldn't quite un-think: a sensor.

Something about the shape, the symmetry, the beveled edge, the way Max touched it absently, grazing it with his thumb strikes her as familiar. It reminds her of the cockpit.

Tiny devices, like the one around Max's neck, are embedded in modern aircraft, slim, innocuous sensors that track vitals, proximity, and body temperature. These devices also don't look like devices. Max's pendant has that same sleek look, as if it was designed in defiant opposition, erasing any imperfections created by humans.

He touches it without thinking, a habit she's caught before.

"What is that again?" she asks, feigning casual.

He smiles, too quick, too smooth. "A gift from a friend."

Then, as if nothing's off, he stares into her, as if trying to reset a spell. "Shall we head to dinner? I made a reservation for us at the Speckled Boar."

She nods, pulling the towel tight around her chest. But even as she moves toward the closet to dress, her mind lingers on the box of photos of the women, the blood running down her leg in the shower. His pendant.

Every nerve in her body hums like it does in the cockpit when something is off, but the gauges haven't caught it yet. Max is keeping secrets. Of that, she's certain. And this time, she isn't going to ignore them.

CHAPTER SEVEN

Brothers

The phone rings twice before a voice answers, low and unhurried, with the clipped edges of a British accent.

"'Ello."

Karolina's finger still hovers near the call button as if she might hang up before the voice can fully settle in her ear. Her breath becomes shallow. The kitchen around her is dim, the silence brittle. Her hand trembles slightly, not from cold, but from something deeper, something coiled inside her since the moment she typed the number.

"Hi there... is this Arthur?"

"'Tis."

She hesitates. Her mouth is dry.

"Hi Arthur, it's Karolina, your brother Max's wife." The other end of the line goes quiet.

"Hello?" Karolina's pulse quickens, worried he has hung up.

The silence stretches just a second too long before it breaks.

"Ah, yes, sorry, right, Max." He doesn't add anything more.

She lets out a breath that doesn't quite settle.

"I hope you don't mind my reaching out," she says. "It's just... when I visited your parents recently, it's clear there is some distance between you and Max. And it breaks my heart, honestly. I thought maybe… I don't know. Maybe I could help."

That is the story she has rehearsed, harmless and earnest, the kind of thing a caring wife might do.

But underneath the script, a different motivation pulses. One she hasn't spoken aloud, not even to herself fully. Her body is changing in quiet, irreversible ways, pulling her into a future she hasn't decided she wants. Her dreams have stopped. And Max… Max has started to feel like a stranger in their own home. He's always been enigmatic, but now he seems to be imitating himself, smiling on cue, saying the right things, and none of it lands right in Karolina's body. He's become a man who watches her more than he speaks. Who smiles at the right moments but with eyes that don't move. He disappears for days at a time under the banner of his "documentary." Something in her, something instinctual, has begun to pull away from him.

"Have you spoken to Max about this?" Arthur is curt. His friendly tone is replaced with something more formal.

"Well, you know Max," she says carefully. "It's difficult to get him to open up sometimes. I thought I'd start with you first."

"The softie, eh? That's me. Always has been. The emotional one. The one who caves first." Karolina tastes a tinge of bitterness in his words.

"I get that," she says. "I'm the same way."

"That's probably why my brother chose you."

The words land with a weight she can't quite deflect.

"I suppose opposites attract," she states.

"Maybe," Arthur says. "But with Max… it's never about difference. He's always drawn to people who reflect something back at him. Who mirror what he's trying to become." Karolina feels a small catch in her breath. "He has this way of wanting what others want," Arthur says. "Not because he wants it, but because they do. That's the trick. Desire doesn't start with him; it starts with someone else. Then, he mimics it so well, it feels like his own."

She says nothing, but her mind reels.

"I always thought desire was personal," he continues. "But with Max, it's contagious. He watched what I had. And he didn't just desire it; he wanted to take it from me. Because I was capable of something he wasn't."

Karolina stares at the floor. *He wanted to take it from me.* The phrase lodges in her like a splinter; it's only human nature, after all to desire what others have, but Arthur seems to be hinting at something darker.

"I know I've only known him a few years," she says carefully, "which must seem like nothing to you. Growing up together as twins."

Arthur laughs softly, but there's no amusement in it. "People think twins are natural mirrors. Like that's something beautiful. But being identical doesn't just breed intimacy. It breeds obsession. Especially when you're unsure where you end and the other begins. We were competitive, of course. But it wasn't normal competition. With Max, rivalry didn't come from being different. It came from sameness. The closer we were, the more he wanted to take. Not because he hated me, but because he needed to prove he was better."

Karolina's stomach twists. "What do you mean?"

There is a brief rustle on the other end of the line as if Arthur is leaning back, gathering his thoughts.

"Max was fearless, even as a toddler. He would climb anything, jump off anything. He rarely cried and never flinched. He would light things on fire: papers, toys, even his own blanket once, and just watch it all burn. He seemed mesmerized by the destruction he created."

A chill passes through her.

"I am the opposite," he continues. "I have too much fear. And I would always trail behind him, trying to put things out, fix whatever he destroyed."

She can hear something in his voice now. Resignation, maybe.

"And with girls," Arthur says, "he always had a type. They were smart, compassionate, and incredibly curious. The kind of girls who could easily lose themselves in the mystery of him. I think he enjoyed confusing them, watching them struggle to find out who he really was."

Karolina doesn't respond.

"I started warning them by the end of high school. Not that it did much good. No one ever listens to the overly sensitive twin."

"Were you ever close to him?"

"We were always close," Arthur says. "Too close. People thought it was sweet. But Max needed me in ways I didn't understand until later. He didn't want to be like me; he wanted to be me."

Her mouth goes dry. "Did he ever act on it?"

Arthur laughs softly. "There was a girl. Madeline. My first real love. He didn't just steal her, he studied her. He studied me. And then, one night, he took my place."

"He stole your girlfriend?"

"It's more the way he went about it." Arthur's voice is hushed. "He slept with her, pretending to be me."

Karolina's voice drops. "He slept with her pretending to be you?" She echoes his words back in disbelief.

"Yes, he let her believe it. Let her kiss him like she was kissing me."

A shiver runs through Karolina's body. She sees it again, the image that flashed before her in Max's parents' living room: the twins as teenagers, a girl standing between them. Max's expression is unreadable. Arthur is almost lost in his shadow. A cold sweat breaks across her skin.

Arthur continues. "He watched me fall apart after I found out. It was all a game to him."

"Did you ever confront him?"

Arthur lets out a sound that isn't quite a laugh. "Of course, but it didn't seem to affect him. For Max, it wasn't just about winning. It was about unraveling me. Proving he could take what I love and ruin it."

"Is that why you stopped speaking to him?" she asks.

"No, but it tipped me off to something deeper going on with him. We got into a massive row. I never saw him the same after that. But that's not why we stop speaking. That's when I realized we were entangled. I didn't just fear losing myself to him. I feared I could be like him. That my identity wasn't mine at all."

From the other end of the line, a child's cry rings out.

"How are your kids doing?" Karolina is grateful to change the subject.

"They're exhausting but brilliant. They keep me honest."

Karolina presses her palm flat against the counter. Her other hand drifts, unconsciously, to rest against her lower stomach.

"Do you know why your parents separated you and Max into different cribs?"

Arthur's voice grows quiet. "They used to wake to me screaming. My parents would come into our room to find Max on top of me, biting my neck. They said he would never make a sound. He would just look up at them, calmly, while they pulled him off of me."

"How old were you?"

"Babies, not even two, I'd say."

Karolina feels a flutter low in her abdomen. Something she doesn't want to feel.

"Has Max ever told you what he actually does for work?"

Arthur's voice dips. "Let me guess. Something with Oneness University?"

"Yes, he said he's directing a documentary for them," Karolina confirms.

Arthur lets out a sharp laugh. "Of course, he did."

"What do you mean?"

"He's not being truthful, Karolina."

"About his career?" Karolina asks.

Another pause. This one is deeper, more final. "About who he is."

The words hang in the air, colder than any silence.

Karolina's mind races with images she tries to unsee. Her chest feels tight. She has one last thing to ask.

"When I visited your parents recently, something stuck with me. I thought maybe you could clear it up."

"Go on."

"Max told me your mum has Alzheimer's," she says, keeping her voice even. "But when I spoke to her, she denied it."

"He told you that?" Arthur's voice sharpens, the words clipped. "Bloody hell. She doesn't have Alzheimer's. Never has. Why would he say that?"

Karolina doesn't speak; she can't. The words hit her like a sudden drop. She knew it, she'd felt the truth in her body the moment Mary looked her in the eye and laughed it off. She just hadn't wanted to believe it then.

Karolina presses the phone tighter to her ear, the silence stretching.

When Arthur speaks again, his tone is lower, more deliberate. "He's good at hiding things, Karolina. And he's even better at hiding himself."

Karolina stares at the darkened window, at her own reflection, blurred and rippling across the glass. The truth hums through her now, steady and quiet. She drops her gaze to her midsection, the part of her body that is starting to betray her secrets. She's become good at hiding things too.

CHAPTER EIGHT

The Speckled Boar

The Speckled Boar had once been Zoe's favorite restaurant in Los Angeles until she learned about the photographer who had assaulted women on the third floor. He had turned the private room into a makeshift studio for photo shoots. The police had recently caught him, thanks to an anonymous witness who'd had a close encounter.

Since then, Zoe had lost her appetite for dining there. But Max's friends, whom she'd never met, had picked the restaurant, and Zoe said yes before she could stop herself. Since their trip to Big Sur, she told herself she would leave Max, just not quite yet. Their relationship was quickly turning from romance to reconnaissance.

Zoe enters and scans the room for Max and his friends. The Speckled Boar buzzes with energy. Waitstaff circle tables, eager to appease the guests. The first floor features a tall oak bar, low tables, and benches tucked along the walls. The vibe is halfway between a grandmother's basement and a London pub. The walls are cluttered with art of all kinds: illustrations, paintings, and ceramic sculptures venerating the pig. She catches sight of a small drawing of a blushing pink pig and thinks of her favorite childhood book. Her mother read it to her at bedtime, and little Zoe always cried at the end.

She approaches the hostess stand. "Max Furtherlore."

"Right this way." The hostess leads her up three flights of stairs. Zoe hesitates as they reach the third floor. The knowledge of what happened there clings like mildew in the air. They come to a wooden door labeled *PRIVATE*. The hostess knocks, opens it, and steps aside for Zoe to enter.

Inside, cigar smoke hangs in the air. A long mahogany table, the only one in the room, is crowded with glasses, candles, and half-eaten appetizers. Max's friends sit around it. They're all dressed the same, in khaki pants and patterned button-downs, like they've stepped off the cover of an Ivy League alumni magazine. There's something coded and performative in their style: perfectly shined loafers, tightly parted hair, a whiff of cologne. It seems to Zoe that nothing about them has evolved since they were teenage boys in prep school. Above them, ceramic pigs crowd the beams. A watercolor of a pig grazing in an open field hangs above the fireplace.

And then there's Max, seated at the head of the table. His hair is a wild mop of curls, his beard is thicker than usual, and instead of pressed khakis, he wears dark jeans and a black shirt with rolled sleeves.

Max rises and takes her hand.

"Chaps, this is Zoe."

One by one, the men stand.

"Ed."

"Ollie."

"Nick."

"Tony."

She smiles politely as she shakes their hands. Zoe would never be drawn to someone like Ed or Ollie or Tony—men who are too polished, too curated. But Max? He's messy and magnetic, like a brilliant, mysterious mind only half-tethered to the earth.

"The boys just got back from hunting pheasants," Max says.

"You didn't join them, my dear?" Zoe turns to him. She can't stand hunting.

"Not enough of a challenge. They bring the birds in cages and then release them."

"To then be shot down?" she replies.

"Better than chasing them in the wild," Ed cuts in. "My family's been hunting pheasants for generations. It's tradition."

The room is darker than she remembers, darker than any restaurant has a right to be. The men at the table look up at her one by one. There's a pause, barely perceptible, but Zoe feels it. A beat too long.

"Zoe," says Tony, pushing back in his chair. "It's lovely to finally meet you."

Nick offers a quick nod. Ed murmurs hello. Ollie raises his glass in a silent salute, eyes sharp and curious.

Zoe sits next to Max, pretending not to notice the flicker that passes between Nick and Tony when Max introduces her. The men settle back into their chairs, conversation picking up again, but Zoe feels the undercurrent of something else. It's not hostility but something closer to calculation.

"So, you're really a journalist then?" Ollie says too loudly. His mannerisms echo old-world entitlement with his elbows perched and fingers steepled, like he's at a mock UN summit, not dinner.

She smiles. "Yes. I'm actually a journalist."

"Print or TV?"

"Both. But I mostly write now."

"Are you working on anything at the moment?"

Zoe meets his eyes. "Always." Each question directed at her is casual on the surface, but underneath, she can feel it. This isn't small talk. It's an inquisition.

Max shifts beside her. He hasn't said much since the introduction, but Zoe can feel him watching her carefully.

"She freelances," he adds, as if that clears anything up.

Ollie tilts his head. "That must be... flexible."

Nick studies her over the rim of his glass. "Must make dating interesting."

Zoe bristles. "Sometimes. But Max seems to manage."

A smirk twitches at the edge of Tony's mouth. Ollie leans forward, elbows on the table.

"And how did you two meet again?"

"Casa del Sol," Max answers smoothly. "I was waiting at the door, just hoping to meet someone like her." He turns to Zoe and winks at her.

Zoe notices that flicker again as Tony and Nick exchange a glance. Ollie is still watching her like a cat with a twitching tail.

The waitress returns to take orders. The moment she leaves, the men talk about their hunting trips, obscure geopolitical gossip, and casually mention colleagues using surnames alone. Zoe tries to fade into the background.

Until Nick turns to her again. "Do you believe in intuition?"

Zoe blinks. "Excuse me?"

"Intuition," he repeats, swirling his wine. "Gut instinct."

"I think it can be useful."

"Even professionally?"

"Especially professionally." She hesitates. "What are you getting at?"

Nick shrugs, but his gaze holds. "Just wondering."

Max finally intervenes. "Zoe's intuition is part of what makes her good at her job."

Nick's smile doesn't reach his eyes. "I bet."

They move on, but Zoe doesn't. Her skin crawls. Something is off. She glances at Max. He's charming and relaxed. But the others? They're watching, listening, weighing her every answer.

Nick turns to Max. "How's Karolina these days?" he asks casually, his fork pausing mid-air.

Zoe blinks.

Max doesn't miss a beat. "She's doing well," he says smoothly, yet jaw clenched. "Still in Europe, working on her own project."

Zoe smiles politely, masking confusion. The name hits her in the chest like a breeze that's colder than it should be. Karolina. Max has never mentioned that name before. Why now, and why here? It's as if Nick was dropping bait just to see what Zoe would do with it. She doesn't bite; instead, she sits in silence, patiently calculating. She catalogs the name, as well as the tenor of Max's answer: it was too smooth, too rehearsed.

Tony glances at Max briefly, almost imperceptibly, and takes a long sip of his wine.

The conversation shifts back to safe terrain: a recent documentary exploring the CIA experiments on psychic spies done during the Cold War. Someone makes a joke about Project Stargate. Zoe mentions the Stanford Research Institute's work on remote viewing, and the table laughs.

She leans back in her chair, watching the men chuckle, watching Max shake his head in laughter. But something feels different now. The mention of Karolina hangs in the air like smoke that won't clear.

The table quiets. Max squeezes her leg under the table. "What's everyone getting to eat?"

The topic shifts to the Harvard–Yale football game. Zoe listens in silence, picking at her cheeseburger.

"How's the documentary coming?" Nick asks.

Max shrugs.

"Still about Oneness University?" Tony presses.

Nick jumps in. "Tell me they're not still working on Sympara."

Zoe's head snaps up. "Sympara?"

The men glance at each other. Tony leans in with a smirk and says, "Has Max not told you?"

Zoe tilts her head slightly, her expression hovering between curiosity and amusement. It's best to let them think she's new to all this and have them underestimate her. That's how Zoe gets the best material. The truth is that she knows more about Sympara than anyone at this table. More than Max himself, she knows. More than Tony with his well-oiled smirk and Ollie with his polished Ivy League sneer, she knows. She reads every leaked memo, every patent application buried in obscure Honduran business registries. She maps out the shadow companies tied to Ryan Sowell and the trial zones where the "neural tech" is being discreetly tested on small, isolated populations.

"Sympara," she says softly as if trying the word on. "Is that the city the tech billionaires are building in Central America?" She raises her eyebrows just enough to pass for intrigue.

Tony nods eagerly, leaning into the void she creates for him. "Exactly. A kind of libertarian paradise, with all private contracts and biometric tracking. It's like... Dubai, but with brain chips."

Zoe laughs lightly, eyes wide, like she's hearing about it for the first time.

"It's a startup city down in Honduras," Ollie adds. "Supposedly, it's built for innovation. It sits in an autonomous zone where there's no government regulations, no FDA or any other alphabet agencies, and of course, no red tape."

Then, Ed jumps in, "It's one big tech hub. They're touting it as the frontier of human optimization. Rumor has it they're embedding neural tech in people. Brain interfaces, emotional enhancement. All sorts of creepy shit." He leans back in his chair, and she sees it just under the open collar of his linen shirt, a pendant, small and triangular, shining like a mirror. It's identical to Max's.

Her pulse skips. "Sounds like something out of a sci-fi novel," Zoe plays along, eyes on Ed's chest.

Max watches her. She can feel his gaze sliding along her cheekbone, trying to decipher whether she's playing dumb or if she's just dim. She doesn't look back at him.

Let them keep talking. Let them believe they're the ones holding the knowledge. Meanwhile, she's already two steps ahead of them, writing a different version of this story in her mind in real time.

She lets her gaze drift back to Max. His pendant is tucked under his shirt now, hidden from view, but she remembers the weight of it, the chill of it against his chest when she touched it. She thought it was unique. Apparently not.

She leans in and lets her voice dip low, like she's trying to be part of the club. "I saw one of those pendants before," she says, looking back at Ed, almost lazily, as if she's trying to remember a dream. "It was yours, Max. And I think it had something written on it? Latin, maybe?"

Ed stiffens. Max stills. The others pause, but it's Ed's expression she clocks. It's too practiced, too careful.

She continues, eyes on Max. "It said something like *We observe... We imitate... We conquer?*"

The table falls unusually quiet.

Max offers a small laugh, too late and a little too flat. "Just an old boarding school motto," he says, brushing it off. "Some joke from our debate club, I think."

Ed jumps in quickly. "Yeah, something like that. It's meant to sound dramatic, to scare off the other schools. Blokes being blokes, what have you."

Zoe nods slowly, smiling like she believes them. "Hmm. Sounds pretty intense for a school motto."

Tony tilts his head, watching her too closely. Ollie's eyes dart between faces.

Max reaches for her hand under the table. His thumb strokes across her palm, steady and calming. But her body feels cold.

When the bill finally arrives, Zoe and Max say their goodbyes to the group. As they walk back to Max's apartment, Zoe's phone buzzes. A text comes in: "Hi. I have a story I'd like to discuss with you. Can we meet in person?"

Max sees her glance at her screen.

"Who's that?"

"Just work," she says, slipping her phone back into her purse. "I'll answer it later."

Venice Beach after dark is never entirely quiet; it has a way of feeling deserted and crowded all at once. Zoe and Max walk side by side down a cracked stretch of sidewalk, weaving past shuttered storefronts, old Craftsman houses converted into startups, and low-slung apartment buildings that look abandoned but aren't. The night takes on a strange, electric stillness.

A flickering streetlamp buzzes overhead. Across the street, a man stands swaying near a palm tree, mumbling to himself. His shadow elongates across the pavement. Farther down, a group of skaters clatters past, their collective laughter rising and falling in the air. Someone pushes a shopping cart slowly across the road, its wheels squealing.

Max walks with his hands in his pockets, his head slightly bowed, his eyes flicking to the shadows without concern. There is always a tension to Venice at night, a strangeness that doesn't feel entirely physical. Something in the mix of the old and the new, the decaying and the polished. Art murals fade under salt air. Glass-walled tech hubs hum with glowing servers inside. The ghosts of bohemia and the glint of surveillance all tangle together.

They pass a former bookstore converted into a wellness studio; its neon sign still lit reads *Breathe*. The front window is empty. Zoe's stomach twinges. The silence between them stretches too long, and she has something she needs to share with him.

"I've been asked to cover a story. It'll only be for a few weeks," she says. "It's about the woman who disappeared in Big Sur."

Max doesn't look at her.

"Oh?"

"One of the editors at *The Daily Quest* reached out. They want me to retrace her steps and write a long-form piece."

He nods as if she's said something obvious.

"Well, are you going to take it?"

"Yes, I think so." She has already accepted but lets him think her decision is still up for discussion.

"Good. You should." His tone is brisk.

Zoe blinks. Isn't he going to ask questions? She is going to the last place the woman had been seen. Alone. Shouldn't he at least ask if she'll be safe?

"Well, it's settled then," she says, trying to keep the edge out of her voice.

"When are you due to leave?"

"Tomorrow."

They walk past a mural of a woman's face, her eyes covered by white paint. A tangle of fairy lights blinks half-dead over the patio of an empty café.

"So," Max says after a moment, "are you going to go missing on me now, too?"

Zoe stops. Just slightly. Enough to glance at him sidelong.

"Too?" she echoes. "What do you mean?"

"Nothing." His voice is smooth. "Sounds like you have everything figured out, my dear." He smiles casually, easily, but there is tension rising from the corners of his mouth. His right eye twitches, then glitters with something that looks like amusement. Or maybe delight. She can't be sure.

Zoe forces a smile back and keeps walking.

Back at Max's loft, they fall into a rhythm of silence and red wine, the kind of intimacy that can feel comforting or suffocating depending on the angle. Zoe wanders into the bedroom to change. She begins unbuttoning her jeans and pauses. Something gold glints near the leg of the dresser. She bends down to look closer, it's an earring, a small gold hoop. Zoe doesn't wear gold. She swallows hard.

Zoe hesitates, then steps closer. She picks the hoop up; it's light and delicate, the kind of jewelry you wear daily, not for fashion but out of habit. The kind you barely notice until it's gone. She places it in her pocket. She turns and sees Max standing behind her, silent. He reaches for her wrist, the same one that she used to pocket the earring, not roughly but not gently either. The grip is precise, practiced. He holds it there for a beat too long. Her heart begins racing.

Then, just as suddenly, he lets go of her wrist. "Come," he says softly.

She follows him down the hallway to the living room, her senses bristling with the strange blend of fear and trust that always seems to accompany his presence. He opens a drawer in his desk and pulls something from it. It's a simple bracelet with dark wooden beads strung tight, and he slides it onto her wrist without asking.

"For protection," he says.

"From what?" she asks, her voice barely audible.

He doesn't answer.

Zoe turns the bracelet slowly on her wrist, the beads still warm from his hands. She watches him for a moment, the way he moves with an ease that borders on theatrical. And then, before she can stop herself, she blurts out, "Who's Karolina?"

Max looks up, blinking once as if startled by the name. His expression is unreadable for a second too long.

"A friend," he says.

Zoe nods, but she sees it, just barely, the faintest glint in his right eye. A twinkle, not of fondness or nostalgia or fear, but of something else. Something sharper, brighter pulses behind his eye. It is a flicker of pure delight, like a kid caught with his hand in the cookie jar.

"Is she someone you dated?"

Max meets her gaze and doesn't blink. "No," he says simply. "Why would you think that?" The air between them feels heavier for a beat, and then he smiles, as if the moment never happened.

She turns the bracelet again. The beads clack softly in the silence between them. But Zoe is rarely satisfied with silence. She can feel a warm tingle beneath her skull, the spark of a question carving a path across her synapses, a path her mind will travel again and again, determined to get a clear-cut answer from him.

"Did you work together then?"

Max's smile falters. He leans back just enough to create distance, his eyes holding hers for a beat too long. "Zoe," he says slowly, "I'm not one of your little case subjects for an article. Don't treat me like I am under some sort of microscope." His voice stays calm, but there's a cool undercurrent running through it now. "This isn't some game of gotcha, and if it is, you're wasting your time."

"I'm just asking questions, Max." There's a flicker of heat low in her belly, a familiar sharp warmth she gets when a source confirms there's something worth digging for. Her pulse beats hard in her throat. "Listen, we're not exclusive yet, but if you're seeing other people I'd just like to know."

Max's expression softens instantly, as if she's wounded him. "Zoe," he says, voice low and warm, "I don't want to see anyone else. Karolina is no one. She was barely even in my life, and she's certainly not in it now. You're the one I want a future with." His thumb traces the inside of her wrist where the bracelet sits, lingering just long enough to feel like possession. "I'm not playing games. I'm here, with you, and I want this to be just us."

His words are perfect, practiced, like the kind of confession meant to be replayed in her mind on a loop. But Zoe caught the faint delay before he said *Karolina*. The way his pupils dilated just slightly when she said *exclusive*. His words don't match his body language, Zoe realizes as her stomach tightens. She feels like she may be sick.

This isn't the start of a love story, at least, not anymore. Something colder has taken root deep inside of Zoe. Max is no longer just a man she's casually dating; he's the key to something bigger, something darker. And she won't walk away. Not until she has the answers she's looking for.

CHAPTER NINE

Sketching

The police had not informed anyone initially about the missing woman, neither the press nor the public. The woman's name and even the location of her disappearance had been withheld. But Karolina had said the headline out loud weeks ago, during her first meeting with the detectives:

WOMAN DISAPPEARS IN BIG SUR

The words came to her like a powerful current, a flash before her eyes. A headline that hadn't existed until now. When she saw the headline in actual print, it stopped her cold.

She knew this moment was coming. She knew it back then, the second she had said the words aloud. But seeing it confirmed, now etched in ink on paper, validated by the outside world, shook her to the core. It made her question what else she might know, and what kind of responsibility that carried.

Her ability scares her and at times feels like a burden. But recent events have made one thing clear, she can no longer ignore it. She doesn't need to ask why the detectives called. Karolina already knows.

The missing woman is real. And now, they need her.

The police station is cold, and the smell of urine is poorly masked by Lysol still hanging in the air. Karolina swallows, trying not to breathe too deeply. A sweetness coats her tongue, and a metallic taste fills her mouth. She can hear metal clanging, doors slamming shut, footsteps quickening, keys jangling. She sits up taller in the metal chair. The footsteps get louder, and the door opens.

Detective Alvarez steps inside, his kind eyes softening as they meet hers. "Thanks for coming in again," he says with a faint smile.

Karolina nods, her voice steady but low. "I saw the headline. I had a feeling that's why you called."

Detective Grey walks into the room, exchanges a glance with Alvarez, then looks at Karolina, impressed. "It's the exact words you gave us before the story ever broke. How did you know about the case?"

Karolina's spine stiffens. "The headline just came to me, in my mind. But I only saw the words. I didn't know who or what it was connected to."

Grey nods, slowly this time. His voice lowers. "I didn't believe you back then, about the flash. About seeing the headline in your mind. I thought it was just a wild coincidence. But then you were also right about the photographer from the Speckled Boar."

Karolina says nothing.

He exhales, as if letting go of something he's been holding onto. "I was wrong."

Alvarez also gives her a small nod of confirmation. "That's why we asked you back. The case just broke to the public, and we think you can help us find her."

Karolina hesitates; she feels a weight pressing at her chest, not just from them but from deep within. "Is the photographer involved?" She asks.

"He's not talking, but he was in our custody when she went missing, so he couldn't have any direct involvement in her disappearance." Grey furrows his eyebrows.

Karolina feels the familiar swell of uncertainty rising in her throat. But this time, it's met by something else. Not doubt or fear, but something steadier. She had seen the headline before the world had. And now the world was catching up to her.

She draws a breath, and as she sinks back into the chair, a flicker of an image rises behind her eyes. Not the woman's face, but the sensation of being watched, distantly and deliberately. She can't picture it fully just yet.

Grey and Alvarez exchange a look, one that confirms they know more than they're saying. Karolina senses there's something about this case they haven't revealed. Something bizarre. Her pulse ticks upward, curiosity edging her on.

"I'm willing to help," she says quietly. "Tell me everything you can."

"The less you know, the more you can help us." Grey walks toward her and Karolina looks at him, eyes wide. "Let me explain," he says as he sits across from her.

Karolina raises an eyebrow, skeptical. "How exactly would this work if I don't know anything about the case?"

"We will train you," the other detective, Detective Alvarez, cuts in confidently, like they've done this before. "Detectives rely on hunches, and psychics use their intuition. Hunches, gut instincts, whatever you want to call it, we all depend on it. And you have a more finely tuned intuition than anyone we've encountered. We believe you can help us find the missing woman."

Since their first encounter, Detective Alvarez saw the potential of working with her on cold cases. He was more open to parapsychology than his partner, and Karolina's ability to sense things, though unexplainable, was undeniable. She could potentially help them find missing people, children, murderers, abductors.

"But I'm not psychic," Karolina says. She always flinched at that word. *Psychic.* It sounded theatrical and fraudulent. As if it belonged to a late-night hotline, neon signs, and crystal balls, and not at all to what she experienced. Her impressions were raw, visceral, and inescapably real. Her knowing came like a hum in her bones, a sudden tightness in her chest, a flash behind her eyes. It wasn't something she summoned. It summoned her.

Alvarez isn't giving up. "Well, in some cases, complicated ones that require out-of-the-box thinking, police turn to intuitives. In New Jersey, a psychic, sorry, an intuitive, has helped solve over 4,000 investigations.

We've spoken with law enforcement officers there about the protocol. It's surprisingly simple."

The label intuitive, a rebrand of psychic, made her wary. She didn't want to be dismissed or, worse, believed too much. But she was curious. She looked up with wide eyes, silently willing them to continue.

"To produce useful information, some intuitives need a photo or article. The New Jersey psychic only uses a birthdate and the date and place last seen. But we..." Alvarez hesitates.

Detective Grey jumps in. "We're keeping details tight. The best way to brief you is not to brief you." He lowers his eyes toward his hands.

Karolina's jaw drops. "I'm not sure I can help," she admits. "This isn't something I can just summon. It doesn't work that way."

"Trust us, the less you know, the more you can tell us," Detective Grey says, sliding a blank notepad in front of her. "In these sessions, it's essential to prevent frontloading. An excess of information wouldn't let your subconscious work freely and independently, and your thinking, rational mind would begin to take over, leading us down the wrong path. If we give you the woman's name or what she does for a career, then the analytical part of your brain, the left side, would create an inaccurate story based on preconceived notions you've picked up throughout your life. For these psychic sessions, it's crucial we only provide limited information to help you get to the truth." He places a pencil beside the pad. Karolina doesn't reach for it.

She crosses her arms, suddenly cold. Her chest tightens. What if she can't access anything? What if she gives them nothing? Or worse, what if she's wrong?

Then again, they seem so sure of her.

"This is a protocol used in remote viewing," Grey continues casually as if describing the weather. "It was developed during the Cold War. Intelligence agencies, the CIA, and the KGB dabbled in it. The idea was to locate people, places, or objects from a distance, using only mental perception. No technology, just trained intuition."

Detective Alvarez offers a pleasant, practiced smile, sidestepping the word. "We like to use the term 'intuitive intelligence.'"

Detective Grey leans in. "The protocols work sometimes. The research has never been fully shut down, and in certain law enforcement circles, they've been quietly adapting intuitive intelligence for civilian use."

Karolina doesn't respond. She just stares at the blank page in front of her. She remembers reading about remote viewing once in a book she pulled from a shelf on a whim, thinking it would be absurd. Sketches. Sensory impressions. Latitude and longitude whispered into dark rooms. At the time, it felt like science fiction. Like playacting for spies who'd run out of real-life options. Now, they were handing her the pencil.

A chill passes over her. This isn't theoretical anymore. Her mind is miles away. She is thinking of her grandmother and the way she used to braid Karolina's hair and say, *"Some things you keep quiet. Some things you carry alone."* Except for her abuela, Karolina's gift had always been a secret, one she often even kept from herself. It was something sacred, unspoken, and even feared. It was never meant for police reports or courtroom evidence.

And what would Max think? Would he laugh? Would he try to explain it away with one of his theories about brain chemistry and pattern recognition? Or worse, would he become fascinated by it? Would he try to turn it into something linear and useful? Karolina clenches her fingers together in her lap. Would she even tell him?

There's a part of her that feels like she's trespassing or betraying some hidden promise she made to herself as a child. If she did this, if she let anyone in to use her ability, she would no longer be able to claim it as her own. Would it become tampered?

She feels the pencil in her hand. The paper is smooth beneath her fingertips. She could walk out now. Say no. Blame jet lag. Pretend none of this happened. But something stops her. The woman. The disappearance. The ache in her ribs that hasn't left since she first read about the case. The headline came to her for a reason.

She takes a breath. "I'll try," she says. But what she's really thinking is: *If I open this door, I'm not sure I'll be able to close it again.* "How will you train me?" she asks carefully.

"Simple," Alvarez says, sliding a second sheet of paper toward her. "By drawing."

She tilts her head. "Drawing?"

"Ideograms," Alvarez explains. "Fast, instinctive marks. It's not art. You'll be drawing symbols repeatedly. The action of drawing bores your analytical mind until your subconscious kicks in."

"So, wait, symbols that stand for something bigger?" She pauses. The glint of Max's pendant appears in her mind, hitting her sharply behind her eye.

"Exactly. We'll say a word, a coordinate, or even just an intention. You close your eyes; don't try to understand, and don't think too much. You'll just let your hand move. That's the whole trick, try not to think or judge what you're doing, and definitely don't analyze."

Karolina hesitates. The pencil feels cool and unfamiliar in her fingers. The pad stares up at her like a dare. Her breath slows. The detectives tap the paper in front of her again. She tells herself she can stop at any time. But something inside her stirs, the same pull she gets right before the knowing starts.

"Ready?"

Karolina nods, though her throat feels tight. She closes her eyes. Detective Grey's voice drops to a hush. "35.2674° North, 120.6747° West." A pause. Then, her hand begins to move in slow, drifting strokes across the paper, like her fingers are responding to something just beyond reach. The room quiets. Even the faint hum of the overhead lights seems to recede. For a moment, there's stillness. Then, a flicker of something colder, foreign.

"You can open your eyes," Grey says softly. "Tell us what you see."

Karolina blinks at the page. It's filled with squiggly lines, curves, and jagged peaks. Shapes that seem to suggest more than they show.

"Water?" she asks. "It looks like I drew waves. There's a body of water, an ocean, maybe. And then that could be a mountain." She points to a jagged line ascending over a cascade of squiggly ones and a cliff.

Grey and Alvarez glance at each other. Grey nods. "That's good. Let's move to the next phase."

She glances at Grey. "There's another phase?"

"We call it sensory immersion," he says. "You're not just looking anymore; you're stepping into it."

"You mean like... imagining myself there?"

"Not exactly," Alvarez says. "More like letting the environment come to you. Through your five senses: sight, sound, smell, even taste or temperature. You stay quiet. We'll prompt you, and you just say what comes to you, even if it makes no sense."

Karolina needs clarity. "You'd like me to feel a place in my mind?"

Grey nods. "That's the idea. Your body might remember something your conscious mind doesn't. And your senses don't lie."

She takes a breath, then closes her eyes again. "Return to the location you drew," Grey says. "Don't try to control it. Just let the impressions come."

There's silence. Then, it hits her. "I feel wind," she whispers. "Salt. My hair's moving. It's cold." She pauses, allowing herself to take in more. "There's something else," she murmurs.

"What is it?"

Her nose twitches. She grimaces. "There's a smell. At first, I thought it was just here in the room; it's so strong. Lysol, maybe?" She opens her eyes for half a second, glancing at the sanitized interrogation room. "But now I'm not sure." Her eyes flutter closed again. "It's sharp; it's not fire or smoke. It's something chemical. I can feel it burning my eyes."

"Keep going," Alvarez gently pushes her to continue.

She inhales again, instinctively trying to separate memory from sensation. She starts coughing.

"It's like something was scrubbed or covered up. But the cover isn't enough. There's something underneath it, it feels faint, wrong." Her stomach turns, and she suddenly feels nauseous. Her hand goes still. The pencil drops to the table.

Detective Grey doesn't move. "You're doing fine."

But Karolina isn't so sure. Because whatever that smell is, whether in the room or in her mind, it's still in her lungs. And it doesn't feel like it's going away.

She coughs and closes her eyes again, trying to erase the smell from her mind. Then, an image appears before her: a woman with long reddish-blonde hair whipped by the wind, her pale, freckled skin glowing against a wash of gray sky. She stands near the edge of a jagged cliff, the Pacific crashing far below. She's wearing a green linen shirt, loose-fitting, caught in the gusts, and narrow black jeans tucked into boots. Her posture is poised, her shoulders pulled back, and her chin lifted toward the horizon as if daring the sea to reach her. Karolina moves closer in the vision. Her heartbeat quickens. The woman's face turns, her eyes vivid, deep brown, and a knowing smile plays at the corner of her lips.

Then, Karolina feels it. A rush of blood floods her chest. It isn't fear; it's exhilaration. A wild, electric surge that climbs her spine and pulls her forward. The hairs on her arms lift. Her legs sway slightly as if she, too, is standing at the edge, staring into the wind.

She clutches the table for balance. The pull, the thrill—it's electric. Then a whisper saying: *what if you just… stepped?* Karolina blinks hard. The woman's image sharpens. Her presence is intoxicating. She seems brave and bold, but something in her eyes wavers, something masked by the smile.

Karolina grabs the pencil and begins to draw fast and intuitively. She stops, opens her eyes, and hands the sketch over, her fingers trembling.

The detectives exchange a look, and this time their expressions sober. They know exactly who it is.

"Let's call in the profile artist," Grey stands. They sit her with the artist. He refines the drawing, asking Karolina to describe the woman she sees in her mind. The artist works on the sketch and shares it with Karolina. She nods at the final version. A familiar face stares back.

The detectives quickly take the sketch and place it in a manila folder. They both stand.

"Thank you, Karolina. This is fantastic."

"Wait, who is she?"

The detectives look at one another. Detective Alvarez begins, but Detective Grey cuts in. "It's a high-profile case. We may release her name later after we speak with the family."

"You can't tell me her name now?" Karolina is anxious and irritated.

"Sorry. We can't." Detective Grey opens the door.

"Is there anything you *can* tell me?"

Silence hangs in the room.

"Only if it stays confidential." Grey shuts the door. Karolina nods. "There is no suspect and no body so far. She was last seen near a cliff. There was no suicide note. We've found nothing conclusive. Which is why we called you in."

Karolina watches him closely. "And the coordinates you gave me? Where are they?"

Detective Grey looks back to Detective Alvarez, who finally answers.

"The Salenan Institute in Big Sur."

The name lodges in her chest. Karolina's heard it before. And it wasn't from the news. She's been there, with Max.

CHAPTER TEN

The Salenan Institute

The car veers right off Highway 1, the tires crunching onto a narrow road flanked by redwoods and mist. The Salenan Institute comes into view slowly, at first just slivers of wood and glass glimpsed through the trees, then fully emerging like a mirage built into the cliffside. A sprawling wooden structure with clean Scandinavian lines sits at its center, surrounded by smaller cottages clinging precariously to the edge of the bluff, like they might slip off into the Pacific at the first strong wind. Zoe's stomach clenches before she even knows why.

The Institute is a refuge for artists, philosophers, and academics seeking the next edge of human consciousness. Now it feels like a relic trying to remake itself as a wellness sanctuary for tech billionaires and ex-founders suffering from a different kind of spiritual crisis. Salenan dangles two hundred feet above the ocean on thirty acres of California coastline in Big Sur, hugging Highway 1, perfectly perched and waiting to be exposed. This is the last place the missing woman is seen, standing alone on a cliff, facing the sea.

Zoe's editor at *The Daily Quest* had warned her how difficult a missing person story is to cover; they are rarely straightforward. They warp time. Investigative journalists, like detectives, can become obsessive and lose themselves in the search for someone else, becoming mirror images of the person they're chasing. Especially when the trail goes cold.

"She could be dead, Zoe," her editor had said. "Or she could just not want to be found."

The woman's name still hasn't been released. Law enforcement won't confirm whether they even know it. But Zoe has a hunch, an instinct she can't explain, that if she retraces the missing woman's steps, she will find what she's looking for.

She steps out of the car, gravel shifting beneath her boots. Her suitcase bumps against her side as she approaches the entrance. Two men stand on either side of a pair of enormous oak doors, dressed identically in khaki pants and pale blue polos. One of the men gestures for her to enter as he opens the door. He smiles broadly and bows a little, still holding the door; his skin is so smooth it looks as if it is made of wax.

"Welcome back to Salenan, Madam," he says in a slow, affected drawl.

Zoe hesitates. *Back?*

As she stares up at the property, Max's words flood back to her: *Are you going to go missing on me now too?* She had brushed it off at the time, but now the words clang around in her head like a gong. Why "too"? Did he know more than he was letting on? Or was it just another one of his glib, offhand remarks, the kind that always left her off-balance? A chill runs down her spine. Max said it so casually, like it had happened before. She smiles politely at the valet and walks past him without correcting the mistake.

Inside, a manufactured scent of honeysuckle and vanilla, cut with salt, fills the air, mimicking an ocean breeze so precisely that it makes her skin itch. She scans the space. In front of her are two winding staircases, curved upward from either side of the foyer, white marble stairs lined in sea-glass green carpet. They are perfectly symmetrical. She climbs the right staircase, pulled forward by something she can't name.

"Namaste, nice to see you again." The man behind the check-in counter's eyes widen as Zoe approaches. He looks like someone who lives off the grid most of the year with his linen pants, mandala tank top, sun-darkened skin, and a crystal swinging gently from one ear. His hair is tied back in a messy topknot, strands bleached out at the ends like he has just returned from a week at Burning Man.

"First time, actually," Zoe says.

He blinks, clearly thrown. "Oh, sorry, you just look... familiar."

It's not the first time. Her years in TV news left a strange residue. People sometimes recognize her without knowing why. A segment they half-watched, a voice they remember from disaster coverage. But this feels different. His eyes don't just register familiarity; they register something that looks closer to fear. His face goes ashen.

Zoe opens her purse, reaching for her wallet, but the beaded bracelet Max gave her snags on the zipper. Something jolts in her. Blood drains from her head. A memory flashes, sudden and sharp: the cliff in Big Sur, wind slicing through her jacket, Max's voice still echoing, but there's no sign of him. Just his absence. Her knees weaken, and she grabs the desk to steady herself.

The man stiffens. "Apologies again. You just remind me of one of our recent guests." His voice speeds up, and his eyes dart. "Checking in, then?"

Zoe studies him. Either he has made a simple mistake, or he is lying—and maybe he thinks she is, too.

"Yes, checking in." Zoe pulls out her wallet and glances around the lobby in search of a mirror. There isn't one. Maybe they have removed all mirrors, a gesture Zoe imagines is meant to sever guests from external validation, from the outside world, from their outer identity, which she is apparently here to shed. *At Salenan, you'll feel so seen you won't ever need to look at yourself again.* Zoe invents the tagline in her head and almost laughs.

"Name on the reservation?" the concierge asks, cutting through her musings. His voice is hushed as if he's handling something sacred.

"Zoe Harrison."

He nods thoughtfully. "We like to use aliases here. It helps our guests shed their outer identity. Could you choose a different name for your stay?"

Zoe pauses, her mind goes empty for a moment too long, as if the part of her responsible for making decisions has stepped aside. Then, a name surfaces, fully formed and uninvited.

"Alessandra," she says.

The concierge freezes, just for a second, but she catches it: a twitch in his jaw, the faintest recoil before he recovers.

"Beautiful choice," he says. "Welcome, Alessandra."

But his words don't match his body. His voice is smooth, yet his body is stiff, betrayed by the tremor in his fingers as he reaches beneath the counter. The concierge's hands shake as he fishes for the key to her cottage. His face flushes red, and he begins to shuffle papers, too many, it seems, and too quickly. One slips free and flutters to the floor.

"I've got it," Zoe says, automatically crouching.

"No...," he says sharply, too late.

She picks up the paper, a standard sheet of printer paper, edges curled slightly from handling. A woman with long, straight blonde hair and wide, searching eyes stares back at her—two versions of the same face, one hand-drawn, the other computer-generated. It is a missing person flyer.

The concierge swallows hard, words tumbling out. "I'm sorry, I'm supposed to put these around the hotel, the police asked, but management doesn't... they don't want to alarm guests. Can I please..." He reaches for the flyer, but Zoe doesn't let go. Her fingers stay clenched around it as her eyes scan the rest of the page. Something inside her begins to twist.

```
For Immediate Release
Missing Persons Alert

Last seen on a cliff in Big Sur, California, at
the Salenan Institute.

Identifies as Female, Age 37, Hazel/Brown eyes,
5'3", 120 lbs., long reddish-blonde hair.

If you have any information, please call 650-555-
5555
```

Zoe stares at the flyer. The photo composite is uncanny. She leans in, eyes narrowing. The woman's features strike a chord: wide, doe-like eyes and bold natural eyebrows. Her eyes dart back and forth between the two versions of the woman on the poster. One image is a loose sketch, raw and vulnerable: there's an intensity and urgency behind its rough outlines. The other is a digital rendering, oddly polished, glossy, and lifeless, like a video game avatar. It's unsettling in its precision.

A tingle hums at the base of Zoe's skull as she pulls the flyer closer. Plenty of women could match this description—five-three, fair skin, hazel eyes, long reddish-blonde hair—but this woman looks just like her. Too much like her. The same heart-shaped face. The same russet undertone in the hair. Even the faint shadow beneath one eye hinting at a tiredness, or maybe a knowing.

A strange dissociation opens inside of Zoe, as if she's looking at a version of herself rendered from someone else's memory. This isn't just resemblance; it feels intentional, like a warning. She pinches her forearm. The sting grounds her, but her thoughts spin. *Max knows this woman.* The thought arrives uninvited. He's never mentioned anyone like this, but Zoe feels it in her chest, that dense, pressurized knowing. The woman's features are not just similar; they're familiar. She imagines it's her face, her energy staring back at her from the poster, mimicked by a computer rendering. This can't be real, but could it be possible?

Zoe rereads the alert, focusing on the last line: *If you have information, please call 650-555-5555.* She fishes into her purse, her hands trembling slightly as she pulls out her notebook. She flips to the number her editor gave her for the police contact, scanning it. It doesn't match. Not even close.

She glances at the flyer again. A different number. A different search? A different handler? Her pulse quickens. There's someone else looking for this woman. Or hiding her. Then, she notices something else: there is still no name for the missing woman. Not even an alias. Why would the police continue to withhold that?

Zoe's journalist brain kicks into overdrive. A few possibilities take shape. The first: maybe the police still don't know her name. Unlikely, because someone must have reported her missing. They would have provided an ID. Maybe the woman is someone well-known, a public figure, and the authorities are trying to avoid a media circus. That's possible.

Or perhaps they're protecting her privacy: a suicide, maybe or a nervous breakdown. The Salenan Institute draws the kind of guests who might want to disappear quietly. Or maybe, Zoe swallows, someone with powerful ties doesn't want the woman to be found. That thought lodges in her mind. Then, another thought creeps in, less plausible but harder to shake. What if this is more than just a missing person's case?

"I can understand why management doesn't want to alarm people." Zoe holds the paper out in front of the concierge. "May I?" She gestures toward her bag.

He nods a little too quickly. She folds the flyer and tucks it into her purse, then meets his gaze again, steady this time.

"Was she a guest?"

"I really can't say, Madam, not until I hear back from..." His walkie-talkie crackles. Someone calls his name. He glances away from her, relieved. Zoe doesn't press. She understands the hotel has its rules. Discretion is the currency here. Still, the silence around a missing woman feels curated. Intentional. *Especially* if she had been a guest here.

The concierge slides a document across the desk. It's a waiver. She skims it.

"No photos or videos during your stay," he says, tapping the clause. "Especially near the hot springs." His tone shifts: it's rehearsed, but with a trace of warning. "Nudity is welcome. Photos are not."

Zoe raises an eyebrow, then keeps reading. The next paragraph is even stranger. The hotel assumes no responsibility for guest safety around the hot springs, the cliff walks, or the beaches.

"The beaches are restricted?" Zoe asks.

"Yes, unfortunately, the ones the public isn't allowed on are the most beautiful."

"Why wouldn't they be allowed?"

He gestures toward the cliffside. "Boulders. They can fall at any time. And the tide, it comes in fast. If people don't get out in time, then they're toast." As if on cue, waves crash violently in the distance. It's not a gentle rhythm but more like a threat. Zoe wonders if the missing woman found her fate on one of the forbidden beaches. She signs the waiver, and the concierge asks if she'd like a tour of the grounds before heading to her room. Zoe hesitates; she's exhausted, but she's also here on assignment.

"I'll take the tour." A bellhop takes her luggage and disappears silently down a corridor.

"The Institute was founded in 1965 by MIT graduates," the concierge explains, leading her down a long, carpeted hallway. "They were interested in exploring human potential through psychology, spirituality, and now, of course, through technology."

Zoe stops mid-step. "But I thought the Institute believes in detoxing from technology?"

He snaps his head back, facing her. She sees a flash of something in his eyes.

"Not that kind of technology," he says, waving his hand as if swatting away 5G electromagnetic rays. "We focus on human transformation technology."

Zoe scrunches her face; the phrase doesn't compute. Reading her confusion, he continues, "We believe in synthesizing ancient wisdom and spirituality with emerging technology, you know, neurofeedback, guided self-optimization, that sort of stuff, to change humanity for the better."

"Who's we?" Zoe's throat tightens. She doesn't know why.

"You certainly ask a lot of questions." He smirks.

"Well, I am...," Zoe starts to say "journalist," then thinks better of it, "...here to learn."

He nods, satisfied, and leads her into a large dining hall made of redwood beams. The space is cavernous, lined with long wooden tables that give it the feel of a cafeteria or a mess hall.

"Guests dine together here every night," he says, walking toward the open industrial kitchen. A chef glances up and waves, his apron smudged with something dark. "The food's cooked fresh from our organic garden on the property," the concierge continues, gesturing to a small table at the entrance. "And here's our famous hand-baked sourdough rye bread. The chef bakes it nightly, and by morning, it's risen. The salt and moisture from the sea air create the perfect fermentation; it's like nothing you've had before."

Zoe steps closer. The loaf looks dense and a bit cracked. There's a faint sour smell, stronger than expected. He lifts a small jar of jam.

"I recommend it with our homemade blood orange jam," he says, swatting at a few fruit flies circling the rim. "Shall we go outside?" He doesn't wait for her answer.

Zoe follows him onto a massive, manicured lawn that stretches to the cliff's edge. The drop beyond is abrupt and dizzying, two hundred feet straight down into the crystal blue ocean. There are no warning signs or railings, just a low wooden fence barely three feet high. She pauses. The grass is damp beneath her shoes. She can see how someone in the wrong state of mind could easily slip. Or jump. The ocean crashes below. The sound is thunderous, rhythmic, and violent. She feels it reverberate up through her legs and into her spine, and her whole body pulses with it.

"For guests who enjoy chess," the concierge says, motioning toward a human-sized chessboard in the center of the lawn. The pieces are nearly as tall as Zoe. "Do you play?"

She shakes her head, glancing back at the towering black queen behind him. They pass fire pits and then curve toward several porcelain tubs clustered in a stone alcove. A sharp, eggy stench rises, the smell of sulfur.

"And these are our hot tubs," he says. "They're fed by underground springs." The water bubbles gently, unlike the rage of the ocean below. "Don't let the smell throw you," he adds. "The springs are magical. The Cold War ended right here in these tubs."

Zoe lets out a dry laugh, and then it hits her. Max. On the road to Big Sur, the top down, his sunglasses reflecting sea light. *I bet you didn't know astronauts ended the Cold War,* he'd said with that dry half-smile of his. She'd laughed then and rolled her eyes. She'd thought he was kidding. A weird joke. Or one of his cryptic metaphors. But standing here now, looking out at the tubs, the cliffs, and the looming black chessboard pieces, she's realizing he knows more than he's said.

The concierge spins suddenly on his heels and opens his arms wide as if to present the entire coast. "And that's the tour. You'll find me in the lobby if you have questions. Your cottage is this way." He points to a small cottage just ten feet from the cliff's edge, perched across from the massive chessboard. Zoe follows slowly, the sharp scent of sulfur thick in the air. It clings to her skin and follows her like breath on her neck. Salenan will be her home for the next few weeks. She better get used to it.

The concierge runs up to her, "Wait, I almost forgot!" He hands her a key to the cottage. Zoe notices it has a tiny flashlight on it. "Guests spend their days and nights shifting between sessions, hot springs, and the large dining hall. It can get very dark out here, so this is helpful when you want to walk around." Zoe thanks him and heads toward her cottage.

Except something feels immediately off.

She rounds a hedge-lined path and finds Cottage 7; the number on the key she was given is marked clearly on the side of a white wooden bungalow with dark green trim. Her luggage is already waiting by the door. She's halfway up the steps when something catches her eye.

Another Cottage 7.

It's across the lawn and identical in shape and color. It even has the same number on the side. She walks slowly across the grass, as if drawn by a magnet. The door is shut, and there are no lights on. She circles it, noticing that this one has no luggage waiting. She feels an empty silence.

Back at her assigned cottage, Zoe pauses again. The number 7 is painted slightly off-center, as if done quickly. She notices a faint outline beneath it, like another number had been painted there and then scrubbed out. Unsettled, she unlocks the door, half-expecting something or someone to be waiting for her inside.

Inside, there is nothing, just the hum of wind. Long white curtains billow gently, and the ocean breeze swirls in the room from a window left open. Everything appears normal, almost too normal. But a whisper of unease tingles in the back of her skull. Zoe slides the window shut; the latch clicks into place, echoing too loudly in the otherwise quiet cottage. The air is thick with salt and redwood, but beneath it, something metallic lingers, like the scent of rusted wires or blood just beginning to dry. She pulls her laptop from her bag, setting it on the desk, the screen casting a blue glow onto her face in the dimming light. This is her favorite part of a story: the beginning, when everything is unknown. When the lines between possibility and paranoia hadn't yet been drawn. When her imagination hadn't yet taken her somewhere she shouldn't go.

There's a missing woman. No name. Few details. No narrative to twist into something tidy; there's just an absence. And absence, Zoe knows, has its own gravitational pull. She opens a blank document, the cursor blinking, expectant. Zoe stares at it, her mind surprisingly still. The Salenan Institute is the last place the woman was seen; that is all Zoe has. And yet, her body already feels pulled toward something, an undertow of implication. Something isn't right here, not just in the disappearance, but in the way this place is built and its history. It feels too curated, too framed.

She has done stories like this before, not a missing person's case, but ones that unravel slowly, luring reporters into the lives of strangers until they are no longer strangers at all. Her editor's warning rings again: stories like this will try to eat you alive. But Zoe believes in her instincts. Her imagination is part of her process, even if it sometimes flirts too closely with delusion. She has learned to walk that line. She closes her eyes, and an image of herself flashes before her. She is behind a newsroom anchor desk, frozen and unable to speak, her voice failing on live television. Her throat tightens at the memory; that shame still lives in her body. But this time, the story will be different.

Zoe focuses back on the task at hand. An average weekend stay at Salenan costs $3,000 a night, more than most can afford. What was the missing woman doing here, and did she pay for the stay herself? Was she craving solitude, and would she find it at Salenan? Or was she here on business? She reaches for the Salenan pamphlet tucked in her bag. The cover is soft, almost fabric-like, printed with a looping serif font: *An alternative educational center devoted to the exploration of human potential through technology.*

Zoe has seen the trick before, most often dubbed under the umbrella of wellness, a spiritual language coopted by tech, used to blur the lines between enlightenment and control. The Institute's mission, she muses, can just as easily read: *A center for exploiting people looking to find themselves.* The irony stings: the very people promising enlightenment and freedom from the ego are the ones most obsessed with scaling their own names into lifetimes of legacy. She rereads the tagline, and her lips curl at the phrase. *Human potential*, the oldest and vaguest promise in the book. Ryan Sowell immediately comes to mind. And then, someone else: Max. And his film project, *Architects of the Mind*. What seems like a vanity project is beginning to feel more like a cover. The documentary, the subjects he insists on keeping secret, his pendant reading *We observe. We imitate. We conquer.* Goosebumps cover her body as the thought strikes her: *Could the missing woman be one of the subjects of Max's documentary?*

She lets the pamphlet fall from her hands and walks to the window, gazing out over the cliff glowing blue in the dying light. And that's when she sees her, a woman sitting in the grass, legs crossed, spine impossibly straight. Her long brown hair is loose and wild in the breeze. Her face is turned toward Zoe's cottage. Her eyes are closed, as if waiting for something. The sight is oddly peaceful.

Then, a deep and impatient voice cuts across the air. "Alessandra, enough already. It's time to leave." It's a man's voice, coming from the porch of Zoe's cottage; it is low and controlled but impatient.

Zoe's heart jumps into her throat. She heads to the door but doesn't open it. Instead, she calls out, "I'm sorry, I think you have the wrong room." Silence. She presses her eye to the peephole. Her vision blurs at the edges and darkness pools in the periphery. She blinks it away and tries again. Nothing. No one is there. She opens the door slowly, scanning the porch, the path, and the grass. The woman who was sitting in the grass is gone. She doesn't see a man. There are no retreating footsteps, no rustle of bushes, just the wind hissing in the trees and the low, rhythmic smash of waves on the rocks below.

She steps outside and sees it on the porch, caught in a swirl of dust and leaves: a tarot card, face up. Three women, arms intertwined, raise golden chalices to the sky. One of them is turned slightly away. Her chest tightens.

The Three of Cups.

Zoe picks it up, a surge of electricity shooting up her back, the card hums in her hand. She turns the card over and reads the caption on the back: "*This card shows the magnetism between women. Beauty, growth, celebration. But beware: the one who turns away may be the one who knows too much.*"

She walks back to her cottage, shutting the door behind her and locking it. She places the card on the nightstand and lies down on the bed, still fully dressed. A strange energy courses through her body: she's unsure why the card was placed on her porch, but it's clear it carries a message. Someone at Salenan has mistaken Zoe for someone else, someone who knows too much.

CHAPTER ELEVEN

Lillian

Lillian pulls her chestnut hair into a loose bun, fingers quick and practiced. Stray strands slip free around her temples as she lowers herself onto a yoga mat placed on the grass, crossing her legs, the earth cool beneath her. In front of her, she lines up three candles, their wicks tilting in the ocean breeze. She lights a stick of palo santo, the flame catching with a tiny hiss, and waves it in slow arcs before and behind her. The scent is sweet, earthy, faintly medicinal. It fills her lungs, unclenching something tight in her chest.

She rests her hands, small and fine-boned, palms facing the sky. Before closing her eyes, she glances down at the wooden bracelet dangling loosely from her wrist, warm from the sun, its weight a familiar comfort. Somewhere behind the quiet ritual, in the cracks between breath and thought, the rest of it presses in. The reason she has come.

Officially, she is here to give a talk on the devastating impact artificial intelligence will have on climate change, the hidden consequences no one wants to face. Unofficially, she is here because she has misplaced a part of herself somewhere between protests, red carpets, and one too many nights biting her tongue for a man who prefers her softer, quieter.

She belongs to a group called Concerned Citizens for Climate Change Rebellion, which works with scientists and technologists to study the effects of climate change on natural and managed ecosystems. Her role is to be a spokesperson to help drive awareness and progress for the climate movement across the globe. After crashing a red-carpet event in Cannes, in the south of France, the group became delegalized and labeled "eco-terrorists" by the French government. That doesn't stop or scare Lillian, she's made it her mission to bring her message to the States. She knows that to affect any change, she will need to follow the money and get in front of tech billionaires. Which is why she finds herself here, at Salenan.

Her boyfriend didn't like it; of course he didn't. He worried her activism put her in danger. He never said it outright; he would joke instead, raising his eyebrows whenever she mentioned Big Sur or Salenan, calling it a haven for washed-up idealists. So, she didn't tell him she was going to Salenan; instead, she told him she was headed to Santa Barbara for a girls' weekend with some friends. It felt safer that way, and easier.

Their relationship had become rocky. He had accused her of having anger issues, and he was right about her being angry, but that wasn't the issue. Indeed, her anger was justified. He was hot and cold and absent a lot—physically, as he traveled for long stretches for work, but also emotionally. When he was at home with Lillian, he didn't seem present. He was distracted, staying up at night and sleeping most of the day. It felt to her as if he was operating in two worlds. As a result, their relationship, a little over a year old at that time, was faltering. She became resentful of how he had quickly blamed her while making excuses for himself.

Some nights, when she wasn't able to sleep, she would catch him staring blankly at the ceiling as if searching for a crack to slip through. She wouldn't ask. She learned to pretend not to notice. Thanks to his steady drumbeat of accusations, Lillian started to believe the lies he had told her. If she changed some aspects of herself, she believed she could improve their relationship. If she could just soften here, polish there... if she could fix herself, she believed she could also fix him, mend them both. It was a beautiful idea, an addictive, intoxicating, and impossible notion.

With this hope in the forefront of her mind, Lillian was looking forward to exploring all this weekend had to offer at the Salenan Institute: a variety of courses designed to help individuals like her achieve their full potential, and Lillian felt eager to try all of them.

Now here, her days are reassuringly packed: a walk around the grounds, an hour-long meditation, a sound bath, a light lunch, a drum circle, journaling, hot baths, and a guided psychedelic experience. The mushroom tea comes highly recommended.

Sometimes, when the air shifts and the light dips, Lillian feels it, a brittleness beneath the beauty, a faintly metallic tang at the back of her throat. Salenan is stunning, yes, but it doesn't breathe the way wild places should. The grounds feel posed and curated. The place is too polished, a little too perfect. Lillian has seen it before, corporations wrapping exploitation in the language of healing, selling transformation as a product. The grounds are manicured like a showroom. Even the air smells scripted.

She brushes the thought away. She isn't here to fight another battle, in this moment. She is here to find her way back to herself. The palo santo burns low in her hand, a thin thread of smoke winding up into the wide, indifferent sky.

Lillian grew up in the mountains of France and always felt a deep connection to nature. Now, as a climatologist, she understands the power of place, the effect nature and our surroundings have on humanity.

She centers herself and closes her eyes to meditate. The smell of palo santo hits her tongue, activating a sensation, the taste of wood, sweet and scorched. Lillian has never eaten wood, although she knows some of her colleagues have done stranger things to feel closer to nature. Tasting smells, seeing sounds, these crossed senses are a gift she has had since childhood.

She remembers being four and seeing a blue square in a book and yelling out, "I taste blue!" Her mother laughed at first, squeezing her hand. "No, Lillian, you see blue."

But Lillian shook her head, stubborn even then. "No. I taste it."

As she grew older, her senses crossed more often, blending sight, taste, sound, and feeling. *Synesthesia*, one of the older women in her village called it. Her mother warned her not to share her ability with anyone. People wouldn't understand. They would look at her differently, dangerously.

So, Lillian learned to hide what she knew.

One of her legs goes numb. She readjusts her position on the mat, sitting taller, breathing deeper, letting her mind travel. The grass hums green beneath her, a low vibration climbing up through her spine.

She sees herself in Toulon, France, standing in line to meet Saint Amma, the Hugging Saint. Hundreds of people waiting for a touch that could heal. St. Amma was known across the world not just for her compassion but for her belief that women carried an untapped force capable of healing the world. A force rooted not in domination but in empathy, vulnerability, and love.

St. Amma traveled tirelessly, embracing millions. Each hug was a transmission of energy, an offer of dignity, forgiveness, unseen strength. She spoke often about the quiet power of the feminine and how true change, the kind that rewires the heart of a nation, begins not with conquest but with connection. In every embrace, St. Amma offered not just comfort but a reminder that strength could be soft, and love could be revolutionary.

Lillian wasn't there alone. The man she was dating had come with her, eager to impress her, though crowds and saints weren't usually his thing. This was her idea. They stood in the heat for over an hour.

When Lillian finally stepped forward, St. Amma's arms wrapped around her, and a wave of warmth and calm flooded her body. Her skin flushed hot; goosebumps raised along her arms. But it was more than comfort. It was something older. Something stronger.

As Amma pressed her close, Lillian felt a pulse of power move through her, a strength that came from stillness. A deep knowing stirred inside her, reassuring her that softness could be a force, that love could be a weapon in the right hands. She didn't have words for it then. She only knew her bones felt heavier afterward, as if some invisible armor had slipped over her shoulders without anyone noticing. As she pulled back from the beloved saint, she felt an overwhelming sense of recognition, a meeting of something deeper.

Then, it was his turn. He politely and cautiously walked closer to St. Amma, standing rigidly in front of her. St. Amma moved closer, wrapping her arms around his torso, her hands on the back of his shoulders. An odd position for a hug, different from the crisscross embrace Lillian received.

Lillian watched as the two seemed frozen in this embrace. It felt like a long time, much longer than eight seconds. St. Amma released her embrace of him, stepping back while he stood frozen, unable to move. Then, something entirely out of the ordinary happened. St. Amma lunged toward him and threw her arms around him again. The crowd gasped as they watched her hug him for a second time. Lillian's heart skipped a beat. She couldn't believe what she saw. This second hug lasted even longer than the first. Then, finally, St. Amma let go of him. She nodded and smiled at him, eyes crinkling at the corner.

When her boyfriend finally staggered away toward Lillian, tears were streaming down his face, his back was convulsing, and he was sobbing uncontrollably. She said nothing. Just took his hand as they walked the grounds together.

But something inside her had shifted, not a thought, not even a feeling, just a quiet weight settling into her bones. She had seen it then, the way Amma had: the hollow space inside him, vast and aching, but strangely untouched by the warmth he was given. It wasn't just that he was wounded. It was that something essential was missing, and no amount of love, whether Amma's or hers own, could ever quite fill it. But it wouldn't stop Lillian from trying.

Later, they found a small kiosk selling bracelets blessed by Amma, slender beads of wood strung together by hand, the kind of token meant to remind you of something larger than yourself. They each picked one, hers a lighter brown, his darker, laughing a little at the solemnity of it all. But she wore hers every day thereafter, the way some people wore armor or a promise they couldn't quite put into words. A tether bringing them together.

Months later, packing for Big Sur, Lillian couldn't find her bracelet. She confronted him, half-joking, half-serious. He grinned, mischievous.

Opening a box on the dresser, it was empty. "I don't know, my dear," he said, slipping his bracelet off his wrist. "Here, have mine. Promise you'll be careful with it." He dropped it into her palm, easy, thoughtless, as if the object itself meant nothing. She slid it over her own wrist without thinking. At the time, it had felt like a gift. She accepted it. Maybe she shouldn't have.

The smell of palo santo thickens. Her feet go numb again. Lillian readjusts her sit bones on the mat, rolling her ankles to bring blood back into her toes, trying to clear her mind, to get back to the missing piece of herself. She takes a long inhale. The scent deepens further, richer, almost metallic at the edges. The air around her tightens, pressing against her skin. The crashing ocean grows heavier, a low pulse hammering behind her ribs. Even the candle flames seem to hum, each one tasting faintly of copper at the back of her throat.

Her senses braid together, a living web of sound, color, taste, and scent. This is how the world speaks when she is still enough to hear it. She lifts her head, the sky tilting slightly sideways. Across the lawn, Cottage 7 stands silent against the dusk. But to Lillian's senses, it murmurs, a low, gray-violet vibration, thick with something she cannot name. She watches it for a long moment, her heart knocking steadily against her ribs, before forcing herself to look away.

Then, a sharp popping noise. Not just a sound, but also a flash of bitter orange on her tongue, the metallic taste of blood flooding her mouth. A crack of violet light seeps behind her closed eyes.

The bracelet had snapped.

Wooden beads scatter across the yoga mat, each clattering with a brittle, metallic sound only she seems to hear, tiny sharp bursts of blue and gray sparking against the dark. They roll across the grass, bouncing and disappearing, the air around her shuddering with faint green tremors she can taste.

CHAPTER TWELVE

Bloodlines

Karolina lets the phone ring on the other end a dozen times before hanging up. Max's voicemail kicks in, warm and performative, the same voice he uses when introducing himself to people he plans to disarm. She sets the phone down on the bathroom sink and lowers herself onto the toilet. Blood slides from her body in slow, thin ribbons.

The cramping has intensified; it's sharper, more final. Her doctor told her that if the bleeding subsided, she wouldn't need to go to the hospital. It's only two blocks away.

She glances around the loft, cavernous and cold, the walls industrial and raw. They've been living here for weeks now, in Max's downtown office, while his Venice Beach apartment is being renovated, though she's never seen or heard of any proof of progress. The loft feels like a bunker or a lab. She despises it.

Another cramp strikes, and she curls inward, wrapping her arms around her stomach. Her hands form fists, nails digging small crescents into her palm. Her toes curl into the tile as she folds into a fetal position; the porcelain of the toilet is cool against her thighs.

The pain passes, but the tumult in her mind doesn't. Max should've been home by now. He said he had a meeting at NASA, then a quick flight back from San Francisco. "Soon," he said. But with Max, soon is just another version of never.

Maybe it's better he's not here. She never knows which version of him she'll get: cold, remote, unreadable Max, or the soft-spoken, tender-eyed man who traces her collarbone while asking about her childhood. Dr. Jekyll or Mr. Hyde. The man who touches her like she's made of glass, or the one who disappears into himself.

Arthur's voice resurfaces uninvited: *He's good at hiding things, even himself.* Karolina shivers. That call was so strange, it had left her not only rattled, but frozen, unsure of what to do next.

Lately, she couldn't trust the shape of things, or herself. Her entire life, Karolina has felt what others feel, but with Max, she was left feeling nothing, just an emptiness.

The night she got pregnant; they had made love. Not sex. Something gentler, or so it seemed. But now, the memory feels flattened, edited, like she'd been watching herself from the outside. Like he'd been watching her, too.

When she realized she was pregnant, she tried to imagine the baby, its eyes, its mouth, the curl of its fingers. But her mind was now blank. Normally a vivid dreamer, her dreams had vanished overnight. She took it as a sign.

She almost told Max after they returned from England. But something inside her whispered: *wait.* Another voice said: *watch.*

The cramps settle. Slowly, she pulls on her underwear, lines it with a pad, and flushes the toilet without looking. She stares at the bathroom wall, her neck rigid, legs trembling and heavy, the blood draining back into her feet.

At the sink, she splashes cold water across her face and brushes her teeth. Her reflection stares back from the mirror, colorless. She pulls her long dark hair into a ponytail with shaking hands. Still no message from Max. Of course.

Max had wanted a baby more than she did. He said having children would make him and Karolina real. It would help ground them. But lately, Karolina wasn't sure she wanted to be tethered to him at all. And now, standing here, she feels a terrible, disloyal flutter of relief. Relief that she would not have to carry forward something that already felt empty inside her. Relief that whatever was missing in him wouldn't be passed quietly down into the hollow of their child.

In the beginning of their relationship, when they first met, she'd felt electric, almost superhuman. Everything seemed to vibrate around her: her skin, her thoughts, the air between them. She didn't need sleep. Her senses dialed up past human. The world looked rendered, almost artificial in its clarity. Max was the trigger, the drug, the lens. She thought it was love. But now she knows it wasn't, it was all a smoke screen, something he deviously designed.

The comedown began about two years into their relationship. Typical tasks drained her, and her thoughts dulled. She couldn't concentrate. She told herself it was hormones, then resolved it must be burnout. But deep down, she knew something had gone quiet inside her. She never blamed Max, which was ironic after all, since she'd given him credit for all her initial ecstasy. Instead, she took the blame for what she was feeling.

She picks up her phone and emerges from the bathroom. Her eyes land instantly on the lion's head. It rests atop the old dresser, mounted, massive, impossibly regal. A real lion. Only the head, no body. Its fur pale with age, its mane, once golden, is now dulled to the color of old wheat. Its mouth is slightly open; lips peeled back from yellowing teeth. Its tongue curls inward like a question mark. The glass eyes are the worst. They're a deep amber, ancient. And somehow, they look wet.

The lion doesn't just watch the room; it seems to sense it. Karolina has seen it in every light: at dusk, by candlelight, in the morning. No matter the hour, the lion, once alive, never looks the same. Its gaze shifts with her mood. Its expression changes when her back is turned.

Max brought it back from England. "My grandfather shot it in Kenya," he said. "Before the regulations. Part of a rite of passage." Then, with a strange light in his eye, he added, "There's a power in killing something so strong." She remembers the way he'd said it, so factually. As if conquest were inevitable because it ran in his blood.

Sometimes, at night, she thinks she sees the lion breathing. The way the shadows move across its ribbed nose. The twitch of imagined muscle near the eye. She tells herself it's just the light. But something deeper warns her otherwise.

There's something beautiful about it, not in a violent, savage way, but in its stillness. Its poise. As if, in death, the lion has become more vulnerable than it ever was in life. It's hard to tell what it is now. Predator? Prey? Maybe both.

She reaches out slowly, fingertips hovering just above its mane. And stops.

Max had once told her not to touch it. "It absorbs things," he said. "Not scent, something else." And she knew, without asking, what he meant.

She imagined the lion was like her, in a way, sensitive to energy, unable to block it out. Karolina had spent her whole life trying to not feel overwhelmed by other people's grief, rage, or desire. The lion had no shield. Just fur and bone and skin. She wasn't sure if touching it would destroy it or undo her entirely.

Her hand drifts back to her side. The lion's amber eyes meet hers. Not accusing, but patient. Like it's waiting for her to decide.

Her phone buzzes in her hand, and without looking at the caller ID, she answers. There's a pause. Then a voice. "Karolina?"

She goes still. It's Arthur's voice, except, wait. No, it's Max's cadence, his breath pattern. The line between the twins frays in her mind.

"Arthur?" she asks, barely audible.

Another pause. "Yes. It's me."

The voice is familiar, but softer than Max's. She stands frozen, with the phone pressed to her ear, the lion just behind her. Karolina opens her mouth to speak trusting she knows who is on the other end.

CHAPTER THIRTEEN

A Different Frequency

"A glass of Sauvignon Blanc, please." The bartender at Chateau Lamont fills the glass and hands it across the bar to Sasha. She moves through the crowd toward her friends, the glass trembling faintly in her hand.

Chateau Lamont sits atop a hill, a Gothic-style castle in the heart of Hollywood. The architect drew inspiration from a French château in the Loire Valley, with accents of Spanish style woven into the interior. The hotel is a maze of cavernous archways and semi-crumbling frescoes, with the faint scent of old wood and damp stone hanging in the air. Chateau Lamont had long since surrendered to time with cracked stone floors and faded murals peeling under the weight of candle smoke and dust.

Sasha looks at her friends, who are circled around a pool chatting. They had dragged her to the party. She hadn't wanted to come. Lately, the edges of the world had started to feel too sharp, too loud. A party in the Hollywood Hills felt almost cruel.

Ever since she heard about the missing woman in Big Sur, a strange heaviness had been growing inside her, something she couldn't explain, something that clung to her ribs and wouldn't let go. She found herself compulsively scouring the internet for updates as if somewhere in the endless scroll, a piece of the missing woman would surface and call her by name. It had become her silent ritual, private and obsessive.

Tonight, the noise of the party vibrates oddly against her skin. Her friends chatter about the latest scandal in American politics, their laughter pealing out in strange, clipped bursts. They sound distant and mechanical, like tape recordings that are playing just a little too fast.

Sasha is operating at a different frequency. Her limbs feel thick, submerged in invisible cement. Even lifting the wine glass to her lips is a force of will. Words form slowly in her mind, dissolving before they reach her tongue. She smiles when she's supposed to. She nods. But beneath the surface, she is sinking. Part of her doesn't mind.

A flash of white light bounces off her glass. She tilts her head back. Above her, the full moon hangs unnaturally bright, casting a cold, watchful glow over the crowd. Sasha wonders if the moon was full the night the woman vanished? The thought strikes her like a cold blade. She reaches for her phone to search for the date and moon again but stops. Not here. She can look later. She closes her eyes. The dream returns, pulling her under. She sees the silhouette of a woman standing alone on a cliff, the vast black ocean roaring behind her. She is poised at the center of a giant, human-sized chessboard, marble squares gleaming under a bruised sky. Wind lashes at the woman's hair and tugs at her clothes, but she doesn't move. She is waiting.

Sasha tries to reach her, to force her own body forward against the howling wind. But each step is heavier than the last. Her feet slip across the marble squares, slick with seawater. The woman starts to turn, but before Sasha can come close to see her face, the world fractures. The cliff vanishes, and the woman is gone.

She wakes up gasping, her fingers curling into fists against the sheet, the taste of salt thick in her mouth, her heart pounding like she's been running for miles. The dreams are too vivid to dismiss now. And yet, Sasha clings to the rational explanations: stress, grief for a stranger, coincidence. If the dream is real, that would change everything. That would demand something of her. And she isn't ready for that.

She shudders and lowers her gaze. That's when she hears it: "Sorry to interrupt, but I wanted to come over and say hi." A soft, melodic voice cuts through the static. Sasha turns and sees a woman, older and sun-kissed, standing beside her. Her eyes are the startling blue of glacier ice. The woman steps closer. The air seems to warp around them. Sasha feels a shimmer along her arms, like electricity before a storm.

"Can I speak with you privately?" the woman asks, touching Sasha's wrist. The contact is feather-light, but electricity jolts up Sasha's spine. Without thinking, Sasha follows the woman to a quieter corner, half-obscured by drooping palms.

They sit. The music and laughter of the party recede as if the air itself has thickened between them. "I do energy work," the woman says. "Normally, I leave it behind after hours. But your energy called to me. I couldn't just walk past you."

Sasha can only nod, the weight in her chest pressing harder.

"Are you feeling like yourself?" the woman asks, studying her with eyes too clear, too knowing. Sasha shakes her head. Words form in her mind, *I'm fine*, but die in her throat. The woman smiles sadly as if she's seen this before. "There's a great sadness clinging to you. But it's not yours. You're carrying someone else's pain."

For a breath, the tightness in Sasha's chest loosens.

"I can see your light underneath it," the woman says softly. "A rare, bright energy. But it's being smothered. And if you're not careful, it will be taken from you."

Goosebumps rise along Sasha's arms. Her heart flutters against her ribs.

"May I?" the woman asks, holding out both hands, palms up.

Sasha places her hands over them, palms down. A warm current flows up her arms, a steady, pulsing thread connecting them.

"You are not like most people," the woman says. "You feel the world in your body. Joy, sorrow, fear. You don't just empathize with the emotions of others, you inhabit them."

"How do you know?" Sasha whispers.

The woman leans closer, and Sasha notices a thin silver pendant resting against her collarbone: it's simple, almost plain, catching the light as it sways slightly. A faint pulse of heat rises along Sasha's arm, but she shrugs it off, focusing instead on the woman's steady blue gaze.

"I see it in your field. I see it in your eyes. A depth that most cannot fathom, and that many often fear."

Sasha pulls her hands away gently, overwhelmed.

"You must be careful," the woman continues. "Darkness will be drawn to your light. Some will covet it and seek to extinguish it."

Sasha opens her mouth. She wants to ask how to protect herself, what to do, but the woman leans in, her voice low and urgent: "She's trying to find you. Don't give up."

A jolt courses through Sasha's blood. For a moment, Sasha feels something loosen in her chest a fleeting, impossible lightness, as if maybe, somehow, she could outrun the heaviness clinging to her.

Then, Max's face crashes through her mind, blank, watchful, the silver pendant at his throat swinging back and forth, slow and hypnotic. A ticking sound follows, deep and sonorous, like a grandfather clock counting down. The lightness the woman brought into Sasha's chest vanishes. A cold shiver races down her spine. The woman grabs Sasha's shivering hands, her voice lowering into something almost musical, something not meant for the ordinary world.

"Not everyone will recognize your gift for what it is," she says, her grip firmer now. "Not everyone will want you to see. But you must. You must protect yourself, even when it hurts."

The space between them feels charged, trembling with unspoken knowledge.

The woman leans in, pressing something into Sasha's palm, swift and deliberate, folding Sasha's fingers around it as if sealing a pact. A hum runs through Sasha's bones, a strange vertigo twisting the edges of her vision.

When she blinks, the woman is already gone. Sasha hadn't even asked her name. There's only empty space where she had been, and the warm imprint of her hands still fading from Sasha's skin.

Sasha uncurls her fingers. A tarot card rests in her hand: three women, arms entwined, raising chalices high under the full moon. The Three of Cups. Sasha recognizes it, but this card is different. It is old, worn, and has a faint crack down its center. On the back, scrawled in delicate ink, are the words: *Not all who toast with you are true.*

The message sinks into her blood. She turns the card again. The women at the front lifted their cups high, faces blurred at the edges. For the briefest moment, Sasha feels the terrifying certainty that some celebrations are only performances, staged for eyes that are meant to devour.

Sasha presses the tarot card against her chest, feeling the tremor still flickering in her hands. The murmur of the party rises and falls around her, laughter, glasses clinking, music shifting gears, but it feels distant now, muffled as if she's listening through a pane of thick glass. Somewhere beneath it all, she hears the faint toll of three soft chimes stitched into the fabric of the night. Not part of this world exactly. It's coming from somewhere else.

CHAPTER FOURTEEN

The Diagnosis

"Karolina." Arthur says her name again, and something in his voice shifts. "I saw the article. The woman in Big Sur. It brought everything back."

It's the guilt in his voice, that's what distinguishes it. Max's voice doesn't carry the tone of guilt. Arthur's voice is different, it's subtle and real.

Karolina exhales, her grip loosening slightly. It's absolutely Arthur on the other end of the phone. "There's something I should've told you before," Arthur says, his voice thinner now. "Something I've been carrying too long. I kept telling myself it wasn't my place to say. That Max deserved privacy. But that was a lie. I was just afraid, afraid of what it meant to admit what I knew. And when I saw that story about the missing woman in Big Sur, there was just something about it. Maybe it has to do with the timing, or the silence surrounding her disappearance, but whatever it is, I've decided I can't stay quiet anymore."

Karolina steadies herself. "Okay," she says. "Tell me."

"Max received his diagnosis before graduating from Oxford."

The words land in Karolina's ear and whirl around her brain like a wasp in a jar. "Diagnosis?" she asks, though she already knows Arthur isn't talking about his brother's ADHD.

"Of course, Max didn't tell you."

Arthur begins explaining: Max was gifted in math as a child. Not just gifted but a savant. Brilliant, different, and, of course, difficult. His parents, especially their father, coddled him. When Max misbehaved at school, his intelligence became the excuse. "He's exceptional," his father would say. "He's just misunderstood."

But Max wasn't just misunderstood. He was calculating. He learned to outwit their father, a stern disciplinarian, before he was ten. It was why they sent him to St. Andrews at seven, far from home, while the other boys stayed at the local school.

By high school, he withdrew. He came home for holidays but spent them locked away in his bedroom, gaming or coding. He was gone. Oxford changed things, but only for a while. The neuroscience program challenged him. It offered a complexity he could obsess over. His studies came wrapped in prestige and mastery. It gave his mind something to grip. It's also where Max met his first girlfriend. She left school after a year with no warning and no explanation. He never heard from her again. He never even said her name. After that, something shifted. He grew erratic, impulsive one minute, unreachable the next. Their parents insisted on a psychiatric evaluation and an fMRI scan of his brain.

"That's when we learned that Max has antisocial personality disorder," Arthur continues. "He's a psychopath. Officially diagnosed. His brain is wired differently."

Karolina grips the edge of the sink. The porcelain is cool, but her skin feels feverish. *Psychopath.* The word lands like a crack in the tile: *my husband is a psychopath.* It's neither an insult nor a metaphor. It's a proper diagnosis, a scientific fact. She was familiar with it and had studied it, dissected it in academic terms: it is an assemble of callous-unemotional traits, lack of remorse, the inability to form real bonds. But hearing it spoken aloud by Arthur about someone whose breath she fell asleep to every night… it doesn't land in her mind. It lands in her stomach.

"It's genetic. If I had to guess, my father has it too. But no one ever dared say the word."

Karolina had always thought Max's father was cold from combat, military trauma, years in war zones. But now it clicks. Maybe he wasn't made numb by war. Maybe he was drawn to it. And maybe Max was, too.

"Was Max ever prescribed anything?" she asks.

"Antipsychotics," Arthur says. "But he didn't take them consistently."

Karolina's chest goes hollow; cold absence opens behind her ribs. It's the same emptiness she felt when the dreams stopped when she became pregnant. She never told Max. The idea of him knowing, of him claiming something within her, had felt wrong in her body, in her blood. And now, she knows why.

Her hand drifts to her stomach, instinctive, automatic. There's nothing there, at least not anymore. She swallows hard. The room is quiet, the air feels thinner now, sharp at the edges, like it's cutting through her. The baby no longer growing inside of her could have inherited not just Max's jawline but his flawed brain circuitry. The miscarriage had protected her, and now Karolina could disappear on him if she wanted to.

"What happened to his girlfriend from Oxford?" she asks.

"No idea," Arthur says. "She disappeared. Max never mentioned her again."

"He's never mentioned her to me. Did he just erase her from his memory?"

"Possibly. But it's more than denial. He has aphantasia, he can't picture things in his mind. No images. No inner visual life. Most people's memories and emotions are tied to images in their mind's eye. But for Max, it's like... nothing sticks. If you're not in the room, you're gone from his mind."

"Aphantasia," Karolina says. The word feels clinical on her tongue. She'd been researching it recently for the missing woman's case; she is struck by the eerie overlap. Arthur keeps talking, but her mind fractures slightly, sliding sideways into memory.

Karolina leans back in the library chair, her laptop casting a cold glow over the spiral notebook sprawled beside her. The search bar blinks, still open to the terms she's been feeding it for hours: dissociative states, emotional flattening, post-stress memory gaps. She was looking for more insight into the missing woman but also parts of herself that had disappeared. A pressure in her chest mounts with each keystroke, a knowing without words, that something about the missing woman was... off. What Karolina felt in her body was not just fear. Not simply a disappearance but an absence. A flatness of something that was once present. As if she had drifted out of her own life long before her body did.

Karolina hadn't told Max. Not about the searches, the strange late-night rabbit holes, the baby. What she was going through was too abstract to explain. She remembered typing one phrase into the search bar almost without thinking: "What happens when you can't picture your own life?" The results had startled her: aphantasia, trauma-induced imagery loss, neural disruption of emotional memory. Buried in the search, one article had hooked her ribs: *"Aphantasia and Altered States: New Frontiers in Cognitive Research."*

The article was dense and clinical. But midway down, something poignant hooked her.

> *Emerging studies suggest that mental imagery is critical for emotional depth and the construction of autobiographical memory. Suppression of imagery pathways, whether through trauma, neurological damage, or deliberate intervention, may blunt emotional resonance, impairing empathy and narrative cohesion, resulting in emotional detachment and vulnerability to manipulation.*

She rereads the phrase: *deliberate intervention.* A slow chill moves through her.

There's a hyperlink embedded in the phrase. Something about neural modulation and emotional regulation trials, conducted by private labs, off-grid, outside traditional regulatory bodies. Karolina stares at the screen, a faint pulse beginning at the back of her skull. This wasn't just about trauma. Aphantasia could be engineered, even induced. The air around her feels heavier.

She minimizes the tab, but the words keep flashing behind her eyes: *Suppression. Intervention. Impairing empathy. Vulnerability to manipulation.* And for the first time, she wonders if the missing woman wasn't just running from something. Maybe she was running from someone. She remembered reading about a Silicon Valley billionaire who had built a visual cataloging app, scrollable grids of people, places, memories. The entire platform had been inspired by his condition, aphantasia. He couldn't picture his mother's face or his child's smile in his mind, so he made a social media app that could. It had become wildly successful. He built a world of images because he couldn't picture any of them for himself.

She wondered now how often Max used that app. If he kept a gallery of photos labeled "Karolina" just to remind himself who she was. Not out of love, but out of necessity. A way to remember the expression to mimic, the look to give back. The thought made her stomach turn, not with disgust, but with grief.

Her memory collapses back into the present. Arthur's voice is low, almost kind. "He doesn't remember people the way we do," he says. "He remembers what they did for him." Her thoughts flick to Max's voice, how it flattened when they talked about memories, how he never told stories, how he lived entirely in the moment but never in her moments. She thought it was trauma. Now she saw it was clear it was something else.

"After the diagnosis," Arthur continued, "he became obsessed with public figures who shared his wiring, CEOs, heads of state, innovators. Their success validated his condition. He doubled down on his studies. Got a scholarship to Yale to study memory and perception. But the diagnosis became a family secret. One I'm done keeping."

Karolina feels her throat tighten. A dull pressure spreads across her chest. "How did I not see this?"

"Don't blame yourself," Arthur says softly. "That's the point of the mask. It's meant to fool empaths like you. *Especially* people like you, people who feel everything and want to see the good in everyone. Max didn't show you who he was. He showed you who you are."

"He used to look at me like I was the sun." A tear slips down her cheek.

"No," Arthur says, "He reflected the shine you give off."

She blinks. The words hit somewhere deep, behind the ribs. What she felt with Max was not admiration, not even love, just mimicry. She hadn't been seen; she'd been studied. Max had held up her warmth, softness, and sensitivity and reflected it back to her like it was his own. She thought she had fallen in love with him. But really, she had fallen in love with the best parts of herself.

Her voice is barely audible. "He never existed, did he? He was just... whatever I wanted to see."

Arthur doesn't answer. He doesn't need to. Her chest aches.

"He's obsessed with influence," Arthur veers the conversation into a different direction. "Always has been. With an understanding of how to control people. The film that he's working on, *Architects of the Mind*, sounds less like a documentary and more like a blueprint. Have you seen any of the footage?"

"No. Nothing concrete at least. Just fragments of experiments he's mentioned, and some interviews with neuroscientists." Karolina's stomach tightens, something cold unfurls in her chest, the words spill out. "Do you know any more stories about women from his past?" Karolina shudders, thinking back to the story of Max sleeping with Arthur's girlfriend in high school by assuming his identity.

Another pause. "I haven't spoken to Max about his relationships in years, but according to my parents, there was one woman he had mentioned. A German woman named Sasha. He bragged to them about how she was a pilot."

"How long did they date?"

"I'm not sure, a year. Maybe two? According to my mom Sasha was super smart, curious... maybe a little too curious for Max."

"Do you still have her contact info?" Karolina asks. She doesn't explain her urge to reach out to Sasha; she doesn't need to.

Arthur waits for a beat, then speaks. "I'll see if I can find it and send it to you."

She hesitates. The next question is one she isn't sure she wants the answer to. "Arthur... do you think he's capable of love?"

He doesn't answer right away. "I believe he's capable of attention. If you're useful. But when you're gone, it's like you were never there."

"Do you ever feel bad for him?"

"I used to. But pity is a dangerous emotion. Max finds people like us, empathetic, cooperative, morally grounded, and exploits our qualities.

He slowly grows to envy us because he wants those qualities for himself, but it's something he can never have."

"So, he tries to destroy the empathy we carry?"

"Yes. But you must stop seeing him through who you are. You must start seeing him for who he is. My brother is a very dangerous man."

Karolina tries to reply. But her throat closes. The words don't come.

Then, the doorbell rings. She jumps. Her heart stutters. She walks to the door and opens it. No one is there. Just an empty hallway, and silence. Then, she looks down. A single tarot card lies face down on the doormat. She bends to pick it up. The card is reversed. On the back, a scrawl of thick black ink: *Scimus. Imitemur. Vincamus.* Her pulse quickens. The words look familiar, although she can't place them. She turns the card over. *Three of Cups.*

It's upside down. Normally, it's a card of celebration, one of connection and sisterhood. The clink of glasses between friends. But reversed, the meaning shifts.

Betrayal. Infidelity. Secrets shared behind your back. The presence of a third.

She stares at the illustration. Three women once toasting under a canopy of fruit, now inverted, suspended in gravity, their goblets emptying instead of filling. Laughter turned into silence. It's a warning.

She hears Arthur's voice echo in her mind. Her fingers tighten around the card. Whoever left it knows something: about Max, about her, and about what comes next.

CHAPTER FIFTEEN

Ambrosia

It's dusk when Zoe arrives at Ambrosia, the iconic cliffside restaurant carved into Big Sur's bones that has been operating for generations. She steps through the heavy wooden doors; their hinges groan softly, and she enters the space. The smell of the kitchen fryer wafts through the air, meeting with the scent of burning wood and something faintly sweet, almost herbal. The interior is made of redwoods, with trunks that are polished but untamed. Floor-to-ceiling windows offer a breathtaking view of the Pacific Ocean, the glass serving as an illusion of a barrier between the sea and the patrons.

Zoe pauses in the doorway. She wonders if the missing woman stood here too. If she looked out at that same horizon. If she knew she wouldn't return. A fireplace crackles in the far corner, casting long shadows. The restaurant is nearly empty. A man in a suit sits alone at the bar, his long gray hair pulled back into a careful ponytail. By the fire, two patrons, a woman in a colorful kaftan, her silver bun coiled low at her neck, and a man with heavy-lidded eyes, speak in hushed tones.

Zoe takes a seat at the bar. The stool creaks beneath her as she picks up a menu offering hearty food without frills: grilled cheese, tomato soup, French fries, and burgers.

"Welcome back," the bartender says, drying a glass with slow precision. His smile is warm, but his eyes scan her face like he's trying to place a memory.

Zoe blinks. She's never seen him before.

"Actually, this is my first time here," she replies, voice light but watchful.

He pauses. His towel stills. "My mistake," he says. "I thought you were one of our regulars."

Zoe smiles, but something in her ribs tightens. "It's so strange," she says. "The concierge at Salenan said the same thing." She lowers her purse into her lap. The flyer, which portrays the missing woman, presses stiffly against her thigh.

"Out of curiosity... do you happen to know her name?" She asks.

The bartender's smile dims. "Sorry, we're not allowed to give out the names of our patrons." He reaches for another glass, wiping it clean, eyes distant. "But," he adds, glancing sideways, "you really do look like her. It's uncanny."

Zoe freezes. A chill darts down her spine. She's about to ask for more about the woman's appearance, hair color, voice, but stops herself. She already knows the answer. All she has to do is look in a mirror. She glances around the bar. No mirror. Just the flicker of firelight in the window glass and the endless night outside.

Then, she sees it, a poster mounted behind the bar, faded and slightly crooked. *The Salenan Institute*. Its mandala-like logo swirls outward in hypnotic symmetry.

"*FIND YOURSELF HERE*," the tagline reads.

Zoe leans closer. The phrase seems to shimmer faintly. For a moment, she can't tell if it's meant as a promise or a warning.

"Have you seen her lately?" Zoe turns back to the bartender.

"Yeah, she was here a few weeks back, having lunch with a British guy." The words whirl in her head, sending her spinning. Zoe clings to the bar stool, wrapping her legs tightly around it to not fall off, and grips the edge of the bar.

"Do you remember what the guy looked like?"

"Not really, just an average-looking guy," the bartender said, casting his eyes downward as he wiped down the bar. "Do you know what you'd like to drink?" She orders a martini, dirty, straight up with three olives. Her eyes follow the redwood beams on the ceiling toward the windows overlooking the ocean. It's too dark to see out.

As the bartender begins making a round of Manhattans for a couple in the corner, seated by the fire, he asks, "So, you're staying at Salenan?"

"I am."

"I bet you're here for the cell service, like most of their guests," the bartender says with a grin. "Funny how many people cheat on their digital detox."

Zoe nods, orders some food from him, and then glances around. The restaurant has filled in without her noticing, a scattering of diners now hunched over glowing screens, their faces lit more by their devices than by the fire or ocean light.

"So," she says, interrupting as he dries another glass, "what's the deal with Salenan?" Good journalists always know bartenders know more than they should.

He raises his eyes toward her, and a mild curiosity flickers. "Depends on who you ask," he says. "Some folks say it used to be a mental hospital. Others swear it was a rehab center. There's no shortage of local lore."

"Actually," a voice cuts in from two stools down, "it was used by the Navy for years. Soldiers were enlisted there." Zoe turns. The man in the suit, with a gray ponytail and sharp eyes, is watching her over the rim of his glass.

She looks back to the bartender. "So, it was a naval base too?"

He shrugs. "Well, not exactly. But you get the idea. Perched up here on the cliff like that, it always gave people the feeling something... official was happening."

A server appears beside them, carrying a plate under a silver dome. The bartender takes it and places it gently in front of Zoe, then lifts the lid. The scent of salt and oil hits her. She pops a French fry into her mouth and bites down, only to wince as it scorches her tongue.

The bartender reaches for another towel and returns to drying glasses, his movements calm and practiced.

"Injured military officers used to come here to rest and recuperate after the war," the bartender says. "Something about the hot springs. They

found it healing. You come into Salenan one person and leave another."
He wipes down the bar as he continues, voice casual, almost rehearsed.
"Later, the place turned into a drug rehabilitation center, run by a cult,
supposedly. That was sometime in the seventies. One of the first rehab
centers for addicts in the country."

Zoe catches the shift in tone. The way he says "cult" with a shrug, like
it's just another historical footnote.

From the bar, the man in the suit unglues his eyes from the TV and
fixes them on Zoe. "Then, the CIA got wind of the property's transfor-
mative effects. Wanted to see what all the fuss was about."

Zoe bristles. She's not a conspiracy theorist, but she's learned not to
dismiss things too quickly.

The bartender nods, picking up the thread. "Yeah, and the training
they used was weird as hell."

"Training?" Zoe asks, instinctively reaching for her notebook. It's
not in her bag; she must've left it at the cottage.

"That's the rumor, anyway," he says. "They ran these sessions on
something called remote viewing. The idea was to train people to travel
through space and time using only their minds. Some real psychic-psy-
chedelic hippie stuff."

"Did it have a name?" Zoe already knows what's coming.

"Project Grill Flame," the man in the suit says.

Zoe scrunches her face. The bartender lifts a finger.

"It also went by another name, Project Stargate."

Zoe's eyes water. A ripple of adrenaline breaks over her, narrowing
her vision. Project Stargate. Max's friends had mentioned it at the Speckled Boar.

"Do you know what remote viewing actually entails?"

"You mean the training?" the bartender asks. Zoe nods.

"I've heard they'd make you sit in a room and draw things over and
over until you hit a trance-like state. That's when the psychic abilities
were supposed to kick in."

Zoe shifts in her seat at the word "trance." It's exactly how she feels
around Max, like her thoughts don't entirely belong to her.

"Were people aware they were being recruited by the CIA?" she asks. She thinks of MK Ultra in the 1950s and 60s, the sex workers lacing drinks with LSD, the one-way mirrors, the American citizens treated like lab rats. The attempt to build minds that couldn't be broken by Soviet control.

The bartender shrugs. "I would assume so."

"One would." Zoe restrains from bringing him down a rabbit hole that would serve no purpose to her story. "So, how long did the CIA use Salenan to train people?"

"I don't think they were doing all the training there; it was more about recruitment. To see who was worth bringing onto the project. According to locals, the project ended in the 1990s. The Government spooks left, and eventually, the Institute returned to its rightful origins."

"Which is?"

"A center for enlightenment." He smiles and winks.

Zoe finishes eating, and the bartender takes away her plate. She turns from the bar, her purse heavy in her lap. The woman in the colorful kaftan is smiling at her, waving her over like she's an old friend. Zoe returns the smile, her pulse flickering. She pats her purse, feels the missing woman's flyer folded inside like a secret, and walks slowly toward the fireplace.

As she approaches, the woman squints. "Oh, my goodness, this is so embarrassing. I waved you over because I thought you were a friend of ours. You look identical to her. I'm so sorry. She's been on my mind lately and... well, I hope this doesn't creep you out."

Zoe feels the same sentence circle around her like it has all week. *You look like her.* "Not at all. May I?" She gestures to the open chair between them.

"Please," the woman says. "I'm Susan. This is my husband, Jack."

Jack nods politely. He's angular, with long silver hair pulled back into a ponytail. His eyes are soft, but something about his posture feels observant, unreadable.

Zoe eases into the chair and crosses her legs. She keeps her purse close. Susan explains that they live in the small cabin attached to Ambrosia. The restaurant was her grandmother's. After she passed, Susan inherited the land, the cabin, and the view.

"We're both artists," she says. "Jack used to work in the Navy. Traveled all over the world."

Zoe nods along, scanning the table. Her eyes catch on a small bottle resting near Susan's drink. "What's that?" she asks.

Susan lifts it carefully. "Ambrosia. It's a special tonic my grandmother created. Been in our family for generations."

"What does it do?"

"It helps you forget your mortality," Susan says, smiling wistfully. "Not in a dangerous way. Just... it softens grief."

"Like a painkiller?" Zoe jokes.

"Not exactly. More like a way of loosening sorrow's grip." She taps the glass. "It helps the energy leave the body."

Zoe hesitates. "Does it work?" She reaches for the bottle, turning it over in her hand. Forgetting her own mortality sounds nice. But what if our human form, our mortality, is the only proof that we exist? What if erasing it with the promise of living forever is not the point?

Susan holds her gaze. "Depends on where you want it to take you."

Jack adds, "It's natural. Psilocybin, a bit of THC, CBD, some other herbs." He grins until Susan elbows him gently.

"Don't give away the recipe," she chides. "Please, feel free to take it."

Zoe chuckles, holding the bottle closer. "How much do I owe you?"

"Nothing. I give it to those who need it. Especially guests from Salenan. It makes the stay more... meaningful." The word hangs between them a beat too long.

Jack leans forward, cutting through her gaze. "So, what brings you to Big Sur?"

Zoe swirls her martini. The glass feels suddenly too cold in her fingers. "I'm a journalist," she says slowly. "I'm investigating a disappearance at Salenan. A woman, I don't have a name, and she left with little trace."

Susan's face goes still, then flickers in the firelight. "I told Jack last night," she says. "I'm afraid the missing woman might be someone we know. A friend. We haven't heard from her in days."

Zoe leans forward, every muscle tightening. "The one you mistook me for?"

Susan nods. "Her name is Alessandra."

Zoe's heart skips, then falters. *Alessandra.* The same name she chose without thinking when she checked into Salenan. No reason. No hesitation. Just instinct. A strange quiet falls inside her. The restaurant doesn't feel real anymore, like a set for a movie that could slide away at any moment. Her hands find the edges of her chair. A cold ripple moves through her chest, and for a moment, she feels it, the boundaries of self-blurring. She plants both feet on the floor. *She's not Alessandra. She's Zoe.* She's sure of that. But for a second, she imagines she is Alessandra, sitting here, sipping a martini, slipping the bottle of Ambrosia in her purse. Laughing, waving, forgetting, disappearing. Her pulse skips. She blinks hard, grounding herself. No. She's here to find Alessandra. She's not her.

She is Zoe.

"Honestly," Jack says, watching her wide-eyed, "you really do look like her."

"You're not the first to say that," Zoe murmurs. "Actually... almost everyone has." The fire snaps. Zoe lifts her drink and takes a long, cold sip, letting the silence press against her skin.

Susan leans in. "It's your eyes. Alessandra's eyes were wide, brown, and delicate. Like yours. Doe-like."

"Do you know what happened to her?" Zoe abruptly moves beyond the focus of shared appearances.

Susan shakes her head. "No. It's as if she just vanished into the night."

"Why was she staying at Salenan?"

"She said she'd been invited to a workshop. Some kind of special program. But she wouldn't say more. Everyone used pseudonyms. Even the facilitators."

Zoe leans forward. "Do you know what it was about?"

"She never told us," Jack says, his voice softening. "But she always carried this book. It had a blue cover. She read it constantly. I think it was tied to the workshop."

"You know, we got along so well," Susan says, her voice wistful. "There was something... intense about her presence. Alessandra had this way of watching people as if she were collecting them, their moods and thoughts. She once told me she was beginning to feel other people's emotions in her body. She said that it was exhausting. Big Sur helped quiet it, she said. It gave her space to just be."

Zoe shifts in her seat. The description doesn't quite match the version of Alessandra she has begun to construct in her mind.

"Do you think she could have..." Zoe doesn't finish the question.

"I suppose anything is possible," Jack replies. "But no, I don't think she would've taken her own life."

"She was driven," Susan adds. "Focused. She was not always easy to read, but it was as if it was purposeful. She had plans. She said she felt a sense of calling, like there were things only she could see clearly. I think it was hard for her to explain that to other people without sounding... intense."

"Work?" Zoe asks.

Susan nods. "She loved animals. She gave Jack a hard time about having gone to the circus once, said it was unforgivable, even though it was decades ago."

"The last time we saw her," Jack says, "she'd just gotten back from a safari in Africa. Told us she'd slipped away from her family to confront a poacher, alone with no warning."

Zoe lifts her eyebrows.

Jack shrugs. "Her father was furious. But that wasn't unusual. They clashed all the time. She said he didn't understand her, that he was part of the problem."

"They had very different ways of seeing the world," Susan agrees. "She said she was trying to undo damage wherever she could."

Zoe cocks her head. "Who's her father?"

Jack meets her eyes. "John Wilder, the CEO of Tex Chemical."

The name crashes through her body. Zoe's pulse spikes and nausea rises, bitter and sudden. The subject line from the anonymous email she received that night at Moffet Field, flashes in her mind, *Tex Chemical files*. It had no attachments, and a dead-end reply. Was Alessandra trying to get in touch with her? Was she the anonymous source? Had the email been intercepted by someone? Her brain reaches for headlines surrounding Tex Chemical, press releases, SEC filings, but one thought cuts through them all: Max had admired him. He'd brought up Wilder casually during their road trip in Big Sur and called him a visionary. And Zoe had nodded complicitly, pretending to not notice how rehearsed it sounded.

She grips the edge of the table. Her fingers go cold. If Alessandra is Wilder's daughter, and Max already knew that, then this feels like more than just a disappearance. It feels like a trap, a trail Zoe's been walking without realizing she was being led.

Did Max know she'd choose to cover this story?

A chill needles up her spine. Zoe fumbles in her purse, pulls out the flyer, and holds it up. "Is this her?"

Susan covers her mouth, eyes wide. She nods.

Zoe grips the flyer tighter. The paper suddenly feels heavier than it should. The missing woman finally has a name. *Alessandra Wilder.*

CHAPTER SIXTEEN

Pulled

Sasha wakes to the sound of her phone buzzing. She stretches her arm across the nightstand and silences it without checking who's calling. She already knows it's Max.

He's been unusually fixated on the pendant lately. Every night for the past week, she's asked him to take it off before bed. He always hesitates—just for a moment—before obliging. Last night was no different. He pulled the chain over his head and set it gently on the nightstand beside her. Then, just before sunrise, he kissed her forehead and slipped out to edit the documentary.

Alone now, Sasha shifts under the duvet, relishing the quiet. Her phone buzzes again. She reaches for it, her fingers brushing the pendant's cold metal surface. It feels colder than it should. She picks it up. Etched in the silver are the words *Scimus. Imitemur. Vincamus.* She stares at them. *We watch. We imitate. We conquer.*

A tremor runs through her. She scrolls through Max's texts:

> *"I left my necklace on the nightstand this morning, Fraulein. Can you please make sure to place it somewhere safe? It is very valuable to me."*

"Hi, my dear, do you see the necklace there? I want to be sure I did, in fact, leave it at home."

"I'm going to come back home this afternoon to get the necklace. Again, it needs to be somewhere safe. It has sentimental value for me. Thank you, my dear."

His insistence is strange. Desperate, almost. As if the pendant were alive. Sasha frowns, holding the pendant in her palm. It feels dense, like it's storing something. What is Max's obsession with this necklace? A tinge of jealousy stirs in her. How is it possible to feel second-rate to an object?

She turns the pendant over again. *Scimus. Imitemur. Vincamus.*

Then, like a flashbulb in her mind, she remembers the tarot card. She yanks open the nightstand drawer and pulls it out. The Three of Cups. A smiling trio of women raising their chalices in celebration. She flips it over. *Scimus. Imitemur. Vincamus.* Her chest tightens.

She crosses the room and opens Max's laptop on the desk. She's never done this before; she's never felt the need. But now something is telling her to look. The screen wakes with a soft glow to a desktop cluttered with folders. One catches her eye, barely visible in the corner: FinalReel_Version3.mov.

Her heart skips a beat. Max is notoriously evasive about his documentary, always vague, always deflecting. She's never seen a single second of it. She double-clicks. The screen goes black. There is a faint scatter of stars. Then footage begins, there's no title, no branding, just a voice.

Max.

"Some minds aren't broken. They're just built... differently. What if we stopped trying to fix them and started learning from them?"

Sasha freezes. The music rises beneath his voice, ambient, metallic, eerily familiar. She closes her eyes. The private room at the Speckled Boar. That same music was playing faintly through the speaker overhead the last time she and Max were there. She thought it was just background noise.

The footage cuts to aerial views of a pastel-colored town: it's sanitized and curated, too perfect. She recognizes the bright, cheerful buildings, the central square, the Mexican restaurant, the walking path. Oneness University, where Max brought her on their third date.

The drone glides toward the edge of the campus, where a massive dome sits, metallic and skeletal, like the ribcage of some extinct machine. Pathways crisscross its surface like neural grooves.

Max's voice continues: "*At Oneness University, we believe in mirroring brilliance. Deep circuit learning allows us to model not just behavior, but intuition, empathy, and emotional reaction.*"

The camera pans to a woman walking alone down a corridor. She has long strawberry-blonde hair and graceful, measured steps. Sasha's pulse hammers. She pauses the video and leans closer. She presses play. The woman turns and smiles at the camera.

Max's voice continues: "*We study the architecture of exceptional minds. Not to replicate—but to understand. Empathy. Intuition. Control.*"

Then a beat. "*Watch. Imitate. Conquer.*"

The screen goes dark. Sasha slams the laptop shut. She rushes to Max's closet and pulls down the box of Polaroids. She digs until she finds her. Strawberry-blonde hair falling over her collarbone. A half-smile that doesn't quite meet her eyes. Scaffolding looms in the background, curved and metallic. And around her neck: the same pendant. Silver. Etched: *Scimus. Imitemur. Vincamus.* Sasha holds her breath as she flips to the next photo. It's the same woman. But this time, she's not alone. She's with Max.

It hits her all at once, not just in her mind but in her body, like a current ripping through her chest, her spine, her gut. This is the same woman from her dream; the figure on the human-sized chessboard cliff always turned away and unreachable. Sasha could never make out her face in the dream, only the outline.

But now, she knows. It's her. The missing woman. The one Sasha had felt in flashes and fragments, chased through her sleep, and searched for without knowing. Her breath comes fast, and her vision blurs. This isn't just obsession surrounding a mystery in the media. It's something deeper, older, a recognition inside of Sasha that has bypassed logic and memory entirely. Her body knew this woman before her mind did. And now it's undeniable.

Sasha glances at the photo again. The woman has her arms around Max. His signature crooked smile. The loose curl that always falls over his brow. Tears rise, fast, hot. The pendant is heavy in her palm. *We watch. We imitate. We conquer.* A line she once thought was branding. Now, it feels more like instruction.

A wave of dizziness crashes over her. The room tilts. For a second, she's not in Max's apartment anymore, she's on a cliff. Wind whipping her hair. The chessboard beneath her feet. The woman's silhouette at the edge, turning just as Sasha reaches out, and then vanishing. Sasha gasps and blinks hard, gripping the pendant in her hand like a lifeline. Her chest aches. Her body is trembling. She wasn't just dreaming about this woman. She was being pulled toward her.

CHAPTER SEVENTEEN

An Enigma

Most people are creatures of habit, and Alessandra Wilder was no different. Even on vacation, she likely followed a daily routine. Zoe grabs her notebook and steps out of her cottage, heading for the lobby. The concierge is behind the desk. He smiles as she approaches.

"Good morning, Alessandra."

Zoe jumps slightly, momentarily forgetting who she chose to be.

"Morning..." Her eyes search his linen shirt for a name tag. Nothing. "What's your name again?" She hadn't asked the first time they met.

"Cody," he replies with a smile.

"Is that your real name?" Zoe asks, studying him. The Institute's fondness for aliases and pseudonyms seems designed to keep people just a little bit apart.

Cody gives a half-smile. "What is real?" He holds her gaze a moment too long. There's something performative in the way he says it, like he's quoting a line from a script he doesn't quite believe anymore.

Zoe arches an eyebrow. "Is that how you answer all personal questions?"

He shrugs, almost sheepish. "Only the ones that matter."

It's too early for riddles. Zoe exhales and glances away, trying to re-orient herself.

"Reality is in the eye of the beholder, I suppose," she says finally, the edge softening in her voice. "Anyway, I was in a rush yesterday and didn't get to properly introduce myself." She extends her hand. "Zoe Harrison. I'm a journalist. I'm here to investigate Alessandra Wilder's disappearance, and I'm hoping you might tell me more about her." Zoe holds his gaze now, steady, clear.

Cody's smile falters. He blinks, visibly nervous. "I'm sorry. Our policy is not to speak about guests." His eyes lower. "It's about respecting their privacy."

Zoe leans in, closer. A tingle sparks at the base of her skull. She knows this feeling. It climbs upward, hot and prickly, like an electric current threading through bone. A lump forms in her throat, and she fights back tears, sadness engulfing her. Her eyes drop to the floor beneath the counter, where a small dog bed sits beside his stool, overflowing with chewed-up toys.

"I didn't know you had a dog here," Zoe says softly, the back of her neck radiates.

"That's Henry's." Cody's voice dips. He glances at the bed, then quickly away. "He died last week. I haven't had the heart to throw it out." His voice catches.

Zoe follows his gaze to the tangle of worn-out toys. "I'm so sorry," she says, her voice low. She looks down at her hands, blinking fast. "Losing a pet is one of the hardest things. They're part of the family."

"He really was." Cody wipes at his eye with the back of his hand. "He was here with me every day. He loved this place. We all did... once."

Zoe nods, about to turn and let him be, when Cody speaks again, softer now.

"You know, Henry loved her. All animals did. She was like a modern-day Snow White."

There's something wistful in his voice, but then he trails off. His eyes drift upward. Zoe follows his gaze. A tiny black dome camera, nestled in the ceiling corner, blinks silently above them. Something flickers in Cody's expression: hesitation, fear, maybe guilt. His voice is even quieter when he speaks again. "Care to go for a walk?" Before she can answer, he grabs a pen, scribbles a note— "Be back in 10"—and presses it to the desk.

As they step outside, the mood shifts. The air feels cooler. They walk briskly toward the fire pits, shoes crunching the gravel. Cody glances over his shoulder, then back at her.

"Ask me anything," he says, voice clipped, urgent. "We never had this conversation. And it's off the record." His jaw tightens. "I can't afford to lose this job."

"You have my word," Zoe says, exhaling. Relief loosens her spine.

"What have you found so far?" he asks, eyes anxious.

"There's no suspect. They searched the bottom of the cliff but found nothing. There's no body, no note and no signs of foul play." Zoe hesitates. "But the longer I stay here, the stranger this place feels."

At the fire pit, Cody gestures for them to sit. She lowers herself first. The bench is cool. He joins her.

"They didn't find a note?" he repeats.

Zoe shakes her head.

"She wouldn't have taken her life," he says firmly. "That I'm sure of."

"How well did you know her?" Zoe thinks of Jack, Susan, and now Cody, all insisting Alessandra wouldn't have ended her life.

"How well do we ever know anyone?" Cody murmurs. "But I'd say I knew her well enough. She didn't commit suicide." He tosses a stick into the fire pit. They both watch as it blackens, curls, and disappears. "She loved animals. She was kind and brilliant. She studied neuroscience at the Stanford Research Institute. She had so much to give."

"What do you think happened?"

"I don't know." His voice is low. "She was here a couple days. Maybe a week."

"That's a long time at a place like this. How could she afford it?" Zoe says, calculating the cost.

"She had family money. Her father's a billionaire. He runs some global chemical company."

Zoe nods. Tex Chemical. She pulls her notebook from her bag. "Mind if I take some notes?"

"Just don't record."

She starts scribbling. "Do you know how she spent her time here?"

Cody lays out Alessandra's routine: hiking Devil's Slide in the morning, lunch at Ambrosia, meditation sessions, and a dip in the hot springs in the afternoon. A pattern forms a path for Zoe to retrace.

"Do you know who reported her missing?"

"I did," Cody says. "She didn't show up to a session."

"What session?"

"Something about artificial intelligence and emotional intelligence."

"Did it have a name?"

He hesitates, eyes dart to the sky, trying to remember. "Something around synthetic consciousness."

Zoe stills, her mind flashes to the first night she met Max, when he was surprised to hear that she knew what the Singularity was, when technology surpasses human intelligence, evolving faster than we can understand or control. Synthetic consciousness is a term that is synonymous with the Singularity, perhaps just a more poetic way to talk about technology overtaking humanity.

"Why would she be interested in that?" Zoe asks.

"Shouldn't we all be?" Cody checks his watch. "I should get back."

Zoe reaches out to shake Cody's hand. He takes it but lingers for a beat too long. Then, just before turning away, he says, almost casually, "By the way... you're staying in her cottage."

Zoe blinks. "What?"

Cody nods toward the main lawn. "That one." He points straight at her door.

Zoe follows his finger. A chill runs up her spine. "That's where Alessandra stayed." His tone is flat, almost too even. "Right up until the day she vanished." Then, he turns, without waiting for a response, and walks back toward the lobby. Zoe is left standing alone, staring at the cottage she's been sleeping in. Her legs feel rooted. The grass beneath her might as well be quicksand. The silence of the lawn presses in from all sides, thick and buzzing. Her heart begins to thud, not fast, but heavy.

She takes a single step toward the cottage. Then, another. Alessandra's cottage. Zoe can't move any farther. She sinks down onto the lawn. Her breath comes short, shallow. Her editor's words echo in her mind: *Some journalists lose themselves in these cases. Keep your feet on the ground.* But the ground doesn't feel solid anymore.

Zoe exhales slowly. Then, rises. She needs to write her editor, so she walks to Ambrosia for cell service. Inside, Zoe orders black coffee and toast with jam. The smells of bacon, redwood, and palo santo wrap around her. She listens to the waves hitting the cliffs, and for a moment, she can't tell if it's the physical force or the sound vibrating through her.

She opens her laptop and types into the search bar: *Feed the World.* Tex Chemical's tagline. She scoffs. A corporate euphemism for chemical warfare. The company specializes in pesticides, engineered toxins dressed up as progress.

What had Alessandra thought about her father's company? Had it eaten away at her? Zoe begins digging into IRS records, donation disclosures, and nonprofit affiliations associated with Tex Chemical. She scans line by line, chasing threads, half-dreading what she might find. Then, she freezes. Her eyes lock on the name. Oneness University.

A donation from Tex Chemical to Oneness University for $3 million. Then, the next year, $16 million. A 500% increase. She reels back in her chair. *What the hell…?* This wasn't a partnership. This was an investment. Or worse, collusion. A fresh wave of nausea curls in her stomach. *What did Alessandra know? Was she about to blow the whistle on her father's company?* Susan's voice flickers in her mind: "She was trying to undo damage wherever she could." What was the damage? And why would Tex Chemical funnel millions into Oneness? The same "tech incubator" backing Max's documentary. Her thoughts lurch sideways. *What exactly does Max know?*

She walks in circles, pacing through the cafe as if her thoughts might burn a hole in her skin. She grabs her notebook and begins writing the story backwards, first scribbling potential headlines, her handwriting jagged:

WOMAN WITH TIES TO TEX CHEMICAL
GOES MISSING FROM GALENAN INSTITUTE

POLICE WON'T IDENTIFY WOMAN MISSING
FROM BIG SUR WITH TIES TO TEX CHEMICAL

None of the headlines mention Oneness University. Not yet, because Zoe doesn't quite know how it all fits together. A cold thought slinks in: *Max is the key.* She stops pacing. Her eyes flick to the vintage poster hanging behind the bar: *Find Yourself Here.* Zoe yanks open her purse, frantically searching until her fingers close around the crumpled Salenan pamphlet. She flips through the course list, eyes scanning.

The Mind Reclaimed: Welcome to the Age of Synthetic Consciousness. She reads the description, her pulse a tight drumbeat under her ribs: *A cutting-edge seminar exploring the convergence of neuroscience, artificial intelligence, and spiritual cognition. Participants will examine how emotional intelligence can be modeled, enhanced, and even transferred through advanced brain-computer interfaces. Drawing on principles from neuroplasticity, predictive coding, and empathy-based learning systems, the workshop challenges attendees to consider: What is the self once consciousness can be simulated? Can intuition be engineered? And how do we protect or upgrade the mind in an era where even thought can be replicated?*

This was the class Alessandra signed up for. This wasn't just a weekend getaway at a wellness retreat. Max had pitched his project to Zoe as a documentary, but now, she wasn't sure it wasn't something else entirely. She fumbles for her phone in her purse; it's gone. It's in the cottage. She throws cash on the table, jams her laptop into her bag, and rushes for the road. Her feet slam the pavement.

Zoe returns to her small cottage at Salenan, kicks off her shoes, rolls her sore neck, and something catches her eye. She sees it sitting neatly on the edge of the desk. A book. It's not hers and wasn't here when she left. She stares at the title on the cover, *The ESP Algorithm* by Dr. Elaine Powers, its edges are worn and there's a faint ring of a water glass on the back. There's something eerily familiar about it. Not just the subject matter, but the quiet fact of its presence. It feels deliberate.

Jack's words come racing back, "Alessandra always carried this book. It had a blue cover; she read it constantly. I think it was tied to the workshop." A chill works its way up her arms. She picks up the book and flips it open. Inside the margins, someone has scrawled notes in a looping, careful hand: "Telepathic resonance = pattern recognition?" "Not a gift, a skill cultivated." "Emotion as frequency / clarity vs noise."

And in the upper right corner of a chapter: "Watch the women." Zoe's pulse jumps, and she slams the book shut, stuffing it into the night-stand drawer.

CHAPTER EIGHTEEN

Profiling

"Today's training will focus on the psychological profiling of our target."

Karolina opens her notebook and writes the date. The detectives had called again. They asked her to attend a behavioral profiling session with a psychological profiler to help in the case of the missing woman. Her eyes scan the room, expecting other invitees but she is alone.

The instructor, an older woman with slate-gray hair pulled into a low twist, stands at the whiteboard. Her expression is impassive, but her eyes are sharp behind frameless glasses. Her presence is grounded and economical.

"We will discuss a scenario based on the missing woman's case in Big Sur. I'll run through the basic details, and you'll learn to build a profile of our target." She speaks with a precision that slices as if each word is weighed before being released.

Karolina lifts her head from her notebook. "Target?" The word strikes her as cold. "Do you mean a profile of the person who has disappeared or the potential perpetrator?"

"Often, we profile both. First, we work with what we know, that a woman has disappeared in Big Sur."

"So, we will profile the victim," Karolina says.

"To start, yes. We begin with what we call a victimology report. What do we know about the missing woman?"

"Some of her basic physical characteristics." Karolina replays what the police confirmed: "The person identifies as female, thirty-seven years old, with hazel-brown eyes, petite, around 5'3" and 120 pounds, and long reddish-blonde hair. Last seen on a cliff overlooking the Pacific Ocean at the Salenan Institute."

"Good. And who is the last person to have seen her?"

"I don't know. The police haven't shared that."

The instructor frowns slightly. "Who is most likely to be the last person to have seen her?"

"If she was here on her own, then a staff member or guest. If with someone, then whoever that person was."

The instructor writes "no known suspect or person of interest" on the board.

"What do we know about the Salenan Institute? What draws people there?"

Karolina has done her research. "It was founded in the mid 1960s as a sort of social experiment. It is an oasis in Big Sur, claiming to help people reach their human potential."

"To transform their lives," the instructor adds.

"Not just individual lives, the collective too."

The instructor writes "human potential" on the board. "Would it classify as a cult?"

Karolina knows they're role-playing now. "No, not technically."

"Why not?"

"It lacks a charismatic leader. There's no single doctrine, and while it offers self-improvement workshops, there's no centralized indoctrination."

"Good." The instructor writes "*cult?*" and then crosses it out.

"How long has the woman been missing?"

"Two weeks."

"Have you looked into what events were occurring at Salenan at that time?"

Karolina reads over her notes: "The Salenan Institute held an invite-only conference the day she disappeared. I hit a roadblock when I tried to learn more about the conference. Several videos had been taken down from the Institute's website. I reached out to someone who attended the conference and read their blog post, but no response. The conference itself has an elusive nature to it. It seems strange."

She hesitates, flipping a page in her notebook, rereading the title: *The Mind Reclaimed: Welcome to the Age of Synthetic Consciousness.* The words make her stomach clench. There's something disquieting about it, something that sounds familiar.

Max had been working on his documentary almost obsessively, yet he hadn't told her much about it, just the title, *Architects of the Mind.* He'd been unusually tight-lipped, more guarded than usual. Whenever she asked, he'd smile vaguely and say, "You'll understand when it's finished."

Karolina hadn't pressed. But now, seeing this title in front of her, she feels a warm heat rise from her belly. *The Mind Reclaimed.* The language and the framing were too aligned to be a coincidence. *Architects of the Mind.* He'd spoken of the mind as a blueprint, something to be redesigned, improved, perfected. Its message had been both seductive and sterile: the future of humanity depended on the engineering of consciousness.

She hadn't thought much of it at the time; his ideas had always hovered at the intersection of philosophy and tech. But now, in the cold light of this profiling session, she wonders if it was more than just a metaphor. What if this workshop was inspired by Max's film? Or were they both drawing from the same source, the same ideology? Had Max been more involved in Salenan than he'd admitted?

She hesitates, flipping a page in her notebook, and rereads the title. *The Mind Reclaimed: Welcome to the Age of Synthetic Consciousness.* Her stomach tightened in more knots. There's something chillingly hollow in the phrasing, something orchestrated. It didn't sound like a transformation. It sounded like mind control.

"Were you at least able to determine the topic of the conference?" the instructor asks.

"Yes. It was called *The Mind Reclaimed: Welcome to the Age of Synthetic Consciousness*."

The instructor stops writing and cranes her neck up toward the ceiling. Karolina follows her eyes to trace a tiny green light in the corner of the room, high above, in the foam panels.

"Soon, artificial intelligence will be doing my job."

"To conduct psychological profiling?" Karolina asks.

"Yes. The FBI began profiling in the seventies, around the same time Salenan took off. Psychology was booming, and institutions wanted to harness it. For years, profiling was a deeply human skill. But now, AI is learning faster. Of course: it can build profiles from reams of data, online behavior, biometrics, images, and synthesize it instantly."

"But profiling depends upon body language. Micro-expressions. How can AI sense the human element?" Karolina asks.

"It can't, at least not yet. That's why we're here." The instructor smiles faintly. "So, we assume the missing woman checked in for soul-searching or to attend the conference. Why might she have disappeared?"

"I'm not sure."

"Money and love are the biggest motivators. Follow the money, follow the heart and you'll find the why."

Karolina draws a Venn diagram: a heart intersecting a dollar sign.

The instructor uncaps a marker with a practiced flick and turns to the whiteboard. "As profilers, we'd recommend detectives check for life insurance policies, request the guest list and conference attendees at Salenan, and pull any CCTV footage."

Karolina leans back slightly in her chair. "They don't have cameras. They've banned technology. And they'll probably require a subpoena for the guest list." She pauses, her voice tightening. "They're like the Speckled Boar, ultra-discreet." The mention of the name sends a ripple through her spine. Max loved both places.

The instructor turns, brows lifting. "How do you know this?"

Karolina meets her gaze. "Places like that all operate the same. They protect their high-net-worth guests."

"What else can we infer?"

"She's likely independently wealthy, on business, or has family money. Salenan runs $1,500 a night."

"What about her psychological state?"

Karolina hesitates. "I wouldn't know."

"Have a guess."

"She could've been there post-breakup, to detox, for work, to get away, to get in shape..."

"Exactly." The instructor taps the cap of her marker against her palm. "AI would parse her digital footprint and build a psychological profile."

Karolina straightens in her chair. The idea makes her stomach twist. She wouldn't want anyone profiling her based on her Big Tech search history. It would be all wrong. "I'd suggest detectives retrace her steps in person," Karolina says, her tone more forceful now. "See what sessions she attended and if she spoke with anyone. Ask about any personal issues."

The instructor nods once. "Send out a human team."

Karolina flinches inwardly at the phrase. A human team. She draws a slow breath and adds, "The police have chosen to hide her identity from the public."

"To protect her?"

"Yes. Or because she's well-known. Or... to protect whoever took her."

The instructor pauses mid-sentence, marker hovering just above the board. She turns her eyes back to Karolina, a spark of interest lighting her features. "Let's move on to the perpetrator. This is where things get interesting."

Karolina's hand tenses around her pen.

"Usually, we'd have a crime scene," the instructor continues, her tone dropping a register. "But there isn't one. That's where you come in. You bring something more than profiling. You bring intuition." She leans in, eyes locking on Karolina's. "I want you to tap into your subconscious. Use your training. Are you comfortable with moving forward?"

Karolina studies the woman's face for a beat longer than necessary. Then, steadying her voice, she says, "Yes, I'm fine with proceeding."

The instructor slides a blank pad and pencil across the desk toward her. "We are being recorded." She gestures subtly toward the green dot glowing above the camera.

Karolina nods, her posture straightening slightly.

The instructor's tone shifts, measured, almost hypnotic, as she begins the remote viewing session. "Beach. Shoe. Sun. Water. Tree. Dog."

Karolina's hand moves instinctively. Eyes closed, she sketches with a light touch, her breath slowing as the words lull her into a trance. Time blurs.

"Big Sur," the instructor says quietly.

Karolina draws a cliff, then waves curling at the bottom.

"Salenan Institute."

Karolina's pencil moves in jagged lines, erratic, rushed. Without a word, the pencil is gently pulled from her hand.

"You can open your eyes." The instructor's voice is close and hushed.

Karolina blinks, disoriented. She looks down, searching for the pad, but it's already turned over and placed on the far corner of the desk, just out of reach.

"The drawing session is done. Now, we will move on to some basic psychology. Are you familiar with the Hare checklist?"

Karolina shakes her head, still not fully grounded, her gaze drifting back toward the pad.

The instructor explains, "It's a psychopathy checklist first designed by Dr. Robert Hare. It's a twenty-item checklist of personality traits to confirm or pathologize someone who has the type of personality disorder most likely to commit a crime like kidnapping or murder. I will first familiarize you with this checklist since we use it often as profilers." She sets the checklist down in front of Karolina.

She reads each trait slowly, taking them in as if the words themselves are burrowing into her. Lack of empathy. Pathological lying. Superficial charm. Her throat goes dry. Every line leads back to Max.

Karolina blinks hard, trying to focus on the page, but the words seem to swim. She swallows, her pulse quickening. Her conversation with Arthur cuts through her memory. How had she missed this? Or had she always known?

The room tilts slightly. Her body is still in the chair, but her mind feels submerged, as if underwater. Memories are floating up, uninvited. Images half-formed. Feelings she had long dismissed now clawing their way back. She grips the edges of the checklist. Her fingers are numb, and her breath is shallow.

She sees Max again, laughing in the sunlight, telling her that she's his home. She sees him with the same gaze he gave when she told him that she was scared. That unfaltering stare of his, like he was recording her from the inside.

She tells herself to think about the victim, about what might've happened to her. But the space between Max and the missing woman begins to collapse. What if he knew her? What if their paths crossed at Salenan? Max had always been drawn to people in transition, people seeking transformation. And the Institute was nothing if not a crucible for the vulnerable. Her hands tremble.

The checklist lies in front of her like a mirror. Each of the twenty traits is a breadcrumb leading not to a stranger, but to her own personal life. She closes her eyes and forces herself to conjure the missing woman's face, but even then, Max's shadow looms. Was he involved? Or was she just seeing him in everything now? This didn't feel like projection. It felt like recall. Still, she questions herself. What if she's wrong? What if she's catastrophizing? Looking for evidence to match a fear? But her body says otherwise. It knows; it has always known. It knew the first time she pulled away from his touch and told herself she was just tired. It knew every time she gaslit herself into believing the burden of unease was hers to carry.

She glances up. The instructor is speaking again, but Karolina can't quite make out the words. The voice sounds far away. Focus. She tries again. The missing woman. A thirty-seven-year-old who vanished during a tech-spirituality conference in Big Sur. *But what if she didn't vanish? What if she was erased?*

Karolina's eyes dart to the checklist again, inhaling sharply as she re-reads the list. She envisions Max's pendant, the interface device he wears around his neck like a relic. She wants to run, to scream, to rip the paper in front of her. But she sits still, shoulders tight, spine straight. She tells herself she's profiling a suspect. She is. She just never expected it might be the man she married.

Karolina's voice breaks through, soft. "How do you know when it's not just emotional immaturity or a trauma response? How do you know it's pathology?" She looks up at the instructor, eyes wide but focused.

The instructor answers gently, breaking away from her role. "Because they don't get better when you love them harder. They just get better at hiding."

Karolina nods, barely. She has stopped blinking. Each trait triggers a memory, a sensation, a flash of her husband. Her breathing shifts. Her limbs feel foreign. Her mind pulls her toward the missing woman and then back again to Max.

"When in the presence of a psychopath, which many of these perpetrators are, there are some key characteristics you will notice if you know what to look for. First, the difference in their speech." The instructor says smoothly. Max's stilted speech and mumbling drop into her mind. Conversations with him left Karolina confused and her mind spinning.

"Psychopaths speak differently than the rest of us. It shows up as more '*ah*s and *um*s,' their conversations are more disjointed, and there isn't a natural flow to them. The disfluency in their speech can often mimic a stutter but goes much deeper than a speech impediment. Neuroimaging research shows structural abnormalities in the brain of psychopaths, which leads to problems with speech and understanding certain words. Psychopaths' word patterns are very cause-and-effect and primitive, focused on their immediate needs: food, sex, money. Their use of language is driven by their subconscious and shows how they operate on a predatory, rational level."

The vision of the lion's head appears to Karolina, and she swallows hard. She shifts slightly in her seat; pencil paused above her notebook. "Why does the conversation lack a natural flow?" she asks, her brows drawing together.

The instructor leans back, fingers steepled lightly. "It's all about control for them. They will suddenly shift the topic of conversation when they are not in control. Or if an emotional word or topic surfaces that they really don't understand, they'll switch the focus."

Karolina taps her pencil against the edge of the desk, lips pressed in thought. "What are some other elements you notice when around a psychopath?" Her tone is casual, but there's an urgency beneath it now. She's become more focused on figuring out if Max fits the profile than on the missing woman she's supposed to be studying.

The instructor studies her for a beat, then leans forward, hands folding on the table. "You've been studying body language, yes?"

Karolina nods, almost too quickly.

"So, you are familiar with micro-expressions, which are registered in our subconscious. So, often, when people say they 'have a bad feeling' about someone, they are likely picking up on the other person's micro-expressions. You have to be fast to pick up on these micro-expressions because they happen within the blink of an eye—quite literally. When someone is angry, they will furrow their eyebrows or snarl their lips, but it will happen in a fraction of a second, and then they will regain their composure."

Karolina leans over the notebook again, her hand already sketching. "What are the most common micro-expressions beyond anger?" she asks without looking up.

"Surprise and shock, which is usually expressed with a raise of the eyebrows and widened eyes. But you might not always see these micro-expressions consciously, so you must pay attention to your gut feelings around a person. Their micro-expressions will enter your subconscious, so you must trust what or how you feel around them."

Karolina draws a face with raised eyebrows and wide eyes, then another with furrowed brows and an upturned lip beside it. Her pencil slows. She wonders if machine learning and AI will one day be able to register a gut feeling. The thought unnerves her. She silently hopes it won't be able to sense or replace human intuition.

The instructor is still speaking, her voice quickening now, animated by the rhythm of her own thoughts.

"There is also something called the 'psychopath stare.' This is the opposite of a micro-expression. It's generally described as a prolonged, predatory gaze or as a fixed stare, one that leaves you unsettled and uncomfortable. Maybe you pick up on the fact that someone's watching you and you catch their eyes every time you look up. The suggested reasons psychopaths use this stare may vary. It could be to dominate, threaten, seduce, or all three simultaneously."

Karolina shudders. When they had sex, Max stared at her without blinking. It left her feeling empty and her thoughts disorganized. Almost as if she was in a trance. She thought his gaze was an awkward romantic attempt taken too far, but she now knows there was something else behind the stare. And still, she whispers inwardly: focus on the missing woman; focus on the case. But Max's name is already etched into her neural pathways.

The victim and the profiler, the past and the present, the mask and the man. Karolina checks her watch. The training session has been going on for three hours, and the instructor notices her looking at the time.

"Ah yes, our time is up." She leans her head back, raising her eyes again to the ceiling. "We can stop the recording now." The green light turns off.

Karolina begins gathering her things and reaches for the pad with her sketches. The instructor gently places her palm on the pad, holding it firmly.

"We'd like to keep this if you don't mind," the instructor leans closer. "The police don't randomly pick someone to do this sort of work. You realize this, Karolina. They chose to work with you for a reason."

Karolina nods. Her cheeks warm as she reaches for the door handle.

"Before you go, I want to ask you something." The instructor flips through the notepad to the last sketch, the one about Salenan. She holds it up for Karolina. Instead of a landscape or a symbol, letters stand out.

"Do you know who this is?" The instructor points to the letters Karolina had clearly spelled out.

Max.

CHAPTER NINETEEN

Synthetic Consciousness

Zoe wakes, realizing she has an hour left before the workshop starts. She pulls the book from the nightstand and stares at the blue cover, taking in the title, *The ESP Algorithm*. She opens the jacket to see a photo of a woman in her late fifties, elegant and focused: Dr. Elaine Powers, a neuroscientist formerly affiliated with Harvard Medical School and a researcher in consciousness and telepathy. The photograph alone unsettles her; this wasn't some fringe theorist. This was someone credentialed, someone who had walked the halls of establishment science and still dared to ask the question: what if Extra Sensory Perception is real?

Zoe bends the spine of the book and reads: "Extraordinary psychic phenomena shouldn't be dismissed simply because we don't yet understand them. They may be signals, not symptoms." Why had Alessandra been carrying a book exploring telepathy, remote viewing, and the neurobiological basis of intuitive knowing while staying at Salenan?

She rereads the first line: "ESP may be a latent human ability, a sixth sense tied to mirror neurons, quantum consciousness, and a nonlocal mind." Zoe recalls Max and his friends' conversation at the Speckled Boar, their scoffing at Project Stargate, the military's psychic spy program based on remote viewing. But this book isn't fantasy. Dr. Powers collaborated with Stanford physicists, studied autistic savants, and suggested that the human brain might be a transceiver, both sending and receiving information from beyond conventional perception.

Zoe flips to a highlighted section: "When tested under controlled conditions, some children, particularly those with heightened empathic circuits, have demonstrated the ability to access information from other minds. These findings challenge the notion that consciousness is confined to the brain." This wasn't just pseudoscience. It was a map, a framework for how someone like Zoe might have been understood. *Why would Alessandra be reading this book now?* Maybe she wasn't just reading it, maybe she was using it.

Zoe closes the book, places it back in the drawer, and heads toward the main lodge for the workshop, *The Mind Reclaimed: Welcome to the Age of Synthetic Consciousness.*

Zoe enrolled in the month-long series Alessandra had been invited to right before she disappeared. She had used her credentials as a journalist to gain permission to attend the weekend sessions, but the facilitator made it clear she needed to maintain a cover and not reveal her identity to protect the comfort level of the attendees. The workshop is invitation-only and confidential, including the identities of those in attendance. The added layer of confidentiality surrounding the workshop lends to an air of importance and exclusivity for the attendees. Zoe wonders if the secrecy is purposeful and meaningful from a security perspective or a promotional stunt to sell more tickets. Perhaps a bit of both.

Beneath her journalistic curiosity lies something more personal. Zoe isn't just searching for Alessandra; she's trying to understand why the concept of synthetic consciousness disturbs her so profoundly. The words tap on the core of her identity, revealing a deep-rooted fear. What if the qualities that define her - her intuition, empathy, and imagination - could be replicated, and exploited for harmful purposes? And yet, a part of her is drawn to it, too. If Alessandra saw promise in this place and in this technology, then maybe Zoe needed to see it for herself. Maybe some part of her wants to believe that consciousness *can* be reclaimed or at least decoded.

Either way, Zoe has agreed not to share any details about the event in her coverage. But that's not stopping her from trying to understand what kind of future we are stepping into and whether it's already begun to shape us from the inside out.

Zoe walks onto the lawn atop the cliff and sees twenty or so people sitting cross-legged in a giant circle around the chessboard. The facilitator stands in the middle of the board. She glances in Zoe's direction and waves her into the circle. The participants are a mix of tech executives and retired hippies, spanning generations and fashion choices.

"Welcome," the facilitator says to the group while looking directly at Zoe. "We will start our session with a five-minute silent meditation and follow with a land acknowledgment."

As Zoe centers herself, resting both palms on her knees, legs crossed, she closes her eyes. The waves crash against the cliff, vibrating up into Zoe's body. Five minutes float by, and the facilitator breaks the silence by introducing herself: she is the head of Deep Think Tank, a tech start-up focused on the future of artificial intelligence and technology. Zoe stifles a laugh at the name of the new business enterprise.

"Let's go around the circle and state your chosen name for the weekend. Some of us may want to refrain from using our given names to maintain privacy and anonymity, so please respect that. I'd also ask you to state a one-word intention for the workshop and share a little about yourself." The instructor gestures toward Zoe. Her stomach tenses.

"My chosen name is Alessandra, my intention is truth-seeking, and I am a writer." She doesn't announce to the other attendees that she is a journalist; after all, she isn't reporting on the workshop.

"Oh, I should have mentioned we don't talk about what we do for work. We focus on who we are." A writer is who Zoe is; a journalist is what she does for work. The two are almost impossible to distinguish in Zoe's mind.

The facilitator glares at Zoe. "Are you an attendee, or are you a participant?"

"What is the difference?" Zoe asks, wondering if the question is meant for her.

"Are you here to participate or observe?" the facilitator presses.

"Participate," Zoe shares a half-truth.

A woman with brunette hair turns to speak. "My real name is Lillian, and my intention is also truth-seeking." She pauses, stretching her neck toward Zoe. "I'm a climatologist, and I am here as a participant."

Zoe smiles at her; she can hear a slight French accent, and an overwhelming sense of familiarity washes over Zoe when she catches Lillian's eyes. For a split second, Zoe feels the oddest pull, as if she's met this woman before.

Everyone has introduced themselves, and the facilitator begins to pace the chessboard. Zoe adjusts her posture on the grass. Her fingers absently brush over the soft clover beneath her knees. She scans the circle of attendees again. While Zoe is rarely intimidated, the mix of power and eccentricity among the attendees is unnerving. The air buzzes with a strange blend of anticipation and performance, everyone eager to be seen thinking differently. She exhales slowly, aware now of the tension gathering in her chest, a low hum of vigilance she knows not to ignore. She is still unsure whether she is here as herself or as a version of herself she's invented for this search.

"You may be wondering why you've been selected to participate in this session. This workshop is hosted by a coalition of technology leaders and researchers. Some of you were hand-picked to start a new conversation about the next wave of consciousness and to begin to determine how our human potential might elevate and integrate with artificial systems."

Zoe's body freezes at the term *integrate*. She feels the weight of it settle in her chest. This isn't about resisting technology; it is about blending with it.

The facilitator steps beside a towering chess piece. "What is the greatest threat to humanity?"

A voice calls out: "artificial intelligence!"

Some chuckle. Others nod solemnly.

"And what is the greatest threat to artificial intelligence?" the facilitator asks, stopping beside a large-sized chess piece. She rests her hand lightly on the crown of the king.

Lillian raises her hand. "Humanity. Our own blindness. Our tendency to create tools more powerful than our ethics."

The facilitator smiles. "And yet we keep building."

Zoe speaks, her voice quieter but firm. "The Singularity is the greatest threat to humanity." The circle freezes.

The facilitator's hand slips from the king's crown; she turns slowly, locking eyes with Zoe. "That's why we're all here," she says sweeping her glance over the entire group, "Right?" A ripple of nervous laughter passes through the circle of attendees, the silence breaking just slightly with nods of affirmation. The facilitator's smile settles into something rehearsed. Zoe feels the weight of the circle's attention shift, recalibrated by the tension her own words introduced. The grass beneath her palms feels suddenly damp, grounding her. She resists the urge to look away.

The facilitator gestures toward Dr. Owen. "I'd like to introduce Dr. Judy Owen, who specializes in empathy research. She is the author of several books, including *The Conscious Empath*, *Empathy is the Answer*, and *The Empathy Quotient*. Dr. Owen, would you join me on the board?"

Dr. Owen rises and walks to the center slowly. Zoe's breath falters. The bone structure. The voice. Even the tilt of her head when she listens. She looks exactly like the author photo from *The ESP Algorithm*, the same poised calm, the same intensity around the eyes. Could she be using a pseudonym too? Zoe narrows her gaze, heart ticking faster.

"I'm here to better understand how artificial technology will affect our brain circuitry," she says. "Our brains constantly search for efficiency. They build shortcuts. If AI grows advanced enough, we may offload even basic forms of cognition to it, reducing our own neural engagement. The result? A quiet kind of downgrade."

A man in the group raises a hand. "Are you saying we'll get... dumber?"

"I wouldn't say dumber," Owen says, smiling faintly. "But certainly number. If you're not emotionally present, you're easier to steer."

Zoe watches the facilitator's eyes flicker, not with surprise, but with calculation.

"And who would be steering?" someone asks.

"Anyone with access to Artificial Intelligence programming systems. Hostile foreign governments can use artificial intelligence to take over a country; companies can use it to co-opt consumers. That sort of stuff." Owen delivers the response as if it is all casual knowledge. She walks off the chess board and sits back down next to Zoe. A heaviness comes over Zoe, thinking of how the future has already arrived and of the danger that lurks around every corner when it's been designed by men like Ryan Sowell. Sympara has already been built, the streets have been paved, the lights are on in the buildings.

"And this is precisely why Deep Think Tank was created." The facilitator says, beaming, her smile widening as she seizes the moment to push the promise of the latest technology product to change the world as we know it. Zoe can smell a pitch a mile away, it comes with a hollow, tinny electrical current, an excitement that circles around the person selling something, but never quite reaches out past their own circumference. She watches in mild amusement as the facilitator stands tall and begins promoting the premise of her company.

"Deep circuit learning is part of the broader field of machine learning that uses artificial neural networks, which are computer simulations patterned after a human brain. Deep learning includes aspects of machine learning algorithms, neural networks, and AI. The artificial neural networks created from these components are where the field of AI comes closest to modeling the workings of the human brain. Improved mathematical formulas and increased computer processing power are enabling the development of more sophisticated deep-learning applications than ever before. Deep learning, also called structured learning and hierarchical learning, is the kind of machine intelligence used to create AIs that beat humans at the game of chess." The facilitator spreads her arms wide, hovering over the chess pieces.

Zoe tries to follow, but the jargon hits her like a fog: convolutional networks, biomimetic clustering, recursive self-training. She leans back into the grass and closes her eyes, listening to the roar of the waves crashing against the cliffs.

This session is less about preventing human downgrading in a world that is ever increasingly controlled by technology and more of an investor pitch to get these top-level tech executives in Silicon Valley to buy into Deep Think Tank. This isn't about reclaiming anything, Zoe thinks. It's about selling a future to people who already own it. An image forms. It's the hollow dome of Hangar One, flickering like a digital brain, synthetic and breathing. Why would Alessandra have been invited to this? Zoe mulls the question over. Perhaps she had investment money that the Deep Think folks would be attracted to?

"What does any of this have to do with empathy research?" Zoe blurts out, wondering why Dr. Owen is there. The circle of attendees collectively shifts their focus to her, and the facilitator eyes her.

Dr. Owen responds, "Right now, the average personality profile of an artificial intelligence program is the same as a human with empathy deficit disorder." Zoe raises her eyebrows. The doctor continues, "meaning AI lacks emotional intelligence and empathy, which means it is similar to the brain patterns we see in psychopaths, sociopaths, and some narcissists."

"That's terrifying," another attendee says. The group collectively nods.

Dr. Owen explains, "For psychopaths, empathy operates like a switch, a circuit breaker that they can turn on or off. They are equipped with cognitive empathy—not somatic empathy."

"Empathy that they can intellectualize with their mind, but not feel in their body," Zoe adds.

"Precisely." The doctor shoots Zoe a knowing look.

As the facilitator takes over and begins talking more about Deep Think, Zoe leans back into the grass and closes her eyes, drowning out the sales pitch. She takes a deep breath, and the sulfur from the hot springs burns her nostrils. Bubbles swirl, the color of steel-gray rust, like molten metal. She's reminded of the colors of the dome on Moffett Field.

The Singularity terrifies Zoe. But more terrifying is the possibility that technology, in whatever form it takes, might one day *feel*. Not think, but *feel*.

She's pulled back to reality by the facilitator's voice. "Time for a lunch break. The dining hall will open in twenty minutes. You're welcome to walk the grounds."

Zoe rises, brushing the grass from her pants. She finds the facilitator and walks beside her. "Thank you for the session. I was curious... have you seen or heard of an attendee named Alessandra Wilder?"

The facilitator stiffens. "Is that the pseudonym she used here?"

"No. It's her real name."

The facilitator hesitates, then turns sharply toward the lodge. "I'm not sure."

Zoe watches her disappear into the main lodge.

There it was again, that sudden tension, as if Alessandra's name was an incantation or a trigger. Why was everyone here so cagey about her? Not simply forgetful but guarded. The facilitator's reaction felt strategic. As if she had been trained to reroute questions she didn't want to answer. It wasn't the first time Zoe had seen this maneuver. She recognized the choreography of avoidance: the exact moment when someone exits the conversation to preserve a lie.

She turns to a bench overlooking the sea and pulls *The ESP Algorithm* from her bag, thumbing back to a dog-eared section. She re-reads the inscription at the upper right corner of the chapter. It's faded, almost translucent, the three handwritten words etched in hurried, narrow script: *Watch the women.*

Was it a message for Zoe to watch the women? Or was it a warning, that she is the one being watched? The boundary between insight and imagination thins, she can't tell if she is decoding something real or playing out a story her mind has already written for her. She flips the page and rereads a sentence that has been underlined in pencil: "Intuition is often the brain's way of recognizing a pattern faster than conscious thought." The irony isn't lost on her, it's as if the pages of the book had read her mind.

Then, something catches her eye inside the front cover: a faintly penciled triangular glyph. It takes a moment to register in Zoe's mind. It is the same shape as Max's pendant. She remembers the words etched on it: *We watch. We imitate. We conquer.* Zoe takes in a thin, unsteady breath. This book didn't just belong to Alessandra. It belonged to someone close to Max. Or to Max himself.

A shadow falls beside her. "Are you enjoying the book?" a voice asks, even but watchful.

Zoe looks up. It's Dr. Owen, or Dr. Elaine Powers, rather. The resemblance is impossible to ignore. Her imagination surges with conclusions. *It's her. It has to be. Who else would recognize the book?*

"Is this yours?" Zoe asks, raising the book.

Dr. Owen smiles with a slight nod. "Do you mind?" she asks, gesturing to the empty bench space.

Zoe moves over. "Please."

Dr. Owen lowers herself carefully, brushing a leaf from the bench before settling in. They both stare at the ocean for a moment, the whitecaps glinting beneath the midday sun.

"How did you get invited?" Dr. Owen finally asks, keeping her tone light, but Zoe detects something more deliberate behind the question, a measure being taken.

Zoe exhales, debating how much to reveal. "I'm a journalist. I asked to attend... to learn."

Dr. Owen doesn't flinch, but her lips press together thoughtfully. She reaches into her bag, removes a thick ivory card, and hands it to Zoe. "This was my invitation."

Zoe turns the card over in her hands. The gold-lettered script reads:

> *"You have been hand-selected to impact the trajectory of the next wave of consciousness."*

She blinks, letting the words settle. "I'm most definitely not a tech leader," Zoe says quietly.

"Neither am I," Dr. Owen replies. "A handful of us were chosen because of our expertise in empathy." She smiles at Zoe. "They are looking to see if it's possible to embed emotional intelligence and empathy into artificial intelligence. We were chosen because of our knowledge of the subject." She pauses, then adds, "Or because we make excellent subjects."

Zoe turns toward her, her breath catching slightly. "Subjects?"

Dr. Owen smiles faintly as if amused by Zoe's reaction. "You'd be surprised how valuable certain neural profiles can be when they're designing synthetic models. The more complex the circuitry, the more useful the map."

"Who are 'they'?" Zoe asks, needing to hear the answer out loud, that is, outside the spiral of her own suspicions. The question sits heavy between them, and for a moment, she wonders if it's too direct of a question, especially at a place like Salenan.

"The sponsors of the event." Dr. Owen seems to be holding back. Zoe bores into her eyes, and she specifies, "The board members of Oneness University."

"Of course, that makes sense." Zoe's journalist instinct flickers. "Do you know Alessandra Wilder?"

Dr. Owen tilts her head slightly as if weighing what to say. "I've heard of her. Many in the empathy research community were eager to meet her."

Zoe leans in, her pulse quickening. "Why?"

Dr. Owen opens her mouth to respond but glances toward a group of attendees gathering by the chessboard. "She went through some preliminary brain scans. I can't share specifics due to patient confidentiality, but there was something there. Something worth looking into. Her results raised a lot of interest in our field."

As she speaks, Zoe notices a man sitting just outside the group. He's dressed like a participant but silent, always watching. He's wearing a thin black band around his wrist. It reminds her of Max's pendant, it's not exactly the same, but unmistakably familiar.

"Some of the early tests," Dr. Owen adds, "weren't just theoretical. We've seen promising results in more flexible jurisdictions."

Zoe narrows her eyes. "What kind of jurisdictions?"

Dr. Owen's smile is gentle but unrevealing. "Places where oversight doesn't hinder innovation."

Zoe's pen freezes over her notebook. That sounds a lot like Sympara, she thinks, too much like Sympara.

Down the path, one of the TED-famous technologists, the silver-haired one who'd introduced himself as a digital ethicist, mutters to another attendee, "They're not ready for Phase 2."

"What?" the other says.

"Nothing," he replies quickly, glancing toward Zoe. She pretends not to notice but scribbles the phrase in her notebook: *Phase 2 of what?*

Zoe exhales slowly. *The Mind Reclaimed* isn't about protecting humanity from artificial intelligence, it's about adapting the human mind to be more machine compatible. Less unpredictable, less emotional and more programmable, easier to control. Maybe Alessandra wasn't here to attend; maybe she was part of the research. A thought floats into Zoe's mind. *They're not studying AI to make it more human. They're studying humans to make us more like AI.*

"Do you know why Alessandra never wound up attending the workshop?"

Dr. Owen shakes her head. "No, but sometimes, it can be too much, the realization of who we are at our core. It's overwhelming, and sometimes people need time to process."

"So, do you believe she dropped out of the workshop?"

Dr. Owen shrugs her shoulders. "It's possible. Or someone in her life didn't want her to continue down this road of self-discovery."

Perhaps Alessandra's father didn't want his daughter to participate in pseudo-scientific research. Maybe she poses a threat to him or his company? Zoe lets that thought linger.

"And why did you come if you're skeptical of technology?" She asks.

Dr. Owen meets her eyes. "Because if people like me don't participate, then people without empathy will shape everything."

Zoe pauses. "Could I be scanned? My brain?"

Dr. Owen smiles. "Absolutely."

Zoe hands over her business card, watching Dr. Owen tuck her card away. A strange vulnerability lingers in the air.

She wonders what her own scan would reveal. She always felt other people's emotions in her body, like a current under her skin. Would her brain scan show a kind of neurological openness that made her easier to influence and control? She used to think her emotional intelligence made her perceptive. But maybe it just made her a better subject.

The dining bell rings. As they head to lunch, Lillian greets them. "Mind if I join?"

Zoe and Dr. Owen nod. The three women find a table. Zoe studies Lillian as she settles into her seat. She has the kind of face that's difficult to look away from, not for its perfection but for its presence. High cheekbones, a sculpted jawline, and shoulder-length brunette hair that frames her face perfectly. There's a polish to her, but it's quiet, effortless. Her eyes, large, dark, and expressive, seem to absorb more than they reveal.

Lillian leans forward, her fingers tracing the rim of her glass as she describes her glacier research. "Most people tune out when you throw statistics at them. Rising sea levels and carbon emissions, they become abstractions. But when you show them a glacier collapsing, the sound of it, like the Earth breaking, it stays with them. People ignore numbers. But stories... visuals... beauty, that gets attention."

Zoe watches her closely, sensing the conviction behind her words. It's not performative. Lillian believes in what she knows and in what she sees vanishing.

Dr. Owen glances between them, squinting slightly. "Sorry, but has anyone ever told you two that you have the same eyes?"

Zoe and Lillian turn to one another. There's a pause, not playful, but quiet and reflective They search each other's faces.

A chill of recognition rolls over Zoe's skin, the back of her neck tingles. She realized now they've both been to the same glacier. Zoe had gone to cover an environmental feature for the network and Lillian was there to gather the footage that no one wanted to fund, footage that still haunted her. Something about the coincidence unnerves Zoe. As if the two women have been circling the same story without knowing it, something larger than them has been drawing them together.

The three women walk along the garden path toward the chessboard, the oversized marble pieces catching the last of the light of day.

"Anyone know how to play?" Lillian asks, resting a hand on a smooth, towering pawn.

Zoe shrugs. "We'd better learn. Before AI beats us." She says it lightly, but the humor falls flat in her own ears.

Dr. Owen walks to the queen, trailing her fingers along its polished edge. "Start with the basics. Then, follow your gut. That's true in chess and in life."

Zoe tilts her head. "Why is the queen the most powerful piece?"

Dr. Owen smiles, but there's something wry beneath it. "Because she's the only one who can move in any direction she wants. The others follow the rules. The queen makes her own."

They head toward the hot tubs. The sulfur smell is sharp. Zoe peels off her clothes and sinks into the warm water. Lillian slips into the tub beside her. Dr. Owen joins the tub next to them.

"This is where we get enlightened?" Lillian jokes.

"No," Zoe says. "This is where the government recruits psychic spies."

Lillian perks up. "What?"

"I've been reading about Project Stargate. The CIA trained people to use extended perception for espionage." Zoe says.

Dr. Owen leans in. "You're not wrong. Some of that happened here at Salenan, it's still classified."

Lillian raises her brows. "Seriously?"

"In the 1980s, there were Soviet-American exchanges taking place here. Astronauts, cosmonauts, the CIA, the KGB, they all met here. They took nature walks, bonded in the hot springs, all in the name of diplomacy. Off the record, of course."

"They believed that if we couldn't connect on Earth, maybe we could connect in orbit," Owen adds. "But they didn't go to space. They came here instead."

Zoe reaches for her water glass. Her beaded bracelet catches the light.

Lillian sees it. "Where did you get that?"

"It was a gift. From my boyfriend," Zoe replies.

"What's his name?"

Zoe hesitates, heart beginning to pound in her chest. "Max."

"Max, what?"

"Max Furtherlore."

Lillian's grip on Zoe's wrist tightens for the briefest moment, her gaze fixed. She doesn't speak. Instead, she slowly releases Zoe's wrist, her fingers slipping away. Zoe's wrist drops and the bracelet strikes the porcelain edge with a sharp crack and then bursts. Beads scatter like shrapnel, vanishing into the grass below. Zoe flinches. For a second, neither of them moves.

"I'm sorry," Lillian says softly, but there's something in her voice.

Zoe looks down at her wrist, bare now. The broken bracelet feels like an omen, a warning disguised as an accident.

Lillian's eyes are fixed on her. "You said his name is Max Furtherlore?"

Zoe nods slowly. "Yes. Why? Do you know him?"

Lillian doesn't answer immediately. Her gaze drops to the shards of beads in the grass. "No," she says finally. "Not directly. But I've heard the name."

Zoe waits, but Lillian says nothing more.

CHAPTER TWENTY

Signals and Stories

The next morning, Zoe finds herself in Dr. Owen's makeshift office at Salenan, sunk into a pastel pink chair made of velvet, designed to soothe. A large monstera plant takes residence in the corner of the room, spreading its Swiss cheese-looking leaves onto both walls, which are painted a limelight green. The space hums with a calm energy, with items curated to regulate the nervous system of its dwellers. But Zoe still feels a sense of unease within its confines, her eyes snag on more items. A deck of tarot cards rests on the corner of Dr. Owen's desk, splayed slightly as if someone had just shuffled them. Behind the desk hangs a framed poster of Abraham Maslow's pyramid of human needs, it's geometry and tidy lines looking more clinical than comforting. Zoe's eyes scan to the left to a quote that stretches across the wall, painted as a mural: *More light, More night.*

"So, the panic attacks began after you met your boyfriend, Max?" Dr. Owen's voice snaps Zoe back into her body.

She grounds her feet on the hard wood floor and shakes her head. "No. They got worse after meeting Max, but it started before I met him." Since she left the anchor desk, Zoe's anxiety seemed to follow her everywhere.

She kept her anxiety a secret, but when she began waking in the middle of the night, covered in sweat and hyperventilating, she knew she couldn't hide it much longer. Dr. Owen raises her eyebrows and makes a note.

"So, when did the first episode happen, in your recollection?"

Zoe grips the sides of the leather couch. "When I was working in TV News. I had a panic attack right before I was about to go on air. I felt as if I was suffocating, drowning. It washed over me. Luckily, it didn't happen live, but it broke my confidence. I became terrified of it happening again. I had to take a leave of absence. Eventually, I left the network altogether to work in print journalism."

"May I ask what story you were about to cover before you went on air?"

"I was covering the story of the tsunami that had just hit Japan."

Dr. Owen's eyes widen. She makes another note. "Well, evolutionary psychologists would say it makes sense that you may have experienced the symptoms of drowning, similar to the victims of the tsunami, and it presented as a panic attack. We'll work through how this happens and why there may be a connection."

Zoe nods. Dr. Owen continues, "I also have the results from your brain scan, and they confirm my original hypothesis about the root of your anxiety."

Dr. Owen has a folder in front of her. Zoe hesitates, staring at the manila envelope. She tells herself she did the fMRI scan for the story, for Alessandra. Any detail, any clue might help her understand what happened to her. But there's another reason, quieter and harder to admit. She wants to know what's inside her own mind. She's spent her life trying to distinguish intuition from imagination, gut feeling from delusion. If there's something measurable, something that explains why and how she feels everything so deeply, maybe she won't have to doubt herself anymore. Maybe her panic will subside, and it will finally make sense.

"Remember how I spoke about mirror neurons, how some people have more than the average person?"

"Yes," Zoe replies.

"Your brain scan shows exceptionally high mirror neuron activity, far more than we typically observe."

"Can you explain more?"

"We now have much more research about mirror neurons and their role. They don't just fire when we see someone perform an action. In some people, they activate emotional mimicry on a deep, bodily level. These individuals can physically feel others' emotions. You, Zoe, show unusually high mirror neuron activation, among the highest I've seen."

Zoe leans back, thoughts racing. She recalls childhood moments, getting sick when others were upset, crying when someone walked into the room angry. This wasn't just emotional contagion. Her body had always been a receptor.

"Would having more mirror neurons also impact my anxiety?"

"Oh yes, it's all connected. You also have a larger amygdala, the part of the brain involved in fear and vigilance. When paired with heightened sensory sensitivity, your brain is wired to detect and respond to threats more intensely."

"That sounds... bad."

"It's neither good nor bad. Just different. From an evolutionary perspective, you'd have been the one to sense danger first, a sort of early-warning system for the tribe."

Zoe thinks of her investigation. She wonders whether this wiring will help her find Alessandra or overwhelm her own brain circuitry, like it used to do on the news set.

"Dr. Owen, what would mirror neurons have to do with a tsunami halfway around the world? I wasn't near it."

"Have you heard of quantum entanglement?"

Zoe shakes her head.

"It's a physics concept that proves two particles, no matter how far apart, can influence each other. Some researchers use it metaphorically to explore consciousness. It's speculative, yes, but it suggests we may be way more connected than we realize."

Zoe's eyes water. A shiver travels her spine. "What connects them?"

"Energy. Consciousness." Dr. Owen states. "We're only beginning to understand how emotion and awareness may ripple across unseen networks."

"Then why wouldn't others have the same reaction I did?" Zoe thinks back not only to her co-workers, who were unwilling or unable to sense what she had, but also to Max. His unflinching, calm demeanor and his almost eerie inability to be startled. Like a boulder, he seemed unmovable, an unshakeable presence even when hit by a tsunami, while she feels more like the ocean, ever movable, ever turbulent.

"You might be more attuned. Others may have felt something but not recognized or paid attention to it." Dr. Owen offers. "With your level of sensitivity, it's possible you registered something deeper."

Zoe hesitates, eyeing the deck of tarot cards, weighing the possibility of what's being laid out before her. "And what about Max? He seems so unflappable, so untouched by things that would startle everyone else. Nothing seems to rattle him." Zoe replays his reaction to nearly running over a hiker on their trip to Big Sur, his hands steady on the wheel, a slight smirk on his face. It was as if the chaos of nearly killing someone had not only not pierced his conscience but had slightly thrilled him.

"Well, again, it may relate to his energetic makeup." Dr. Owen leans forward. "Can you describe him to me?"

Zoe blinks, caught off guard. "Describe him how?"

"Just... what's it like to be around him? What do you feel in your body?"

Zoe draws a slow breath. "It's strange. Around Max, everything slows down. There's this stillness. It's almost serene, like nothing can touch me. I feel... calm, I guess. But detached. Like being inside a snow globe."

Dr. Owen's pen pauses on her notepad. "Detached?"

"Yeah. Not numb exactly, just... quiet. I never seem to feel a sense of panic when I'm with Max; instead, I feel steady, calm, quiet. I guess a bit more like him."

The doctor nods slowly. "That's very telling." She folds her hands. "Without assessing Max, I can't say definitively, but your description suggests he might have a mirror neuron deficiency."

Zoe tilts her head. "What does that mean?"

"People with psychopathy or antisocial traits tend to have extremely low mirror neuron activity, sometimes none at all. They don't emit emotional resonance in the way most people do. So, being near them... it can feel like peace. But really, it's absence. The absence of emotional input. What you're sensing, that stillness, may not be safety. It may be silence."

Zoe's body stiffens. Silence. Of course. Max's uncanny calm, his cool charm, the way he never seemed rattled even when others were panicked. Even when they nearly hit the woman on Highway 1.

She feels the truth drop into place like a stone. The things Max didn't feel. The things he didn't do.

Dr. Owen's voice lowers. "Psychopaths also tend to have a smaller amygdala, the brain's fear center. This makes them less reactive. Less empathetic. Evolutionarily, they were the hunters, the risk-takers. They didn't flinch. And that made them incredibly dangerous, and incredibly effective."

Zoe stares down at her hands. Her breath tightens. The question hangs in the air, unspoken: *Have I been sleeping next to a psychopath?*

"Zoe," Dr. Owen says gently, "you don't need to label him. But it's important to name what your body already knows."

Zoe nods once, letting it sink in. The stillness wasn't safety. It was a warning, masked as calm. She had mistaken the quiet for peace when, really, it was a void. And now, the panic attacks made a cruel kind of sense. Her body had known what her mind wasn't ready to see.

Dr. Owen places a hand lightly on Zoe's file. "You've been absorbing more than your fair share of emotion, Zoe. But they're not yours to carry. They're a symptom of something missing in the other person, not of something wrong with you."

Zoe swallows hard. Now, she wonders if Max's stillness, the silence, was the truest thing about him and what drew her in. "So, Max and I may be opposites, neurologically speaking?"

"Yes. And such extremes often attract each other. And repel."

"How common is this?"

"On either extreme, whether it's sociopathy or extreme sensitivity, it occurs in around 2 percent of the population. The scientific community tends to focus on the psychopathic side of the spectrum. But we're just beginning to study people like you, those with intense sensory perception and empathy."

"What's the term for those of us on the opposite side of the spectrum?"

"There isn't an agreed term. Some say 'hyper-empathetic individuals,' 'highly sensitive people,' or 'sensory processing sensitivity,' while others simply say empaths, but that's not widely accepted in science."

"But we exist."

"You do. And your brain scans prove it."

Zoe feels both validated and uneasy. "So, if I'm absorbing everyone else's feelings... what happens when I'm around someone who is dangerous?"

"It depends on your boundaries. And your awareness. That's what we're trying to understand." Dr. Owen leans forward. "Would you consider joining a clinical trial?"

Zoe shakes her head. "I'd rather not be a test subject. I'll do my own research."

Dr. Owen nods. "Fair. If you'd prefer a non-invasive approach, you could start by listening to your anxiety. Ask what it might be trying to tell you. Your body may already know what your mind doesn't."

"I've always struggled to tell the difference between my intuition and my imagination," she says. "How do you know what's real?"

Dr. Owen looks at her thoughtfully. "It's one of the oldest questions, isn't it? The mind is designed to simulate, to project scenarios, to dream. That's our imagination. But intuition, that's pattern recognition filtered through the unconscious. It's fast, and it's quiet. A knowing that feels immediate, often without explanation."

Zoe nods slowly, absorbing it.

"Think of your brain as a prediction engine," Owen continues. "It's always scanning for what fits, for what matches prior experience, emotional resonance, and sensed energy. When your intuition fires, it's because your subconscious has assembled the pieces faster than your conscious mind can follow."

"But what if I'm wrong?" Zoe asks. "What if I'm just projecting?"

"You will be, sometimes," Owen says with a small smile. "But here's the trick: imagination tends to speak in stories. Intuition, in signals. Imagination asks *what if?* Intuition whispers *this.*"

Zoe exhales, letting that land.

Dr. Owen leans back, her hands folding in her lap. "From a neurological standpoint, your scan shows heightened activity in the insula, the part of the brain that processes *interoception*, our internal sense of the body. That's where intuition often lives. It's also the part of the brain responsible for empathy. If you feel things in your body before you understand them, it's because your brain is translating patterns into sensation."

"So the body knows first."

"Almost always," Owen says. "Especially yours."

Zoe glances down at her hands, folded in her lap. "Then, maybe I need to stop arguing with it."

Owen's smile softens. "That's the beginning of trust, not in anyone else, just in yourself."

Zoe swallows hard. Her intuition is something she had struggled with, often brushing it away. But now, she knows it's more than that. Her intuition isn't a flaw in her system; it is a strength.

Zoe's gaze drifts from Dr. Owen to the wall to her left. She rereads the words painted in black against the pastel backdrop: *More light, More night.* It hits her hard: she and Max are opposites, each hard-wired to attract the other, like magnets.

Dr. Owen catches Zoe's gaze and smiles. "We are living in fascinating times, Zoe. Don't let anyone convince you that your perceptions aren't real. The science is catching up."

Later that night, after the hot springs have cleared and the campus grows quiet, Zoe slips back into the small cottage assigned to her at Salenan. She closes the door behind her and pulls *The ESP Algorithm* from her nightstand. The room hums faintly, as if it's charged. She thumbs through the underlined passages, not sure of what she's looking for, until a scrap of paper slips out from between the pages.

It's a note, handwritten: "Watch the women." Beneath it, a second line, scrawled messier: "They're the prototypes."

Zoe freezes. Her eyes flick across the room instinctively. Something clicks into place like a puzzle piece snapping in backward. She grabs her laptop and reopens the file Dr. Owen had emailed earlier with her brain scan results. They were mostly diagnostic, high amygdala activation, extreme empathic processing, but now something else catches her eye. A folder embedded in the metadata: /salenan/data/models/prototype_f_09.

Prototypes? Why would her scan be labeled a prototype model? She runs a local search and finds a few others: prototype_f_03, f_04_r, f_08_cleared. And then, f_01_a.wilder.

Her stomach flips. Alessandra's last name. Coded. But there.

They've been collecting them. Women. Scanning them. Indexing their neural architecture. She scrolls deeper into the file tree and locates a reference to Sympara. Her fingers hover over the keys, typing in into the keyboard: ./sympara/circuit-design-research/neural-empathy-modeling/. Zoe stares at the screen.

Salenan is not just a wellness retreat: it's a front, an intake site, a soft entry, with Sympara as the lab. This entire workshop was the screening process. Empathy-mining disguised as mindfulness. Human consciousness reverse engineered. Zoe shuts the laptop and paces the room.

Watch the women. What are they building? What is she already part of? Who is behind this? Max. Everything comes back to Max.

Her anxiety. The silence. The eerie sense of stillness around him, like a room with all the air pulled out. And now, these scans. This place. Zoe grabs her notebook and flips back to the page where she'd written the donation amounts.

Tex Chemical → Oneness University
$3 million. Then $16 million.

Why would a chemical corporation, known for agricultural toxins and deep environmental violations, fund a university researching artificial intelligence and synthetic empathy?

Zoe updates her notes: "Alessandra's father is the CEO of Tex Chemical. Alessandra disappears, and her neural scan winds up catalogued in a system linked to Sympara."

Max, who is tightly connected to Oneness University by his documentary, *Architects of The Mind*, never really talked about his funding sources. Zoe flips to another page where she finds scribbled notes from a late-night internet deep dive: *Oneness = Tax-exempt umbrella. Multiple LLCs. Registered in Delaware.* Max's production company had appeared in the same registry... as a subsidiary, a possible shell company.

Zoe closes her eyes and lets the pattern rise; she concentrates on separating the stories from the signals, just as Dr. Owen instructed. The money trail. The brain scans. The documentary. And Max, always hovering around the truth but never touching it directly. *Could Max have known who Alessandra was? What her brain was capable of? Did he study her before she disappeared? Is that what he's now doing with Zoe?*

She thinks of the phrase etched onto Max's pendant: *We watch. We imitate. We conquer.*

A doctrine. A method. And she can't shake the thought that Max is imitating empathy, *her* empathy, wearing it like a skin.

A knock rattles her door. She freezes, her breathing shallow. She cracks it open an inch. It's Cody, the concierge.

"Hey," he whispers. "Can I talk to you?"

Zoe lets him in. He steps inside quickly, glancing over his shoulder.

"I shouldn't be doing this," he says, rubbing his hands together nervously, then he reaches for his pocket.

He pulls out a small flash drive.

"Alessandra left this with me. Told me to give it to someone who asked the right questions."

Zoe takes it, heart pounding. "What's on it?"

"I don't know. I never looked. But someone's been asking about it. Someone from the University."

Zoe starts to ask who, but the sound of footsteps outside silences them both. Cody pales.

"I have to go," he whispers and slips out the door of her cottage into the darkness.

CHAPTER TWENTY-ONE

The Bond of Betrayal

Sasha is folding her uniform into a compact roll when the phone begins to ring again. She ignores it, turning instead to the mirror. Her pilot's jacket is draped neatly over the chair, silver wings glinting in the morning light. It's nearly time to fly back to New York. She pulls her long blonde hair into a low ponytail and studies her reflection with clinical precision, a habit from her pre-flight ritual. The familiarity of it soothes her, even as her mind churns.

She dabs a hint of cream blush on her cheeks, the burnt orange tint warming her otherwise pale complexion. Her fingers move methodically first to her eyes, then cheekbones, then lips. It gives her something to focus on besides the unease building in her chest. Ever since the woman vanished from Big Sur, Sasha hasn't been able to sleep through the night. She keeps dreaming of water, dark, cold and turbulent. And always the same woman, just out of reach.

She picks up her phone. Missed call. Then, it rings again. Sasha hesitates, her thumb hovering; she finally answers.

"Hello?"

"Hi, yes, is this Sasha?" a woman with a soft Spanish accent asks.

"Yes, who is this?" Sasha's German accent is slight but unmistakable, a clipped elegance sharpened by unease.

"My name is Karolina." The line goes quiet. Then, "Do you know Max Furtherlore?"

Sasha sits on the edge of the bed. Her legs begin to shake. A thousand thoughts rush in. The pendant. The woman in the photo. His documentary. The silences. The inconsistencies.

"Yes," she says. "Why?"

"This may seem like a lot, what I am about to share, but I am Max's wife, well, soon-to-be ex-wife, although he doesn't quite know that yet. I still live with him for the moment," Karolina nervously rambles. "Anyway, I've been in touch with his twin brother, Arthur, and he mentioned your name. I wanted to speak with you about your experience with him." Karolina pauses, and Sasha is stunned into silence. Karolina continues, "I don't mean to intrude into your personal life. I am just curious if you had a similar experience with him."

"Karolina, I am so sorry. I had no idea Max had a wife." Sasha apologizes for Max's duplicity, feeling somehow responsible despite being blindsided herself. "We've dated long-distance for so many years, and he travels so much for work. I guess I can see how logistically he could be living separate lives, but I must say I'm in shock."

"Yes, it takes some time to process, at least it did for me. Eventually, you will feel, and this may sound odd... a sense of relief."

A pang of recognition comes over Sasha. Karolina continues: "I was relieved to know the truth because it meant I wasn't making things up. The reality in my mind was accurate. I loved a man I didn't know. He wanted me to question my sanity, to believe I had been crazy, which couldn't be farther from the truth."

A tear rolls down Sasha's cheek. "How did I not know?" Sasha asks both herself and Karolina.

"We knew, Sasha. We always knew. He made us deny what we knew. Don't beat yourself up. This will get easier."

Sasha is stunned by Karolina's sincerity, her lack of jealousy, and how she's not looking to seek revenge. Sasha is the other woman, after all.

Karolina continues, letting Sasha absorb the news in silence. "Sasha,

I need to be sure you will keep this between us. I don't want Max to know we've discovered each other."

"Why don't you want Max to know?" Sasha's surprise is turning into a quiet rage toward Max.

"Well, in my conversation with Arthur, he shared something about Max." Karolina pauses as if she doesn't want to continue.

"What did he share?" Sasha prods.

"Max has been diagnosed with antisocial personality disorder." Karolina lets out a breath. "He is a psychopath."

Sasha digs her fingers into the side of the bed. Her stomach drops. A rush of blood fills her head, and for a moment, everything around her blurs. She can't see. She can't breathe. The only sound is the pounding of her own heart, loud and arrhythmic, like a warning drum echoing through her chest.

She grips the edge of the bedsheet, holding it close like a makeshift life raft. Her eyes drift to the nightstand, to the glass of water she hadn't touched, to the empty space where Max's watch had once rested.

All at once, her dreams come rushing back, the ones she'd dismissed as anxiety, as fragments of memory playing tricks on her. The woman on the cliff. The darkness that seemed as if it was watching her from inside the dream. The shape of a man just out of frame. She hadn't seen his face. But now... she wonders if she'd known all along. Some part of her must have.

Another tear slips down her cheek, but she wipes it away fast, angry with herself for missing it, for ignoring what her body had already been trying to tell her. For letting herself feel safe. She's not sure which terrifies her more—that Max is a psychopath, or that some part of her always knew, but she kept it hidden.

She swallows, her voice barely a whisper. "How could I have let him in?"

On the other end of the line, Karolina is silent for a beat, then says, "You didn't let him in. He got in by knowing exactly how to shape himself into the person you needed him to be."

Sasha presses a palm to her stomach. She feels the coldness there. A slow, spreading dread.

"He used to talk about something called 'Phase 2,'" Karolina adds. Her voice wavers now. "At the time, I thought it was about work, one of his documentaries. But now, I wonder. It always sounded… rehearsed."

Sasha doesn't respond right away. She's thinking about the photo again that she found in Max's apartment. The missing woman. Her dream. And the feeling that the dream would never end, unless she found out who the woman was.

Sasha swallows hard. "Did he share anything about his film, *Architects of the Mind,* with you?"

"Not really, he talked about it in vague terms," Karolina replies. "He would say it was his passion project about the future of intelligence, both human and artificial. But he never showed me any footage."

"I saw a rough cut once, just a few minutes. I was able to find it on his laptop, but he doesn't know I saw it."

"What was on it?"

Sasha hesitates. "It showed the campus of Oneness University; there was a voiceover about neuroplasticity, empathy studies, and synthetic consciousness. There were shots of children hooked up to EEG caps, their faces blurred. One woman was talking about 'emotional imprinting' and… brain mapping. Max had said a good deal of research had gone into the film, but this looked like something other than research used for a documentary. It felt more clinical, disturbing."

"Children?" Karolina asks, her voice fills with shock.

"Yes, I think he's not just documenting something. It seems as if whatever he is working on is bigger than just a film." Sasha whispers. "And he's part of it."

Karolina is quiet for a beat. Then, softly, "Do you think… do you think this project is his way of trying to fix something in himself?"

Sasha exhales, "Like curing his own psychopathy?"

Karolina's voice is steadier now. "Maybe not curing, maybe containing. Or mimicking what he thinks empathy looks like."

Neither woman speaks for a moment. The silence between them stretches thick, an electric expansion.

"If he knows who he is," Sasha finally says, "then, this film... it might not be a documentary. It might be a blueprint."

"A blueprint for what, though?" Karolina asks.

"I'm not entirely sure," Sasha says. "Do you know anything about Max's pendant?" Everything Sasha had stuffed away, pretending to ignore, is now bubbling up.

Karolina lets out a breath over the phone. "The one he never takes off. What about it?"

"He had an odd obsession with the pendant. I researched it, and it's tied to Oneness University. I found a picture of him with a woman wearing the same necklace, standing side-by-side on Moffett Field." A weight lifts. Sasha finally has someone to share her suspicions with. "Did Max ever take you to Moffett Field?"

"Yes, you too?"

Sasha nods. "Yes."

"The woman in the photo, what does she look like?" Karolina asks.

Sasha asks Karolina to hold. She searches on her phone for the picture she had found of the Polaroid of the woman and Max. "I'm sending it to you now." She texts the picture to Karolina. Karolina starts shaking and sweating. She rummages through the desk drawer and pulls out the rendering she did for the police of the missing woman in Big Sur.

"This is going to sound strange." Karolina hesitates.

"We've passed that point by now," Sasha laughs.

"I think the woman in the photo with Max is the woman who has gone missing in Big Sur. Have you heard about the case?"

Sasha's heart beats in her throat; the woman in the photo is the missing woman from her dream. She hadn't been able to stop thinking about the woman, and now she knows why. "Yes, I know about it." Sasha sits back in silence, unable to bring herself to ask Karolina if Max may be involved.

"We need to find her," Karolina says. Sasha searches the box of photos and finds another picture of the woman: this time she is confronting poachers in Africa. She stares at the picture. A man is holding a shotgun in one hand and a lion's head in the other, his face covered. A wave of familiarity comes over her. She takes a screenshot of the photo and throws it back into the box.

"Do you know if Max has ever been to Africa?" Sasha asks.

"Not to my knowledge, but you never know with him. He's impossible to keep track of, and he's been all over," Karolina says.

"Karolina, I have one last question." Sasha remembers the pool party, the intuitive handing her the tarot card with three other women. "Do you think there are more of us?"

CHAPTER TWENTY-TWO

Unmasking Mimicry

Zoe's cottage is silent again. Cody is gone, swallowed by the dark, his hurried footsteps already fading. Zoe locks the door behind him. The latch sounds louder than it should.

She stands for a beat, pulse quick and steady, staring at the drive in her hand as if it might detonate. It's small and innocuous; she's seen drives like this a million times before, but the one in her hand feels electric now, like it contains something radioactive. She moves to the desk, slides into the chair, and plugs it into her laptop, heart thudding.

The screen flickers. A folder auto-opens: /research/archive/early-models/

Inside are dozens of files, each labeled with alphanumeric strings. She clicks on one. A grayscale image loads. It's a brain scan, yet it looks different from the scan Dr. Owen had shown her of her own brain. This one is smaller, much smaller. She looks closer; the structures within the brain look less developed. She clicks another. And another. They are all tiny brains.

The scans are from children, minds still under development. Zoe leans closer, scrolling rapidly now. The metadata includes scan dates, timestamps, neural signature analyses, and then ages. Six. Four. Two. Her throat tightens. These aren't adult profiles.

Why would Alessandra have these? She opens the metadata logs again. A few contain names, but they are initials only. Others include coded references: *mirror sensitivity, anomalous empathy, high EQ projection.* Zoe stares at the phrases. It doesn't make sense. Had these children been scanned for empathy traits?

She finds one more folder: /aether-model/sympara-delta/

It's password protected. She tries *Wilder*, but the screen freezes, then words appear: denied. She tries PrototypeF_09. Denied.

She leans back, her pulse quickening. Was Alessandra about to expose this? A line that had been crossed somewhere deep inside the research. Zoe doesn't know what it means yet. But the implication chills her.

She thinks back to what Dr. Owen had said during the workshop. *"A handful of us were chosen because of our expertise in empathy."* she said. *"They are looking to see if it's possible to embed emotional intelligence and empathy into artificial intelligence. We were chosen because of our knowledge of the subject."* She had paused, then added, *"Or because we make excellent subjects."* When Zoe asked who *they* were, Dr. Owen had hesitated and then said it plainly: *"The Board of Oneness."*

But now, with the flash drive still warm in her hand, something sharp slices through her memory. Max. That night they met at Casa del Sol. The way he'd first approached her.

"Your article on Ryan Sowell," he'd said. *"Was brutal. But brilliant."*

Zoe's breath falters. She turns to her laptop, fingers suddenly clumsy on the keys, and opens a new window: Oneness University Board of Directors.

It loads slowly, and she can feel impatience bubbling in her throat.

There it is: *Ryan Sowell. Director. Investor. Vision Architect.*

Her vision tunnels for a moment. A high, rising buzz in her ears. *How did I miss this?* Her exposé had made national headlines. She knew his history, his voice, his tells. She had mapped his manipulations in print. But somehow, through all the subtle re-brandings and shell companies, she hadn't thought to check here. Ryan Sowell was on the board of Oneness University. He had been hiding in plain sight the entire time.

Zoe stares at the screen, her pulse climbing. Max hadn't just admired her article. He had used it to find her. She slams the laptop shut. Outside, the wind rattles the eucalyptus. A branch scrapes the glass. She walks barefoot across the cool floor. She opens the window. The sea sounds calm, deceptively so. A bright, white light beams down onto the lawn. The moon is full. Her breath steadies. Still, the electricity inside her won't fade. She needs air. She grabs her room key with a tiny flashlight and slips outside. The grass is cold beneath her feet, dew clinging to her toes. The air sharpens her senses.

Zoe walks barefoot across the dew-damp lawn, flashlight beam catching on the silvered grass. Her chest is tight; the contents of the flash drive had rattled her, but it was something deeper now. As she reaches the cliffside bench, she exhales, trying to force out a scream, but no sound comes.

It wasn't just about the data anymore. It was the shape the story was taking. And how it kept pulling her in. Her editor's voice returned, sudden and firm: *Don't lose yourself in it, Zoe.* But what if the source... was her?

She reaches the bench at the cliff's edge and sits, staring out at the dark. One of the first things she ever learned as a reporter: *keep space between yourself and the source.* Between the story and the self. That space is what makes the work possible, what keeps the truth evident and the story clear.

But the more she investigates, the less that space exists. The story keeps drawing her into its folds. She's not just covering the story of Alessandra's disappearance. She herself has been mistaken for her, not just once or twice, but many times.

She tries to ground herself in the cold of the bench, the slickness of the grass beneath her feet. But the knowing is still there. Low and certain. She wasn't just reporting the story anymore. She was beginning to disappear inside of it.

Then, she hears a rustle.

Zoe spins. The flashlight flickers across the trees, nothing. Then, a silhouette steps out from the shadow of the gazebo.

"Sorry," a voice calls softly. "I didn't mean to startle you."

It's Lillian. She's wrapped in a pale wool shawl, her dark hair spilling around her face. Her features are sharper in the moonlight; they look haunted, almost, like she hasn't slept either. She's barefoot, like Zoe, and her eyes shimmer with unshed tears.

Zoe exhales hard. "God. You scared me."

"I couldn't sleep." She moves into the moonlight, her face luminous. "I've been restless. The air is loud tonight."

Zoe doesn't respond right away; she's not sure if she heard her correctly. And something about Lillian's sudden appearance, the timing, strikes her as too convenient. But then, she sees it. Lillian's eyes are watery, not just from the light, but with something else, a strange color-layered perception. Zoe's body warms.

She nods toward the bench. "Want to sit?"

Lillian does, wrapping her shawl around her shoulders. They're quiet for a beat. The ocean roars below.

Lillian speaks first. "Your bracelet... I didn't want to say anything until I was sure."

Zoe watches her closely. "Sure of what?"

Lillian's mouth moves, but no sound comes out at first. Then, finally, she says, "I know Max. I've known him for three years."

Zoe remains silent. Her body is still, but her gaze shifts to the moonlit ocean, to the tips of her fingers.

"I didn't lie," Lillian says, almost too fast. "Not directly." Her composure looks like it's being held in place by a single breath.

Zoe doesn't move. "What do you mean?"

Lillian exhales. "It means I've been trying to convince myself of something for a while now. That I'm not insane. That there was something off with him. And seeing that bracelet on your wrist..." She trails off, then meets Zoe's eyes. "I'm involved with Max too."

The words land with a punch in Zoe's solar plexus, knocking the air from her lungs. "What?"

"We've been seeing each other for about three years," Lillian says, her voice tightening. "He was always disappearing for work. He would never explain much. I thought it was just the artist in him. Or perhaps his stoicism."

Zoe leans back, trying to understand it all. "So, when you saw the bracelet..." her voice goes thin.

"I recognized it. He gave me one, too." Lillian looks down at Zoe's bare wrist. "But it broke the other day when I was meditating."

Zoe's legs feel suddenly unsteady. "Why didn't you say something earlier?"

"Because I didn't want it to be true," Lillian snaps, then softens. "Because I needed to be sure. And then, when you said his name, the way your voice sounded, I knew it wasn't casual, or a coincidence that we met. I couldn't ignore the truth anymore."

Zoe swallows hard, her heart pounding. "He told me he loved me."

Lillian's mouth twists. "He told me the same."

They stare at each other, the night air thick around them, the fire crackling faintly in the distance.

"I think," Lillian finally says, her voice hollow, "we're just starting to learn how deep this really goes."

The words clang in Zoe's chest like a struck bell. The silence that follows feels bottomless. Zoe says nothing. The wind rattles the eucalyptus branches behind them. She stares at the ocean, her hands clenched in her lap.

Zoe finally turns to her. "Did you say the air felt loud tonight? What do you mean by that?"

Lillian hesitates. "I have synesthesia. It's a condition where I see things in color, sounds, and emotions. It's all connected. Tonight, the air is loud; it's jagged, like a burnt orange layered in deep static. It feels like something's off, something's shifting." Lillian's hands tremble in her lap. "When Max spoke... I never saw anything. His voice had no color. Just black. That's never happened to me before."

Zoe's neck stiffens.

"I thought it was me," Lillian whispers. "That I was broken. That I was fading."

Zoe takes her hand. "It wasn't you."

"He told me I was too intense. That I needed to stop projecting. That I imagined things."

Zoe nods. "Same." She leans forward slightly, her voice lower. "Can I ask you something?" Lillian nods. "Did you ever feel like Max wasn't... entirely there? Like you were with a version of him, not the whole person?"

Lillian blinks, surprised. "Yes. That's exactly how I'd describe it."

They sit for a moment in silence, the waves churning below. Finally, Zoe speaks.

"It's wild. What are the odds you and I would meet, here of all places, only to find we're both involved with the same man?"

"It almost feels designed," Lillian says.

Zoe's jaw tightens. She knows it's not fate; it's a pattern that's been prescribed. She shivers.

"He felt cold to me sometimes, like he was a robot trying to mimic emotion," Lillian states.

"I felt that too, all the time. He blamed it on his being British. But it was more than that. He didn't know how to stay in a conversation. It was like... like I spoke a language he didn't understand."

"Every time I tried to talk about feelings," Lillian says, "he looked at me like I was speaking in code. Then he'd steer us somewhere else, somewhere safer, which was usually sex."

Zoe exhales. "It always felt like a performance. Like he was rehearsing being human."

"Zoe..." Lillian turns to her. "Did you ever feel like you were in a trance around him?"

Zoe goes still. "Yes. Like my nervous system shut off. No more thoughts, I was just filled with a sense of calmness, but it almost felt too calm."

"I thought it was love," Lillian whispers. "That kind of stillness, but maybe it was something else."

Zoe nods, eyes wide. "Like your body stopped questioning things. But when he was gone, my anxiety came back. Stronger. I had terrible panic attacks." Zoe inhales. "I had a session earlier with someone. A psychologist, Dr. Owen. She ran a scan of my brain and told me I have an overabundance of mirror neurons."

Lillian raises her brows. "Really? What does that mean?"

"She said it makes me feel other people's emotions in my body. Physically. And she also told me something else." Zoe studies Lillian's face. "That people who don't emit any resonance, when their mirror neuron system isn't really engaging, I can sense it. They feel 'still' to people like me, but really, they're a void. She said that's what it's like being around a psychopath; you can end up feeling strangely detached yourself, almost like you're in a trance."

Lillian goes cold. "You think Max is a psychopath?"

Zoe's eyes glisten. "I'm pretty sure he is."

Lillian doesn't deny it. Doesn't flinch. Instead, she whispers, "That would explain everything."

Zoe leans back on the bench, her pulse pounding in her ears. "I thought it was just me. I thought I was too sensitive, too reactive. But the calm I felt around him, now I know it wasn't a sense of safety I was feeling. It was an absence."

Lillian shifts on the bench, staring at the sea but not really seeing it.

"He had this way of looking at me," she says, her voice far away. "Like he was memorizing me. Like I was some rare bird or exotic animal in the wild."

Zoe nods slowly. "His stare. I know."

"It wasn't lust," Lillian adds. "It was more intense than that. Reverent, almost. I used to think it meant he was really present, that he was taking me in on some deep soul level."

Zoe's throat tightens. "It does feel that way. But that stare, it's not intimacy. It's acquisition. He's watching for patterns, scanning your body, your mannerisms, what lights your eyes up. What makes you retreat in fear. He's not connecting with us; he's collecting information."

Lillian turns to look at her. "And what he gives back to you, the attention, the empathy, the interest, it's not real?"

"It's real to you," Zoe says. "But it's just mimicry. He has trained himself to mirror your values, your humor, your depth. You think you've finally met someone who sees the world the way you do. But really, you're falling in love with your own reflection."

Lillian goes still.

Zoe continues, quieter now. "It's a mask. He builds a version of himself out of your energy, your traits, and your goodness. That's what makes it feel so magnetic, it's you. You're experiencing yourself, reflected back with perfect clarity. And because no one's ever done that before, you think it must be love."

Lillian's eyes are glassy, but she doesn't blink. "It felt like being seen, really being seen for the first time ever in my life."

"I know," Zoe says. "It does. And the moment you start to feel doubt," she adds, "they switch tactics. He'll go cold and disappear. And because you felt such a deep connection, you assume it must be your fault. You double down and try harder. You reach back toward the intensity you had felt with him, not realizing it was never his to begin with."

Lillian's voice breaks slightly. "He made me feel like the most extraordinary version of myself."

"That's part of the manipulation," Zoe says gently. "He studied your light and gave it back to you in a shape you'd fall for. He didn't love us. He *learned* us."

"So it's not love," she says. "It's an algorithm."

Zoe meets her gaze. "Exactly."

They sit, quietly staring at the sea.

Lillian is the one who breaks the silence. "I know I should feel angry," she says, "but what I keep circling back to is... how much I wanted to know him."

Zoe doesn't flinch. She knows the feeling too well, desire threaded with admiration, confusion, recognition, the addiction of solving the mystery of his mind.

Lillian presses her lips together. Her eyes are bright now, not from tears but from the effort of holding herself steady. "I'm not a fool," she says. "I've always been... discerning. Cautious. I don't get swept up in people easily."

"That's why he picked you," Zoe says gently. "That's why he picked both of us."

Lillian looks at her, searching.

"They don't want weak women," Zoe continues. "They want women with super traits. Empathy. Intuition. Loyalty. The capacity to love deeply. Because those are the women who will stay, who will try to understand them, and who will do the emotional labor of holding the relationship together, even when it's tearing them apart."

Lillian looks down at her hands. "It's so strange. I felt powerful with him. Like we were equals. Like he saw how complex I was."

"He did," Zoe says. "But not the way you think. He saw your complexity and knew exactly how to make it work for him."

Lillian's voice is smaller now. "And I wanted so badly for it to be real. I kept rationalizing things. Reframing the red flags. I thought I was being generous."

"You were," Zoe says. "Generosity is part of what made you vulnerable."

Lillian meets her eyes. "And you?"

Zoe hesitates. "I thought I could handle him. If I understood him intellectually and emotionally, I could stay one step ahead. That I could love him without getting lost in him."

"And did you?"

Zoe is quiet for a long time. "No. I thought I was studying him, figuring him out. But I was already under his spell."

Lillian closes her eyes, then opens them. "I keep wondering what it says about me that I was so drawn to him. That I gave him access."

Zoe shakes her head. "It doesn't say anything bad. It says you're wired to connect. That your nervous system is tuned to others. That your instincts are refined, not broken."

Lillian lets out a breath. "So why didn't I see it sooner?"

"Because you're the kind of person who leads with trust," Zoe says. "You weren't blind. You were committed. That's not a flaw, that's your architecture."

Lillian nods slowly, like she's taking that in for the first time.

"He's a psychopath," Zoe says quietly. "But that doesn't mean we were stupid to care. It just means we were targeted for what's best in us. It's like an intense magnetism between two polarities, opposites attracting."

There's a long silence. The air around them feels heavier now, not with pain, but with understanding.

"I won't let him rewire what I know about myself," Lillian says.

"Good," Zoe replies. "Because now we see it. And that means we're not prey anymore."

Lillian turns toward her. "We're the ones who know how he works."

Zoe nods. "Which makes us dangerous."

Lillian lifts her chin toward the ocean, its surface glinting in the dark. "Did Max ever tell you the story behind the bracelet?"

Zoe shakes her head slowly. "No."

Lillian smiles, but it doesn't reach her eyes. "We got them in India. There was a temple, a long line of people wrapped around it like a ribbon. All waiting for one thing, a hug from a woman they called the Hugging Saint. St. Amma."

Zoe tilts her head, listening.

"She didn't speak much," Lillian continues. "Most people got one hug. But Max?" She pauses, the memory curdling into something strange. "She hugged him twice. Back-to-back. No explanation."

Zoe's eyes narrow. "Why?"

"She said, through the translator, that he was deeply fractured. Like something was missing." Lillian lets out a breath. "I didn't believe it at the time. I thought it was part of the mystique."

"And the bracelets?" Zoe asks.

"We bought them afterward, to remember the moment." She lifts her wrist, bare now. "We wore them for months. He said it was for protection."

Zoe glances down at her own wrist, the memory of Max saying the same words to her as he slipped the bracelet onto her wrist before she left for Salenan.

"What does the Saint represent?" she asks.

"Women's empowerment," Lillian says simply.

Zoe snorts. "You're kidding."

Lillian shakes her head. "Nope. The divine feminine, resilience, and boundaries. All the things we ignored, while convincing ourselves he was just misunderstood."

The air has cooled. Without a word, they both rise from the bench, brushing the damp from their clothes. Their footsteps fall into rhythm as they head back toward the cottages, the flashlight beam stretching long across the path. Then, the light lands on something just ahead: the giant chessboard. The pieces stand like statues, regal and unmoved. Zoe steps closer and squints. There's a gap. The queen has disappeared.

CHAPTER TWENTY-THREE

Erased

The next morning, Zoe walks to the front desk expecting to see Cody: his lazy grin, his habit of tapping the counter twice before speaking, the quiet gravity he carried like a hippie from another time, forced into a hospitality uniform.

But the counter is bare.

It's not just tidy. It's been cleared; it shines like it's been sanitized. So glossy she can see her reflection on the wood. She scans the space; there's no mug, no notebook. The old, laminated trail map Cody used to fidget with is gone. Zoe's eyes fall to the floor instinctively to the spot behind the desk where Henry's worn, flattened dog bed always sat. It's gone.

She feels a subtle clench in her throat. Her fingers twitch at her side. She scans the lobby. The Ficus tree still leans toward the sunlight like always, and the fireplace hums faintly, but something feels off, like it's been staged.

A woman she's never seen before stands behind the desk. She has a neat, straight black bob and an unreadable face. Her name tag says Amara.

"Hi," Zoe says. Her voice is light. "Is Cody around?"

The woman pauses, then tilts her head. "Cody?"

"The concierge. He was working here yesterday."

"I'm sorry," Amara says with a slight frown. "There's no one here by that name."

Zoe doesn't reply. She turns toward the hallway leading to the staff cabins, her heart already ticking faster. Her body moves before her thoughts catch up.

The door to the staff cabins creaks as she pushes through it. She walks past the low windows until she reaches the one she knows belongs to Cody. She presses her face close. Inside, everything is still. The bed is made, and the drawers are empty.

Her chest tightens. She presses her hand against the rough wood of the cabin door, like it might offer her a pulse.

Nothing.

His name doesn't register on the staff logs anymore. She checks the keypad by the security office on instinct. Cody's keycard is deactivated. It's not missing; it's been erased.

She returns to the lobby in a daze. Her fingers curl around the flash drive in her pocket. It pulses like a live wire, burning through the fabric. She can hear her own breath now. The muscles in her neck are tight; she's holding herself too upright, the way people do when they feel hunted. Zoe walks back to her cottage, body on autopilot, mind reeling. The light has changed; it's flat and colorless, like the air has been drained of oxygen.

She sits on the edge of her bed but doesn't stay long. Her body won't let her. There's too much charge in her limbs, too much noise behind her eyes. She stands again, grabs her sweatshirt, and slips the flash drive into her sock.

She doesn't knock on Lillian's door so much as hit it with her knuckles, quick and urgent. It opens seconds later. Lillian is barefoot, wearing an oversized T-shirt and sweatpants, her dark hair braided loosely down one shoulder. She looks startled.

"Zoe?"

Zoe pushes past her. "I need to talk to you. Now."

Lillian closes the door behind them. "What happened?"

Zoe turns in a tight circle, scanning the room as if someone might be listening. Her voice comes out in a whisper-shout.

"Cody's gone."

Lillian frowns. "What do you mean, gone?"

"Like, erased. His name isn't in the system anymore. The woman at the front desk claimed she'd never heard of him. His keycard doesn't work. His cabin is empty. And Henry's bed? It's gone too." Her voice cracks on the last word.

Lillian watches her carefully. "Zoe—"

Zoe crosses to the window, looking out at the waves. The sea's rhythm helps her find her breath. Her voice lowers, but the weight of it deepens. "I'm not just here for the workshop. I'm here investigating a disappearance."

Lillian's posture stiffens. "Disappearance?"

"A woman named Alessandra Wilder. She was supposed to be here, attending the workshop. But she vanished. Her room was left untouched. Her things were still in the drawer. No check-out record. She just... disappeared."

There's a pause. Lillian's expression flickers with surprise, calculation, concern. Then, she asks quietly, "Do you think Max had something to do with it?"

"I didn't, at first," Zoe says. "But everything keeps pointing back to him. The people he knows. The places he's been. His connection to Oneness University. Even the way he acts. And... I recently found out something else."

Zoe hesitates, then continues. She reaches into her sweater pocket and pulls out the paperback, *The ESP Algorithm*. She offers it to Lillian without a word. The cover is worn, corners curled.

"It was already in my room," Zoe says. "I was assigned Alessandra's cottage after she disappeared. Everything else had been cleared out, except this. It was sitting on the edge of the desk."

Lillian takes the book gently, like it might shatter. "She left it for you."

Zoe nods. "That's what it feels like."

Lillian flips through the pages. "I've heard of this. It argues that extrasensory perception, ESP, isn't supernatural. It's a kind of heightened pattern recognition. The brain running simulations faster than we can consciously process. Like catching the edge of a lie before it's spoken. Or sensing something's wrong before you can name it."

Zoe leans in. "The author suggests it's more common in highly sensitive people. Especially women. And instead of being studied, we're dismissed. Labeled emotional. Irrational. But really, we're reading something others can't."

Lillian nods, her fingers lingering over a smudge on the inside cover. "When I was younger, I thought there was something wrong with me. Seeing voices. Tasting moods. Now it feels like maybe I wasn't the problem. Maybe I was the system they couldn't decode."

Zoe flips to a dog-eared page. A phrase has been faintly underlined in pencil: "*Watch the women.*"

Lillian stares at it. "Is it a warning?"

"Or an instruction," Zoe says. "I think Alessandra realized the women here weren't just participants. We were the source material. The blueprint."

Lillian's eyes sharpen. "For what?"

Zoe hesitates. "Emotional intelligence. Empathy. Something they're trying to map. Or replicate. Or simulate. I think Max is part of it, he's not just documenting, but embedded in it. And Oneness University is the engine funding all of it."

"You said he knew Alessandra."

"I'm almost certain."

Lillian lowers the book. "Then maybe she started pulling at a thread. And it led somewhere she wasn't supposed to go."

Zoe looks toward the woods, where the outline of Salenan sits heavy and patient. "Someone wanted me in her room. With her book. They wanted me to find that note."

Lillian looks down at the phrase again. Her voice is quiet, but certain. "Alessandra Wilder, is she related to...?"

Before she can finish the sentence, Zoe says, "The CEO of Tex Chemical, John Wilder, yes. He is her father."

Lillian exhales sharply, her posture stiffening. "I know Tex Chemical," she says. "Too well."

Zoe looks over.

Lillian's voice is quiet, but razor-edged. "They ran pesticide trials in rural India about five years ago. I was there, working with an NGO doing water safety testing. The compounds were unregulated, some kind of experimental neurotoxins. Migrant workers were spraying them without masks. Women started miscarrying in the fields. Babies born with no limbs. Stillbirths spiked. And not just in one village. Across the region." Zoe's stomach turns at Lillian's words. "We tried to get it to the press. But the data was scrubbed. The local clinics were paid off. Eventually, Tex Chemical paid a settlement of eighty-six million dollars. But they still operate there, just under a different name. Using the same chemicals, same formulas. Just... new branding." Zoe is silent, the wind knotting her hair across her cheek. "That kind of damage," Lillian continues, "it doesn't disappear. It just mutates."

Zoe thinks of the fMRI scans. The ones labeled only by initials. A series of neural images that looked standard at first, until she realized they were from children. The markings were subtle, like bruises in the tissue. But unmistakable. The scans showed underdeveloped empathy circuits. The mirror neuron systems, dim, almost silent.

"Alessandra's father has been strangely absent from any public statements since her disappearance. No press, no missing person bulletin. Nothing."

Lillian's eyes narrow. "If she was trying to expose something..."

"She's the only one who could," Zoe says. "The only one with access on both sides. She grew up inside that company. And somehow, she's tied to Oneness too. Max must have known her, I'm sure of it."

"But why would a tech incubator want to work with a chemical giant?"

Zoe's voice is low, almost swallowed by the waves. "Tex Chemical made a donation to Oneness University last year for $16 million. No record of where it went after that."

Lillian's head turns sharply, her expression darkens, but she doesn't interrupt. She doesn't move. She looks hollowed out, like something inside her just shifted, permanently.

"Cody shared a flash drive with me that Alessandra had given him. It has fMRI scans on it," Zoe says. "The technology exists. I think they're using people like us, people with sensitivities, as data models. The neural blueprints, I'm just not sure why they are doing this research. There's a bridge between Tex Chemical and Oneness. I just can't see it yet."

Lillian stares into the dark. "Maybe it's not a bridge," she murmurs. "Maybe it's a backchannel. Something no one was supposed to find."

A shiver runs up Zoe's spine. A familiar, ancestral warning. Lillian continues, "Maybe they're embedding those sensitivities into people who don't register emotion."

"People like Max," Zoe says.

Lillian glances toward the Salenan building. "This whole retreat might be a field test." She looks out toward the forest, where the darkened silhouette of Salenan looms. "And if we're right," she says, "Alessandra and Cody might not be the only ones to disappear."

"So... what do we do about Max?" Zoe finally asks.

Lillian doesn't answer right away. Her eyes are fixed on the trees, her profile sharp in the morning light. When she finally speaks, her voice is flat and eerily calm. "Ten hours ago, I might've cried," she says. "Or thrown something. Sent a long, stupid message I'd regret."

Zoe says nothing.

"But now?" Lillian turns to her. "Now I want to know why, why us? Why here? And what is he really doing?"

Zoe nods slowly. "He doesn't choose women randomly. He studies them. Mirrors them. We're not accidents, we're data."

Lillian swallows. "You think we were part of it?"

"I think we are," Zoe says. "He brought us here for a reason. Maybe not just to observe us. Maybe to test something."

The ocean cracks loudly against the cliffs behind them. A wave of cold air curls under Zoe's sweater. She pulls it tighter.

"So, we don't confront him," Lillian says quietly.

"No," Zoe replies. "At least not yet. He'd deny it anyway. Twist it back. Make us question ourselves."

Lillian's jaw clenches. The color returns to her face. "Then, we let him think he's still in control," she says.

Zoe meets her eyes. "Exactly. We stay close, smile, ask questions like nothing's changed."

Lillian's expression flickers, not of pain, but something cleaner, more determined.

"And when the moment comes?"

Zoe looks out toward the looming shadow of Salenan, its windows dark like a creature watching them from within. "We make sure he doesn't see it coming."

Zoe's thoughts are moving elsewhere now, circling, triangulating.

"Have you been to his office?" she says suddenly.

Lillian looks over. "What do you mean?"

Zoe hesitates. "Max told me he kept an office downtown. Some kind of private workspace, he said it was for editing. But there was something about the way he said it, like he was sharing a secret. He was vague, careful about it."

Lillian tilts her head. "He never mentioned it to me. Do you know where it is?"

"I remember the name: The Meridian Works in the Arts District, Downtown LA."

Lillian processes this.

Zoe continues, more to herself than to Lillian. "I think he's hiding something there. Maybe data. Equipment. Or..." She doesn't finish the thought. But the implication hangs there.

Lillian's eyes darken. "Do you want me to go?"

Zoe looks at her, surprised.

"I'm not on his radar," Lillian says. "Not in the same way as you. If he's hiding something in plain sight, he won't be expecting me."

Zoe hesitates. "Not yet. But soon."

She pulls out her phone, scrolls to the contact her editor slipped her: someone working with the police, off the books, who could help her verify leads if she had any. Her thumb hovers over the number.

Lillian watches her. Zoe doesn't make the call. Not yet. A silence blooms between them. Something has shifted, not just between Zoe and Max, but also between Zoe and Lillian. They're no longer strangers; they're tethered now in the shadow of a man who had mirrored them both and who may be trying to erase them.

CHAPTER TWENTY-FOUR

A Call

Karolina's phone rings. An unfamiliar number. She hesitates, her thumb hovering, but instinct tells her to answer.

"Hello?"

"Hi, this is Zoe Harrison from *The Daily Quest*. Would you have a moment to speak with me? I have some questions for the police, and some information I'd like to share."

Karolina tenses. "I'm not supposed to talk with the media. How did you get my number?"

"That's strange," Zoe replies. "My editor said the detectives gave us this number to call if we had information to share." Her tone shifts: it's calculated, but not unfriendly. "Are you a detective on the case? FBI?"

Karolina's grip tightens around the phone. The word "detective" feels too sharp. "FBI" feels laughable. Her title isn't real. Her presence on the case has always felt provisional, as if she's just hovering outside the perimeter, useful but unnamable.

"No. Neither," she says finally. The pause afterward feels like an admission. "I'm... a consultant. Brought in to assist through... alternative means."

"Alternative?" Zoe repeats, not skeptically, but with curiosity. "What sort of means?"

Karolina feels her throat constrict; she hesitates. The line between revelation and risk feels razor thin. She glances at the closed door, as if someone might be listening. It is as if saying it out loud might collapse the fragile permission she's been given to be part of this case at all.

"This conversation is off the record, right?" she says, her voice quieter now. "And you're not recording?"

"Absolutely," Zoe says, without hesitation. But Karolina knows the tone well; Zoe's not just a reporter who hunts down a story; she gets inside of the story and begins to live it.

Karolina exhales slowly, forcing her voice not to waver. "I've been working with the police as an intuitive. You could say... a psychic detective, I suppose." Karolina braces herself for laughter.

There's a pause, but it's not the silence of judgment. Karolina can hear the faint shift of Zoe repositioning on the other end, like someone leaning in, not away.

"We journalists and intuitives are two sides of the same coin," Zoe says. "We both dig for the truth that no one wants to say out loud, letting our gut feelings and our intuition lead us in the direction we need to go. If we work together on this case, I think we can find the threads the police may be overlooking."

Karolina blinks, her chest tight with something between relief and suspicion. Maybe, for the first time in this case, she's not alone.

"A name would help. I still don't know who she is," Karolina's voice sharpens slightly. The secrecy around the woman's identity has gnawed at her from the start.

"I believe her name is Alessandra Wilder."

Karolina's heart lurches.

"I need to call you back," she says and hangs up before Zoe can reply.

Karolina moves to her computer and googles the name. Pictures appear, one after another. She doesn't need to grab the missing poster: the woman she saw in her mind's eye stares back at her from the screen. It's her. Karolina closes the browser and opens a portal that the detectives would rather her not have access to. She hadn't exactly stolen the passcode, she had just memorized it. They'd already told her to stay in her lane. But Karolina never liked lanes. She types in *Alessandra Wilder.*

The data appears in seconds.

No one is anonymous anymore, not truly. Every text, every photo, every offhanded GPS ping maps movements. Every web search, no matter how fleeting or shameful, becomes part of a greater fingerprint. Even DNA now lives in cloud servers and can resurrect ancestors or identify a killer. Everyone is cataloged not just by their choices but by their silences. To disappear, truly disappear, is a dying art.

Karolina pores over Alessandra's emails and phone records. A stack of printed pages rests on her lap, hot from the printer. She flips to the call logs from the week Alessandra vanished, with a yellow highlighter in her hand, finger skimming rows of numbers and timestamps.

There it is, one number. Then, again. Thirty minutes. Forty-five. Over an hour. Multiple days. A pattern. She flips through the stack, the same number repeating until it becomes the final call Alessandra made the day she went missing.

The highlighter squeaks against the paper. Karolina pauses. A chill runs through her arms. She doesn't know why, but something about the number sets off a low buzz behind her ribs, like her body is reacting before her mind can catch up. She pulls the address linked to the number. Her fingers hover over the keyboard. Something about it feels familiar. She can't place it. It's like a trace of a dream or the echo of a half-forgotten voice. A flicker of Max. She had laughed it off then. Now, her stomach tightens.

She dials Zoe. "I have a potential lead."

"I'm ready." Zoe's voice comes quick, firm, already back in reporter mode.

"Alessandra made several long calls to a number in Salinas Valley. It's the last call on record before her phone went dark. The location is a rural property, forty-five minutes inland from Big Sur."

"Salinas Valley?" Zoe asks. Karolina can hear Zoe's pen scratching in the background. "Is that significant?"

"It's farmland, pretty isolated. There's not much out there. I can't imagine why Alessandra would be in contact with anyone there, unless it's part of something we don't yet understand."

"Will the police follow up?"

"I can flag it," Karolina says carefully, "but they've already told me to stay out of traditional leads. They don't like that I'm going off script."

"Then give me the address." Zoe's tone sharpens, not with skepticism but with focus. She's already preparing her move.

Karolina reads the address slowly and deliberately.

Zoe scribbles. There's a pause, just long enough to feel like something unsaid has slipped between them.

"You know," Zoe says slowly, "your voice feels... familiar."

Karolina stiffens. "Does it?"

"Yeah, and your name. It's probably nothing."

Karolina forces a soft laugh. "Maybe we've crossed paths in another life."

But the moment lingers. There's a static hum between them, an unease.

Zoe adds, "I don't mean to sound weird. I just... get a feeling sometimes."

Karolina exhales through her nose, a practiced breath that steadies her when her body knows something her mind won't name.

"I get that," she says. "Sometimes, I just... know things. Even when I have no reason to."

A beat. Then Zoe says it, softly, as if testing the air: "Do you believe people can be connected without realizing it?"

Karolina's breath catches. "Yes," she says, almost before the word forms. "Completely."

Another silence. This one is heavier.

"Sorry," Zoe says with a half-laugh that doesn't reach her voice. "Ignore me. Sometimes I just overread things. It's a reporter habit. And maybe something else."

Karolina says nothing. She feels the same tug beneath her skin. Not fear, but a recognition that's too close. A sense she's circling something she already knows.

They move on, but the air doesn't clear. Something clings to the edges of the conversation, invisible and electric. Neither of them understands it. But the knowing is already there, just waiting for a name.

"Salinas Valley…" Zoe murmurs again.

"What would Alessandra have been doing out there? It must be part of something deeper." Karolina wonders.

Zoe's voice lowers. "Do you know who her father is?"

"No." Karolina straightens in her seat.

"She's a Wilder," Zoe says. "As in John Wilder, the CEO of Tex Chemical."

Karolina blinks. A rush of recognition slams into her. The name, the context, of course.

Karolina had read about him before, maybe in *The Intercept*, or maybe in a court transcript. The company had been blamed for tainting crops, poisoning water supplies, and causing illness in vulnerable communities for decades.

Except Max admired him.

She remembers it now; the memory is sharp and unwelcome. The way Max once spoke of Wilder at a dinner party, calling him "ruthlessly pragmatic." Karolina hadn't thought much of it then, just another one of Max's provocative takes. But now, it lands differently.

Karolina's mouth goes dry. A strange, acrid taste rises at the back of her tongue. It's chemical, bitter, and synthetic. She tastes it because she's been here before, when she first sat in the police station sketching the missing woman. It had crept in then too: the taste, the sense of a looming cloud over everything.

"My husband's always been strangely fascinated by him," she says, her voice more guarded now. "He once called him 'ruthlessly pragmatic.'"

Zoe's voice is steady. "That's so strange. My boyfriend was also fascinated with him. He said how Wilder 'rebuilt a sinking empire.'"

A silence folds over the line. Karolina's tries to write it off as coincidence, but her body doesn't buy it.

Then something surfaces. A flicker from a few weeks ago. Max, coming home late. The way he'd been energized, animated. Talking about a journalist he met at a screening. "*The kind who asks questions like she already knows the answers,*" he'd said.

Karolina hadn't thought much of it. But now, hearing Zoe's voice, the cadence, the confidence, it echoes. Her hands tremble now. This isn't just a missing person's case, this case is tied power, and possibly to Max.

Zoe's voice returns, calm but charged. "I'll head there now."

"Be careful," Karolina says. She doesn't know why she says it, only that she has to.

"I'll message you when I arrive," Zoe says.

Karolina doesn't answer right away. The air feels thick.

"Yes," she finally manages. "Please do."

CHAPTER TWENTY-FIVE

Salinas Valley

Salinas Valley lies inland, northeast of Big Sur, forty-five minutes from the cliffs surrounding the Salenan Institute. But it feels like a world away.

Zoe presses down on the gas pedal, her knuckles white around the steering wheel. Her heart hasn't stopped pounding since the call. She's not sure what rattled her more: the lead Karolina gave her, or Karolina herself. Zoe thinks back to the Speckled Boar, when Max had been asked about a woman named Karolina. This couldn't possibly be the same woman, what are the chances?

But there was something in her voice. Familiar, but not recognizably so; it was more like déjà vu. Like overhearing a conversation, you swear you've had before in a dream. Their exchange left a strange imprint on Zoe. She had the sense they were standing on opposite sides of the same veil, each feeling the other's outline without quite seeing the face. She shakes the thought off and refocuses on the road.

The lush cliffs of Big Sur are long gone now, replaced by dry, sun-bleached monotony. The land has flattened. The palette has faded. It's all sepia dust and skeletal brush, interrupted only by clusters of gas stations and the long gray streak of highway. The Salinas River cuts across the valley to the east, mostly dry this time of year, a pale scar in the dirt. Every so often, a jarring emerald green slashes across the fields, rows of crops so bright and plush they look artificial, almost fluorescent in the haze. Zoe blinks, startled by the contrast. From a distance, lettuce, spinach, and what looks like strawberries, seem to shimmer, looking unnaturally lush against the dust. It's the only color in sight, and somehow, the most unsettling.

She exits toward a small town, the GPS guiding her through a maze of cracked asphalt and faded signage. The main street tries its best to appear cheerful with bright awnings, a hand-painted mural, kids on bikes, but a few turns later, the cheer disappears.

Here, the homes are sagging low to the ground and sunburnt. Roofs patched with tin, shutters hanging off windows. Some yards are crowded with broken-down cars, their engines stripped, wheels gone, resting on cinderblocks like abandoned relics.

Zoe slows the car, the voice in her mind growing louder now. It's not the GPS, but Karolina's voice. Something about the way she said, "psychic detective." It should've sounded absurd, but it didn't. It had felt... inevitable. And then, there was the other thing. The moment Karolina paused, just after Zoe mentioned Max's fascination with Alessandra's father. Zoe had sensed something shifting.

Zoe tightens her grip on the wheel again. She doesn't know who Karolina is, not really. But she knows what it feels like when someone's holding back the same thing you are.

She enters a cul-de-sac and leans forward, bringing her body closer to the wheel and her face to the windshield to see the numbers on the homes. Zoe finds the one she's looking for, in the center of the cul-de-sac, painted an eggshell blue, faded, and yellowed by the sun and the dry heat of the valley. She parks on the road, not in the driveway. She turns off the car's ignition, grabs her purse, and opens the car door, smoothing out the wrinkles that had accordioned in her lap from the drive. Her palms are wet, and her heart is in her throat. She reminds herself she is a journalist; she has done cold calls before. This is what she does. She sends Karolina a quick text, "I've arrived."

Zoe walks onto the plywood porch and stands on a mat, reading *Bienvenidos*. She presses the doorbell. It doesn't ring. She knocks instead, hears rustling inside, and watches as the doorknob turns. The door opens, and a woman stands before her.

She's small, maybe five feet tall, with long dark hair pulled into a loose braid and deep-set eyes shadowed by exhaustion. Her skin is sun-worn, her frame wiry, but there's a steadiness in her stance, a kind of quiet resilience. She looks both young and aged at once, like someone who's lived too many lives in too few years. She looks at Zoe with a flicker of recollection.

She raises one eyebrow. "Can I help you?" The corner of her lip curls. Zoe's stomach tightens; she immediately senses the woman's weariness. It floods her, heavy in her limbs; her body is overcome with a fatigue that isn't hers.

"Hi, my name is Zoe Harrison." Zoe reaches her hand out for a shake as a warm smile spreads across her face. The woman slowly meets Zoe's hand with hers. Zoe continues, "I am a journalist, and I am hoping you'd be able to speak to me about a story I've been working on." The woman's eyes widen and light up.

"Are you here to help us?" the woman says, with restrained hope. Zoe notices the woman's eyes starting to water.

"I'm hoping you could actually help me. I am searching for a missing woman." Zoe doesn't want to give anyone false hope and needs to be honest about the reason she is here.

The woman says nothing and shakes her head back and forth. She tucks herself back into the doorway and begins to close the door. She says something in Spanish that Zoe does not recognize. Before the door shuts, a smell burns Zoe's nostrils. It's sweet, clinging, chemical, sour. She lifts her head to see an opaque cloud hanging in the sky, looming and coming toward the house. Zoe begins coughing and loses her balance. The woman tugs at her arm, dragging her inside the home and slams the front door behind her.

"You can't be outside when they spray," she says. Zoe glances at the woman and then out the window toward the cloud. It hangs over the house. The air becomes misty and foggy. The smell still burns her nostrils. It's not a cloud; it's a dense plume of smoke. Zoe's eyes dart, searching for a bathroom in case she is sick.

"What are they spraying?" Zoe cranes her head to look out the window toward the sky and then toward the two young children playing on the rug in the living room. They catch her gaze and look up at her. Zoe notices they have the same bags under their eyes as their mother.

"Chemicals for the crops," the woman says, picking up a toy in the hallway so Zoe doesn't trip on it. "I will show you in the backyard." They enter the kitchen and lean over the sink, peering out the window facing the backyard of the home. They watch as the white cloud of smoke passes overhead, leaving a thin, dewy, filmlike residue on the picnic table and children's swing set.

"The spray from the chemical creates a cloud that drifts into our homes, schools, and workplaces in the area. Kids playing on playgrounds at school or in their backyards become out of breath. They throw up, and the smell is so strong. It hits your brain and swarms in your head. My son has become so sick from it; I don't let him out now."

"I'm so sorry. This can't be legal. Have you spoken to a lawyer?" A wave of nausea comes over Zoe. She's unsure of its cause, if it's the chemical swirling in the air or the poisonous news the woman is sharing.

The woman eyes Zoe fiercely. "It's legal if it's happening to us. We are migrants, farm workers. We are a poor community: we complain to the police; they do nothing. And lawyers are too expensive. No one cares what happens to us." The woman turns her head toward the kitchen window. "So, are you here to help us?"

"Can we sit down and talk?" They sit at the tiny kitchen table. The woman offers Zoe tea and shares her name, Maria. She is a single mom of three kids at thirty-four years of age. Her husband was a migrant worker in Salinas Valley before he got sick. Fifty farmworkers in the valley became ill, and a number had to be hospitalized after being exposed to a plume of a chemical that had traveled from a neighboring farm.

"It has a strong odor, as you can see, and first, you become nauseous and then start vomiting. That is only the immediate effect; we don't know the long-term effects, but there are some studies." Her husband became so ill he could no longer work, and shortly after, he died. A sense of hopelessness crawls over Zoe's skin. It's more than sympathy; it coils in her gut, a sharp ache like she's inhaling Maria's grief. Her throat burns, even though the chemical cloud has lifted.

Maria goes into the hallway to a desk and pulls out a folder. It is overflowing with research, articles, and notes.

"What is the chemical called?" Zoe asks.

"Chlorpyrifos. It is an insecticide. Indoor use of the chemical has been banned by the Environmental Protection Agency since 2000 because of the extreme risks to children's health." Maria pulls out a research study.

"What sort of health effects?"

"All kinds. Exposure during pregnancy leads to lower IQ, a higher risk of the child having autism, reduced fertility, and, in some cases, miscarriages and stillbirths. If they are born at all, the poison affects their brain development. Children here are regularly vomiting and covered in skin rashes. They scratch their skin until they bleed. Salinas Valley has been the most impacted. Children living within less than a mile from farm fields where chlorpyrifos is sprayed. Our children have been shown to have lower IQs and lower verbal comprehension. But that's not the worst of it…"

She continues listing the symptoms: brain damage, asthma, convulsions, death, and Zoe's pen freezes above her notebook.

"Has this ever been covered in the media?" she asks.

"No." Maria pulls out another study and silently points to it. The insecticide had reportedly been the cause of death of over fifty children in the valley.

Lillian's voice echoes in her mind from one of their late-night talks at Salenan: "*Tex Chemical doesn't just poison ecosystems. They poison memory. They cover up the damage they do, rewrite what people think is real, who's sick, what's sacred, what's even happening.*" Had Lillian known something more about Alessandra? Or had she simply sensed the danger without needing proof?

"I don't understand. How is this still allowed to happen?" Zoe asks.

"Salinas Valley has some of the worst air quality and highest poverty in the country. Our community is primarily Latino and Indigenous. We've tried. No one listens."

"But with these studies and deaths, the EPA must have acted…"

Maria nods slowly, her voice flat. "They did act. For a while. The EPA had installed a ban on the chemical. But recently, they reversed it."

Zoe stiffens. "Reversed it?"

"Tex Chemical claimed the research was inconclusive. Said banning it would trigger a humanitarian crisis due to crop loss. A representative from Oneness University met with the EPA to argue against the ban."

Zoe sits up straighter. *The donation.* The $16 million from Tex Chemical to Oneness suddenly takes on a more sinister tone. Was it a bribe to lobby the agency?

"Do you know what role Oneness University has in all of this?"

Maria's gaze flickers. "They gave farmers new technology. Drones. Crop-dusters. They paid for our medical bills. But then, strange things began to happen."

Zoe's pulse skips. "What kind of strange things?"

"They began asking for brain scans. They said it was to help diagnose the children. But then the scans started going missing. Vanishing from the doctors' offices. No explanation. The staff looked at me like I was making it up."

Zoe's fingers go cold. The scans. Alessandra had them. And now, Zoe does. She kicks herself for forgetting them back at Salenan. She had been in such a rush.

"When did all of that start?" Zoe asks. "Was it around the time you met Alessandra?" Zoe decides to use her name, knowing Maria had received countless calls from Alessandra's phone, to see her reaction.

Maria freezes. "Is that why you're here? Is she the missing woman?" She squints at Zoe, tilting her head. "Wait… you look like her. A little too much."

Zoe blinks. "I've heard that."

Maria nods slowly. "It's in your eyes, and the way you speak. The way you stood on the porch before gave me a chill. At first, I thought… no. But now, I'm not so sure."

Zoe says nothing. A flicker of unease twists in her gut, but she pushes it down.

Maria grips her teacup, her hands trembling. "Please excuse me." She gets up and disappears down the hall.

Zoe's mind races. Alessandra had cared. She must have. Why else would she risk everything?

Maria returns, quieter now.

"How did you meet her?" Zoe asks.

"She came to my house. Just showed up one day and said she wanted to help. At first, I thought she was just another rich white lady trying to help. But she had information. Real evidence. She said she had found an internal research study Tex Chemical had done and buried. She wanted to publish it."

"Did she leave it with you?"

"No. She didn't want that kind of danger for us."

"Or responsibility," Zoe murmurs.

Maria nods, but her eyes linger. "There was something about her, though. The way she talked... it was so precise. Almost rehearsed."

Zoe tilts her head. "Rehearsed?"

"Like she already knew what I would ask before I said it. And she wore this strange necklace, it was silver, shaped like an eye. She said it was for 'empathy,' but... it gave me the creeps."

Zoe stiffens. *The pendant.* Max's pendant.

"Have you heard from her since?" Zoe asks.

Maria shakes her head. "No. That's what I'm telling you. Her disappearance, it's a warning."

Zoe exhales. "Would you ever consider telling your story?"

Maria's voice tightens. "What will they do to me? To my kids? Do you think they'd let me live if I went public?"

A boy coughs in the hallway. He pads toward them and clings to Maria's pant leg. She bends down, her voice bitter and quiet.

"They have billions. We have nothing. And they're destroying more than our bodies. They're destroying the land. The spirit. Our children's minds. Do you think they'll fix it with brain scans? With technology? No. They're just erasing the damage they caused. Sanitizing it."

Zoe's chest constricts, heart thudding, not with her own fear but Maria's. It rises through the room, tightening around them. Her arms tingle. The urge to flee, to protect, to vanish, it's not hers, but it floods her anyway.

She stands. "I understand."

Maria studies her. "Do you?"

Zoe no longer feels sick. She feels sure. She says goodbye to Maria, and as she walks toward the door, she feels Maria's fear lingering in her spine. There was no performance in it. Righteous fury surges inside her. This is why Alessandra disappeared. She got too close to the truth. She was going to blow the whistle on Tex Chemical and Oneness, and they silenced her. Alessandra had wanted to help, and now she was gone.

Zoe opens the door, adrenaline flooding her limbs. She pauses on the porch before getting into her car. A drone buzzes overhead, far enough not to notice at first, but now, its whir cuts sharply through the quiet. It might be nothing. But she doesn't like how long it lingers before veering off toward the fields.

She had to get back to Salenan. The scans were more than evidence. They were bait.

CHAPTER TWENTY-SIX

The Meridian Works

It's late morning when Lillian arrives in Downtown Los Angeles. The streets are empty and quiet, with more buildings than people. She parks on a desolate street, surrounded by a stretch of abandoned industrial buildings a few blocks from Skid Row. Lillian double-checks the address Zoe had given her and gets out of the car, standing before an old building in the Arts District, its brick façade weathered and crumbling, with ghosted white letters still visible above the entrance: The Meridian Works.

The large steel doors creak open to reveal a dim lobby lined with mailboxes. Lillian scans until she finds "M. Furtherlore #301." She eyes the rickety elevator, hesitates, then takes the stairs. On the third floor, the hallway is industrial and bare. Only one unit has a welcome mat, #301. The mat reads *Bienvenidos*. Lillian pauses. Max doesn't speak Spanish.

She knocks, and the cold reverberates up her arm. A lock shifts. The door opens. A woman stands before her with long brown hair and wide dark eyes. They're the same height, and they have the same petite frame. For a moment, it's like Lillian is staring into a mirror.

"Hello," they say simultaneously, both blinking.

"I'm sorry, can I help you?" the woman asks, catching Lillian's French accent.

Lillian hesitates at the threshold of the apartment, already half-turned to leave. "I think I may have the wrong address," she says, her voice thin.

The woman inside tilts her head, eyes narrowing with curiosity. "Who are you looking for?" she asks, not unkindly.

Lillian swallows. "Max Furtherlore."

A flicker crosses the woman's face, something tightening, then stilling completely. Without a word, she turns and walks back inside. The door remains ajar. Lillian stands frozen. The air in the hallway feels too still, the light too cold. Then, drawn by a mix of curiosity, dread, and inevitability, she steps over the threshold.

Her eyes scan the space. The interior is spare, with concrete floors and glossy white walls. A white leather sofa sits in the center of the space draped with a sheepskin rug. Everything looks curated, chosen. It's sleek and sterile. On the far end, beneath a glinting chandelier, a queen bed anchors the room.

This isn't an office, it's a home.

A suitcase lies half-unzipped by the couch, clothes spilling from its edge. The sink overflows with dishes. On the counter: two wine glasses. One rimmed with mauve lipstick.

Lillian steps closer to the suitcase. Right on top is a black V-neck T-shirt, folded with almost obsessive precision.

Then, it hits her, that smell.

A faint trace of his cologne, citrus and vetiver, but warped now by travel, skin, and time. To Lillian, it always carried a flicker of deep navy, the kind of blue that felt like a lie wrapped in velvet. She used to think it was mysterious. Now it just makes her stomach tighten. The scent sharpens in the back of her throat.

This is Max's place; there is no doubt about it.

"How do you know Max?" Lillian asks quietly, nodding toward the suitcase.

The woman opens the fridge and pulls out a bottle of rosé. "He's my husband," she replies, tone even.

Lillian's breath catches in her throat. Her gaze snaps to the side table. A silver frame holds a wedding photo. Max is in a tuxedo, smiling, next to a woman in a white gown, her hand in his. Her legs go weak. She reaches for the table's edge to steady herself.

"Water? Wine?" the woman offers, pouring with a grace that feels composed. A little too composed. Lillian nods, barely. She takes the wine, sits down slowly on the edge of the sofa, and blurts before she can stop herself.

"Your husband is my boyfriend. Or... was. He doesn't know I'm leaving." As soon as the words leave her mouth, the room shifts, and the air thickens. A wave of violet floods behind Lillian's eyes; it's bitter, electric. Her synesthesia sparks, shocking her. The rosé in her glass smells suddenly of iron. Her fingers tingle with pins of orange heat. She knows, instantly, this is a moment she'll remember by the color, not the words.

The woman doesn't flinch. Instead, she reaches out and rests her hand lightly over Lillian's, her touch steady. "I'm Karolina," she says softly. "And I think... we have some things to figure out."

Lillian studies her. She has the kind of beauty that felt both grounded and quietly magnetic. Her hair is a cascade of chestnut curls, thick and effortlessly tousled, framing her face in soft waves. Her eyes are large and dark, with an openness that feels familiar yet also holds something unreadable. She isn't wearing a wedding ring.

Karolina meets her gaze and then speaks quietly at first. "He was always gone. Traveling for a shoot and attending meetings in cities I'd never been to. I told myself it was just the way things were when you're with someone ambitious." She pauses, her thumb absently circling the base of her wineglass. "But over time, it started to feel deliberate. Like he wanted to be untraceable. Like he was becoming tired of having to curate the version of himself I was allowed to know."

Lillian shifts uncomfortably. "I'm... I'm sorry."

Karolina looks at her, eyes steady. "Don't be. The loneliness had already started to calcify. There were things I was going through that he never even noticed. Things I chose to not tell him." Her voice softens, but the weight beneath it deepens. "I think some part of me already knew. Before you. Before this. That something wasn't right. That I couldn't build a future with someone whose inner world felt so... inaccessible."

She takes a long sip of wine. "So no, you didn't break anything. You just confirmed what I'd already stopped trying to deny. You didn't deceive me. He did."

"There's more," Lillian says. "It's not just us."

Karolina sighs. "Let me guess, you know about Sasha?"

"Who is Sasha?"

"Another girlfriend of his. She's a German pilot. Kind, long-distance. When I first heard her name… I don't know how to explain it. My whole body went cold. Like I'd known all along. I thought it was just intuition, but now…."

Lillian stares at her, but her mind has already splintered. Another woman. Of course. She should be numb by now, numb to the betrayals, the lies, Max's duplicity, but this one lands differently. It's sharper and quieter, like a needle beneath the skin.

How many women had there been? How many had mistaken proximity for connection? Something twists in her stomach, shame, maybe. Or recognition. That she hadn't just been misled or betrayed; it's beyond that. She'd been patterned and selected. Folded into some invisible design she hadn't seen coming.

She swallows, steadying her voice. "How many of us are there?" Her eyes search Karolina's. "You must know Zoe, then?"

Karolina frowns. "Zoe Harrison? The journalist?"

Lillian hesitates. "Yes. She's the reason I'm here. I met her at the Salenan Institute. She's been investigating the disappearance of Alessandra Wilder."

Karolina's eyes narrow. "Wait, how did she get this address? Is she also involved with Max? She called me a few days ago about the case."

Lillian's voice is faint. "Yes, he dated her, too."

Karolina stops pacing. Her eyes meet Lillian's. "Then, we're all part of this. All of us."

Lillian's eyes widen. "Why would Zoe have called you about the case of the missing woman?"

Karolina speaks slowly. "I've been consulting with the police, more on the intuitive side of things. They brought me in when Alessandra's disappearance started to show unusual patterns. She is not just a missing person; there are layers, symbols, and strange gaps in time. Things that don't add up through logic alone, and then, of course, the ties to Tex Chemical."

Lillian nods. "Yes. I'm a climatologist. I've done environmental impact research for years. I'm all too familiar with Tex Chemical."

Karolina crosses her arms, unsettled. "I found a number that Alessandra had called, one of the last numbers before she went missing, and traced it to a home in Salinas Valley. I told Zoe, and she went and met the woman who lived there, Maria, who said Alessandra had visited her. That Alessandra wanted to help. Maria's kids had been exposed to pesticides sprayed on the farms near their house. Neurotoxic stuff. The kind that doesn't show up right away but rewires the body from the inside out."

Karolina's jaw tenses as she continues. "The whole town was getting sick. And then, somehow, the brain scans from the children went missing. Just vanished from the medical research archives. The doctors played dumb."

Lillian freezes. "The missing scans were on the flash drive that Cody gave to Zoe. Alessandra had them. Zoe said they were scans of children's brains. Alessandra must have known about the corruption."

Karolina shakes her head. "The question is, what was she going to do about it?"

Karolina opens a drawer and pulls out a worn photograph. "Sasha sent me this," she says, handing it to Lillian. "It's Max and a woman, taken in Africa. A research trip, apparently."

In the image, Max has one arm around a striking woman with dirty blonde hair and intense eyes. Behind them, mounted high on the adobe wall of a thatched safari lodge, is the same lion's head. Lillian's chest locks tight.

"That's Alessandra," Karolina says.

"What is Max doing with her?" Lillian leans in. "Wait—what's that?" She points to something small and glinting around Alessandra's neck.

Karolina narrows her eyes. "It's the pendant. Max's pendant."

Lillian stiffens. "He never takes it off. I thought it was just something personal."

"Looks like she had one too," Karolina says. "Or she was wearing his. Either way, that changes things."

They both stare at the photo.

"She doesn't look afraid," Lillian murmurs. "Not in the way I'd expect."

Karolina studies it again. "No, she looks like she's in control. Like she's watching him."

A pause.

"Do you think she knew?" Lillian asks.

"That she'd disappear?"

"That she'd be the one whose story no one could verify."

Karolina doesn't answer right away. Her eyes flick back to the lion. "I don't know what scares me more, that he did this to her... or that she..." Her voice trails off, and her eyes stay locked on the image of the lion. "He brought the lion back with him. Rested it on top of the dresser like a trophy. Or maybe a warning."

A strange stillness passes between them. The room feels suddenly heavier, as if the lion itself is listening. Karolina moves closer to the dresser. "I've had dreams about it," she whispers. "The lion, watching me as if it were still alive."

"Did he tell you not to touch it too?" Lillian steps closer to the dresser, drawn to the object with a sensation she can't explain. Her fingertips begin to tingle, a slow bloom of heat crawling up her arms. The air smells faintly of ozone. Her synesthesia kicks in like a siren: rust-red pulses behind her eyes.

"Yes, he said it was laced with arsenic. That even brushing it would poison me."

Lillian stares at it, the amber eyes, the frozen snarl. "What if that's exactly why we should?"

They hesitate, hands hovering just above the mane.

"Wait," Lillian says, sensing Karolina's pause. Her fingers tingle, a sharp, buzzing orange that climbs up her wrists. The taste of copper hits her tongue.

Karolina steps back instinctively. "What is it?"

"I think there is something under it, I have a feeling."

They look at each other and land their hands onto the lion's stiff fur, lifting it together, slowly and deliberately. It's heavier than it looks. The bottom scrapes softly against the wood. Beneath it, nestled into a shallow cutout in the wood of the dresser, is a small black flash drive.

Lillian exhales, the air catching in her throat.

Karolina stares at it. "He hid it under what he thought we would fear the most."

They exchange a look, something equal parts awe and horror.

Karolina reaches for the drive. They plug the flash drive into Karolina's laptop. One file loads: Architects of the Mind: V.3 / Subject A.W.

The screen flickers to life. Alessandra Wilder sits in a white room. She's not wearing any makeup, and her dirty blonde hair is pulled back in a clean, efficient twist. The pendant around her neck catches the sterile overhead light, gleaming like a surgical instrument.

She's calm. Unsettlingly so. Her features are delicate, fine-boned, symmetrical, almost classical in their composition. She has the kind of beauty that disarms. But in the video, it's her stillness that is unnerving, the way she holds her body, poised and precise, as if nothing could startle her. As if she's already three steps ahead.

A voice off camera asks, "What do you believe empathy is?"

"You think empathy is a feeling," Alessandra says. "It's not. It's a pattern. A programmable pattern. That's what they'll never understand." There's no visible emotion on display, certainly no evidence of fear, only a glint in her eyes. Whatever this room was meant to expose hasn't cracked her.

Static. Then, the video cuts.

Lillian's body tightens. Her vision blooms violet at the edges. "This doesn't look like an interview," she says. "She looks like she is leading it."

Karolina nods slowly. "She doesn't look coerced at all."

"She looks like she's testing him."

"Or all of us."

Karolina's hands tremble. Lillian swallows. "The question is, why would Tex Chemical care about a consciousness project?"

"What if they weren't just poisoning people," Karolina says. "What if they were tracking the damage? Creating a market for something they had destroyed?"

Karolina opens the drawer again and pulls out another folder; a folded page falls out. It's a sketch, a face drawn repeatedly, layered over itself, each version altered slightly. Beneath it are names: *Lillian, Karolina, Sasha, Zoe*. One name is smudged out.

"What is this?" Lillian breathes.

Karolina lifts another piece of paper; it's a childhood report card. Circled notes: excels in mimicry, poor emotional bonding, low empathy, and conscientiousness.

"How long has he been studying us?" Lillian asks.

"Since before he met us," Karolina says.

Lillian meets her gaze. "He needed us for something." She looks back at the sketch, at the familiar, haunted faces, the deep intensity of their eyes. "I think we were meant to replace what he couldn't feel."

CHAPTER TWENTY-SEVEN

A Strange Stillness

Sasha sits on the couch in the living room of their apartment, waiting. Her fingers press rhythmically into the fabric beside her, finding a pulse in the silence. She watches the door. The light is gray and uncommitted, the kind that makes time feel slow and untrustworthy.

The call from Karolina replays in her head like a broadcast from another reality. It hasn't been long. Just long enough to rearrange everything.

"How could I have let him in?" Sasha had asked.

"You didn't let him in," Karolina had said. *"He got in by knowing exactly how to shape himself into what you needed."*

At first, Sasha was in shock. But then came another phone call and more names. Zoe. Lillian. The overlapping timelines, familiar tones in his voice when she asked too many questions. A recycled tenderness that always felt... off.

She had thought she had been chosen by Max, singular and special. But now she realizes she was just part of a sequence of many women, programmed, tested, and observed. She sees now that every *I love you* was a line read. Every apology was rehearsed. Every tender gesture was a manipulation cloaked in sensuality. And still, she loved him. This is what undoes her the most.

The front door clicks open.

Max enters, strangely upbeat, his face bright with performance. He's holding a bouquet of lilies, bright white. Their smell is sickeningly sweet. The silver pendant swings gently from his neck, catching the low light.

Sasha's stomach turns.

She thinks of the photo he never meant her to find: Max standing beside the woman who has now vanished, her head tilted slightly toward him, her expression unreadable. Around her neck was a silver pendant. The same one Max wears now. The one Sasha always asked him to remove before they made love because it felt like there were three of them in the bed: her, Max, and someone else.

She had recognized the missing woman from her dreams. A confirmation made by Karolina.

"*This is going to sound strange,*" Karolina had said over the phone, voice tight. "*I think the woman in the photo with Max is the woman who has gone missing in Big Sur.*"

And in that moment, everything had clicked for Sasha, the haunting dreams, the soft humming she couldn't explain, the sense that something had been passed down to her from the tarot card.

She clears her throat.

Max walks toward her, leans down, and kisses her. Her lips burn from the disconnect, a memory of warmth now frozen in ritual.

"Hello, my love," he says, voice smooth.

"Hi, my dear," Sasha replies, jaw tight. "Sit down next to me for a moment. There's something I need to tell you."

He settles beside her, jacket still on, the lilies dangling between them like a forgotten prop. The pendant sits centered over his sternum, resting just above the place where she once laid her head.

"I'm leaving," she says plainly. She doesn't explain. She doesn't offer an apology. A pause stretches between them. The air in the room changes; it grows cold, and a strange emptiness takes over her. The hairs on her arms rise. She looks at him.

His expression flattens into something disturbingly neutral. It's not dramatic. Not a flicker of rage or heartbreak. It's colder than that, more efficient. She's seen it before, in flashes. But now he doesn't bother concealing it. He has simply stopped performing for her. The light in his eyes recedes, and the contours of his face slacken. The warmth she once read in his features vanishes like indeed it was never real. The man she loved slips out of view, like a costume falling from a hanger.

Max turns toward her. His eyes have gone dark, not in color but in essence. They no longer reflect anything. It feels like watching a reptile rotate to assess heat, not connection. He is expressionless, devoid of any feeling. She no longer recognizes him.

And suddenly, she understands what she's been feeling for months but couldn't name. It wasn't fear. It was the recognition of absence. Of something that mimicked emotion without ever experiencing it.

"You've made your decision," he says, voice stripped of nuance. His voice is flat, dead. It isn't rage or grief. It's the absence of both. There's no sadness in him. No loss. Just a recalibration. Like a machine adjusting to the absence of a part it no longer needs.

"I loved you," Sasha says. She doesn't know why she says it. Maybe for herself. A heaviness floods her body. The grief that wells up isn't for him.

He tilts his head slightly. "Is this because of that phone call from Karolina?"

Her body stills. "Karolina?" she echoes, carefully. He knows. Or suspects, but she doesn't flinch. She wonders how closely he's been listening. He always knows more than he lets on. But this time, so does she.

Max stands and moves toward the bedroom. Before entering, he pauses, staring at the packed suitcase near the door. "I see you're ready."

"Yes."

He lingers in the doorway, his silhouette rigid, hollowed out by shadow. Sasha feels the panic rising; she should have left during the night. Instead, she gave him this moment.

He turns slowly and walks behind the couch. He places a hand at the base of her neck, fingers resting on her clavicle. His grip is gentle. Too gentle. It's the calm touch of someone assessing vulnerability, measuring how breakable you are.

Sasha jumps. He smirks. "I'll stay at a hotel tonight, my dear. I'll leave you be."

Max turns toward the door. Now she sees what Karolina meant: the hollowness, the repetition, the way he mirrored back whatever she most needed to see. Most psychopaths don't kill with violence, instead they kill with charm and confusion. They rob you of the ability to trust what your body has already told you. And her body had always known. Long before her mind caught up.

Sasha stands. It's time for her to turn the tables on him.

"Max."

He stops. Turns, slightly amused. She walks toward him, slow and measured.

"Before you go..." she says softly. "Let me see you."

She places her hand on his chest, not over his heart but on the pendant. Her fingertips graze the chain. She kisses him, and moves her hand toward his pants, the way he expects. Her other hand moves to the back of his neck, grazing the clasp. In the same breath, she unhooks the chain without him noticing. The pendant slips into her palm like a secret.

She keeps kissing him, gripping the pendant tight, and then steps back.

"Goodbye, Max."

He hesitates. A flicker of something passes through his eyes, but it's too late to track. Then, he turns and leaves. The door shuts.

Sasha exhales for the first time in what feels like hours. The pendant is warm in her hand. Heavier than she expected. She closes her fingers around it. And for a second, she thinks she hears a faint whine, not mechanical but instinctual. Like the cry of something displaced. She doesn't know exactly what it is. But she knows what it represents, the mask he wore for all of them. The wireframe of the person he pretended to be. And now, she has it. It's hers. She opens her palm, staring at the pendant and reads the inscription.

Scimus. Imitemur. Vincamus.
We watch. We imitate. We conquer.

She walks to the bedroom and sits on the edge of the bed. She wonders what it felt like for Alessandra, the moment she realized she'd been
chosen not for who she was, but for how she could be studied, mirrored,
and then undone.

Exhaustion overtakes her. She lies down in her clothes. The pendant
still clutched in her hand and falls asleep.

CHAPTER TWENTY-EIGHT

Rewired

Casa Jay doesn't try to impress. The restaurant lurks just off Ocean Avenue in Santa Monica; an unassuming shack wedged between coastal glitter and Tongva Park's sculpted minimalism. The front sign is crooked. A weathered nautical theme clings to the place like a last breath. Inside, there are red-checkered tablecloths, ship wheels on the walls, and an old marlin mounted above the bar. And, as always, peanut shells on the floor, a tradition since 1959. The walls breathe with a half-century of secrets, and the floor crunches with the shells.

In a place like Casa Jay, the line between truth and performance has always been thin. That's why Zoe chose it. A peanut from the dusty floor of the bar was taken to the moon by one of the astronauts from Apollo 11, an oddity that was so absurd precisely because of how ordinary and other-worldly it was. Zoe thinks back to that night with Max in the NASA barracks at Moffett Field, how she had spotted the PAYDAY candy bar wrapper on the floor of their room. It had struck her back than as odd, perhaps a warning of some kind. But now, in hindsight, it feels like a sign pointing here, a future she remembered then, back to this moment she would orchestrate, surrounded by peanut shells. Max had admitted that night, with a certain softness, that he was allergic to peanuts, that something so small, so fragile, could undo him. Zoe had always known the story she and Max were sitting inside of, it just took a while for the details to unfold.

She scans the dimly lit bar for him and heads to a red vinyl booth in the back, Table 10, the one rumored to have hosted more than one historic handoff. According to legend, this was where a military analyst passed the Pentagon Papers to a reporter from the *New York Times*, sliding the classified documents beneath a beer-soaked napkin in the middle of the Vietnam War. The leak exposed years of government deception, changing the course of public trust in the US government forever. The idea that history could pivot in a moment like that, under flickering lights, over cheap drinks, makes this table feel almost mythic.

Zoe slides into the booth. The air is thick with salt and age, beer and varnish. Goosebumps bubble up on her skin, not from cold but from the charge in her body. He had agreed to meet her here, in a tiny bar designed to keep secrets and betray them in equal measure.

She sees him step into the doorway, sunlight outlining his figure like a crime scene chalk mark. He has a full beard and wild curls. His skin looks tan, rough. She raises her hand, but he doesn't notice her right away. He glances down at the peanut shells crunching beneath his shoes then eyes the basket on her table with a single raised eyebrow and a subtle shake of his head.

"Hi, my dear." He bends down for a hug.

"Hi, Max," she replies, standing to meet him, but only offers her hand. He tilts his head, confused.

"I thought you'd be a little more excited to see me." He slides into the booth across from her, still watching the peanuts like they might rearrange themselves into something ominous.

As a journalist, Zoe understands the power of place. She chose Casa Jay for a few reasons: the astronaut lore, the Pentagon Papers table, and the floor covered in potential death.

She lets her silence and the setting do the work, waiting for him to speak.

"So, how was Big Sur? he asks, reaching for a menu. "Any leads on the missing woman?" Of course, this is his first question, Zoe thinks.

Delivered in a light, casual way like it's all a shared adventure, but she can sense the calculation behind his words. He has no idea how far away she's drifted from him, how much ground she's covered behind his back.

Zoe had kept her distance deliberately with sporadic texts, delayed replies, excuses about bad service at Salenan. It wasn't untrue, but it also wasn't the whole story. She needed space to think clearly, to move without his shadow warping her perception.

Now, sitting across from him again, her stomach turns. His voice feels invasive, like a virus in her bloodstream. The table is sticky under her palms, the air metallic. She watches him, and in a fleeting, shameful flicker, she feels it. Envy. She envies him, the stillness and detachment that surrounds him. To move through the world without fear or guilt, untouched by consequence, unburdened by feeling, what is that even like? To live without empathy for a day might feel like relief to her. She imagines slipping into his skin, just briefly, and the imagined silence inside almost feels seductive.

She reaches for the peanut basket and pushes it to the edge of the table, more forcefully than necessary. Then, without thinking, her fingers hover over one of the shells. She stares at the shell. She imagines at some point, he would get up to use the bathroom and she could easily slip her fingers around the shell, break it open, letting the oil drip between her fingertips and then lightly rub the rim of his pint glass. Maybe he'd go into anaphylactic shock, he'd begin breathing heavy, hands gripping his throat, sweat pouring from his forehead, and she'd wait just a minute too long to help reach for the EpiPen in his pocket. She'd type 911 into her phone but pause before hitting send. And then this whole ordeal would be over, his fate in her fingertips. She thinks back to the mural in Dr. Owen's office in Salenan: *More light, More night.*

But then, she feels Max's pendant, which Sasha had given her, its sharp edge warm against her palm. And she knows she wouldn't last a minute in that kind of emptiness. It's her light that drew him to her, and his darkness that had pulled her in, but she refuses to carry it with her. She could never live with herself: his death would haunt her, eat her from the inside out. She could never let him destroy her light, her empathy, no matter how much destruction he has caused to herself and others. Her hand withdraws from the basket brimming with peanuts. Max notices and smirks faintly, as if he can read the thoughts she's been flirting with, as if some part of him still knows her.

"I can't tell you if I have any leads," she says, finally answering his question, her voice sweet and controlled, "but I can say my recent visit to Big Sur was very enlightening."

The bartender drops off two sweating beers. One spills slightly, puddling at the base of the glass.

"Lovely," Max mutters, wiping at it with napkins. Something flickers across his face. It's not annoyance or frustration, but something colder, almost primal. Then, it's gone.

"How are you? How was San Francisco?" she asks. He looks thinner, stripped down, sharpened. Like something shedding its skin. His muttered response is barely audible. She finds herself needing to re-learn his cadences, like tuning into a frequency she no longer trusts.

"San Francisco was fine," he says, his voice clipped. Then, after a pause: "Are you okay? You don't seem like yourself." He angles his head, performing concern. His words feel like a trap, an attempt to flip the narrative before she can make her move.

Her throat tightens. A tingling sensation rises at the base of her skull. The same electric warning she felt the day she found the PAYDAY wrapper in their room at Moffett Field.

"You seem off," he adds, eyes drifting toward the menu.

"What do you mean?" Zoe asks, testing him, keeping her tone light. He glances up, surprised she called it out. Then he shrugs.

"You're just... different. That's all."

The waiter approaches and takes their order. As she hands over the menu, Zoe keeps her expression blank, but inside, something shifts. Karolina had warned her that Max had asked Sasha questions, strange ones, about a phone call between Karolina and Sasha, one he shouldn't have known about. How much does he know? How long has he been tracing their movements like lines on a map?

She feels a flicker of heat behind her sternum, part fear, part fury. Not just at Max but at herself for ever having mistaken his interest as intimacy instead of surveillance.

As Max returns the menu, his hand moves reflexively to his chest, then stops. Fingers brush against fabric like an old habit but find nothing. Zoe feels her entire body shift. Her hand curls around the pendant in her coat pocket, gripping it like a talisman. The metal presses cold and sharp against her palm, and for a second, she lets herself feel the full gravity of what it represents. Alessandra. The women. The missing scans. The sense of being studied, harvested, mimicked.

She breathes deep, and something inside her locks into place. She says nothing. Slowly, she reaches into her coat pocket and places the pendant at the center of the table. Its cool, triangular edge catches the light like a scalpel. He stares at it. His breath hitches, just barely.

The engraving glints: *Scimus. Imitemur. Vincamus. We watch. We imitate. We conquer.* The motto of a man who learned to mimic humanity from the outside in. Max keeps his eyes locked on it. His breath is barely perceptible, and something in his eyes shifts, just a flicker, but she catches it. A glitch in the program.

"I know about Karolina," Zoe says. Her voice feels distant to her own ears, low and resonant, like it's coming from somewhere deeper than her throat.

Her chest tightens. There's a pressure between her ribs, like a breath held too long. A buzz behind her ears. Her body doesn't just hum; it vibrates with the convergence of memory, intuition, and knowing. Her grip tightens on the pendant. She thinks of Lillian's synesthetic precision, Sasha's dream-warnings, and Karolina's quiet dread. And Alessandra, gone, but not erased. The lies, the rewiring, the empty eye contact. The stillness she's felt around Max since the beginning is now a full-body alarm. Every nerve is tuned to the moment. Her voice, when it comes, is not cool. It's steady and certain. Alive with everything he will never feel.

"And Sasha. And Lillian." Max doesn't move. But something behind his eyes contracts, like the frame of a house realizing it's on fire.

"You're not as hidden as you think." She lets the silence stretch. The pendant stays between them, like a detonator neither of them touches.

She had planned this. No drama. No heat. Just the facts, placed in the light. Psychopaths don't fear confrontation; they fear exposure. They fear convergence. And now, she was the convergence. The women he fractured were all talking. Comparing notes. Holding the same thread of shared intuition. They were the sensors, each wired differently and uniquely attuned. And now, Zoe sees herself among them, she isn't broken. It's quite the opposite. She is wired to perceive what others miss.

Zoe leans forward, voice steady. "Where's Alessandra?"

Max exhales slowly, as if amused. "You've been busy," he says. His tone is almost affectionate, but his eyes are flat. "Connecting dots that were never meant to touch."

He leans back, folding his arms. "You want the truth? You think cornering me makes you immune? I watched each of you scramble for meaning. Karolina clinging to instincts she couldn't explain, Sasha trying to outrun her own dreams, Lillian drowning in color. And you..."

He stops, tilts his head, and studies her. "You were always the most entertaining. The one who felt too much and mistook your wild imagination for intuition. But it's more than that."

And now, she sees it in herself. How quickly she had filled in his silences, mistaking mystery for depth, mood for substance. How many times had she twisted herself to match his tone, to decode what didn't deserve decoding? She had contorted herself to feel for both of them, until she finally stopped. This, right now, was the evidence of that shift.

Zoe doesn't blink. "And still, you followed us."

A smile twitches at the corner of his mouth. "I didn't follow you. I studied you. There's a difference."

Something in her jaw tightens. He still thinks he holds the frame.

Max's gaze drops to the pendant, then back to her. He hesitates. "Alessandra went missing the day we were at Moffett," he says quietly. "We were in the room. I had nothing to do with it."

Zoe studies him. "She was preparing to blow the whistle on Tex Chemical, wasn't she? The missing brain scans of children in Salinas Valley, the ones showing neurological damage from chlorpyrifos, Alessandra had seen them."

Max's expression doesn't change. But he doesn't deny it.

"She had evidence," Zoe continues. "Evidence that could have destroyed her father's company."

He takes a long sip of beer, then sets the glass down, empty. "Possibly."

"What is Oneness University really doing with Tex Chemical?" she asks.

Max tilts his head.

"And don't give me some nonsense about your documentary. *Architects of the Mind* is not about innovation, is it? It's about control, replicating behaviors, and emotional mimicry."

He says nothing.

"You never told me your diagnosis," she says.

His jaw flexes. "What does it matter?"

It matters, she thinks, because it confirms what her body already knew. Long before she understood Max intellectually, she felt it, in her spine, in the prickle behind her eyes, in the way her breath changed when he entered a room. A somatic knowing. It had been her compass before language could catch up.

She thinks of the others now. Lillian, who sees emotion as color and taste. Karolina, whose instincts twitch before logic lands. Sasha, dreaming futures in fragments she can't yet explain. And now herself, the one who feels the world as a full-body frequency. They weren't women Max happened to meet. They were selected, studied, and stalked like prey, subjects for his own personal gain and profit.

"Because you've been spending time at an institution studying the one thing you don't have," she says.

He squints. "Empathy?"

Zoe nods. "Is that why you're involved with Oneness? To study people like us, people who are sensitive, who feel things that you can't? You watch us. Imitate us. And then what, conquer us?" She glares at the pendant.

His lips twitch. Almost a smile, and then his voice softens, unexpectedly. "Being in your presence, Zoe, it's like being near something rare. The way you look at people, the way you make space for them. There's a... clarity to you. A warmth I've never understood. But I've seen how people respond to it. How they lean in. How they open up." His eyes lose their usual edge, just for a moment. "It's magnetic. Magical, even. And I wanted to feel it too. To know what that was like, to have that effect on people."

Zoe feels something in her chest catch, an ache, a shadow of pity. Not because she believes him, but because part of her understands the trap of it. The magnetic pull between people like her, the highly sensitive, those who feel everything deeply and men like him. She's read about it, how those who are hyper-empathic often mistake intensity for intimacy, how they confuse being seen with being safe. Psychopaths are drawn to empathy like moths to flame, not to feel it, but to feed off it. Because highly sensitive people project meaning onto things. They assume reciprocity. They want to believe. That's the hook. That's the hunger. And Max had known exactly how to exploit it: he's been doing it his entire life.

He pauses, his voice shifting into something flatter, more clinical. "Because for me, connection, happiness... those aren't things I feel. Not really, at least not in the way neurotypical people do. What I do feel, what lights something up in me, is watching people give themselves away when they trust me. That's the moment I can gain control. Not because I want their trust, I couldn't care less about that, but simply because I can take it, and get them to do whatever I please."

He shrugs lightly. "That's the closest I've ever come to joy. Whatever the clinicians choose to call it, duping delight, lying or manipulation, they all give me a rush, a thrill. It's the closest I come to happiness."

He looks down at the basket of peanuts. "I've always known something was different in me. They diagnosed me with psychopathy when I was seventeen, but it's not like what you see in the movies. I'm not hiding any bodies in the trunk. In fact, killing someone seems like a real inconvenience to me. Being a psychopath is way more excruciating than murder. The boredom and nothingness I feel on a daily basis fills me with rage. I've learned that I am wired with an inability to find joy in small, mundane, everyday things. I would give anything to feel what that's like. It's something that most people take for granted. I've learned to be adaptable, to wear a mask, to mirror other's emotions and reactions."

He lets the words settle like ash. Zoe leans in, curious as to why he's engaging in this confessional and why now.

"Arthur and I are identical in every visible way. But he got the warm blood, the emotional intelligence, the radar for people. He'd cry at movies, and I'd watch him cry and wonder what that was like or why he was faking tears. It's not that I wanted to feel what he did. I just wanted to understand why it mattered so much."

Zoe studies him. "Does your condition ever make you feel sad?"

He tilts his head slightly, like the question is a piece to some sort of puzzle. "Not in the way you mean. I don't feel sorrow or regret. But I feel the absence. A kind of emptiness where I imagine something should be. I see how connection between people has an effect, but I never really feel it from the inside. That used to bother me. Now it just is."

Zoe studies him for a long moment. "The absence... is that where the boredom comes in?"

Max's mouth twitches, almost like he's pleased by the precision of the question. "Yes. Exactly. Boredom is the background of my life. Most people avoid pain, but I avoid nothingness. Half of the time, I don't even feel like I'm alive: it feels like I'm just getting through the day. That's why I push boundaries, not because I'm just chasing a thrill, but because I'm running from the boredom. You'd be amazed what people like me will do to feel something close to an emotion."

The absence he describes, a numbness where connection should be, rattles something in her. She cannot imagine that life. Her days are colored by feeling. Every room, every person, every silence leaves a mark on her skin. She doesn't forgive him, but for a second, she grieves for him.

"I'm not all bad," he says as if reading her thoughts. "I've been doing the rewiring sessions at Oneness. Trying to learn more about myself, to see if I can change."

"Is that what they're promising you?" she asks. "That they can rewire your brain, give you a conscience?"

His eyes flick to hers, searching for a reaction. "Empathy is just a circuit in the brain. One day, the technology will allow for a neural implant to inject empathy into people like me. But for now, I've learned how to replicate the effects without the ability to actually feel them."

Max drains his beer, tosses a few bills on the table, and stands.

Zoe's voice cuts through the air, low but firm, with one last question before he leaves. "Is Alessandra still alive?"

Max freezes. Not dramatically, just for a beat, like a skip in the rhythm of a machine. "She might be," he says without turning. "But if she is, it's because she chose to be."

Zoe's pulse jumps. Chose? It lands strangely, not just cryptic but pointed. Not like a man talking about someone who was taken, but someone who walked away. A woman who knew exactly what she was doing. A flicker of unease slips through her. Was Alessandra hiding? Or running from something?

"Where is she, Max?"

He finally looks back at her. "You already know where to look."

She searches his face for a crack, a clue but all she sees is the same deliberate blankness, like someone looking at her through one-way glass. "You could tell me," she says.

"I could," he replies. "But I won't."

A pause. Then something flickers in his expression, not guilt, not quite. Something closer to nostalgia. Or it's imitation. "You know, Zoe... the world would be a better place if there were more people like you in it. And fewer like me."

She doesn't answer. Not with words. She lets her hand rest on the pendant and slips it back into her pocket.

Zoe doesn't know if he believes what he's just said. Maybe he doesn't either. But it's the closest he's ever come to the truth. And that's what makes it dangerous. Because if he's telling the truth, it means he knows what the truth feels like. He just chooses not to live by it.

Still, for the first time, she doesn't need anything from him. Not confirmation. Not validation. Not even proof. Because something inside her has shifted permanently. She had once mistaken the intuition in her body for imagination, but now she knows better. This was never just a story. It was a signal, subtle and electric, running under her skin the whole time, the hum she had ignored. Until now.

Zoe had always doubted her sensitivity. Now it's her sharpest weapon. The others, Lillian, Karolina, and Sasha, had taught her that, not only in their words, but in the quiet courage of their perception. This isn't just her story anymore. It belongs to all of them. And she's ready to finish it.

She watches Max walk out across the peanut shells, their brittle crunch echoing behind him. He moves like someone who's never had to second-guess a step, never paused to consider the damage left in his wake. And yet, for the first time, he feels smaller to her, like a figure exiting a stage he no longer controls.

She lets herself feel it, fully and without shame, empathy, her empathy. Not the naive kind, not the kind he once fed on, but the kind that sees clearly. She understands it now: Max's vacancy isn't power, it's poverty. And her own sensitivity, once a source of anxiety and confusion, is what anchors her to the truth.

Finally, she sees herself not as a girl who was fooled but as a woman who has the power to feel and sense her way through the world. She doesn't follow him; he no longer holds the answers. She does.

CHAPTER TWENTY-NINE

Singularity

Zoe stands at the gates of Oneness University, gripping her bag with one hand and the tarot card with the other. The wind carries the scent of salt and synthetic sweetness. It's the same signature fragrance pumped through the lobby at Salenan.

The white metal bars look less like security and more like the frame of a clinical experiment. She tries to quiet the hum in her body. Everything here feels curated and manufactured. Beyond the gate, she sees manicured walkways, evenly spaced trees, and pastel buildings that echo the blueprints of a city she's been researching.

Sympara.

She had spent weeks tracing funding trails from shell companies in Honduras to private intelligence firms in California. Sympara was the prototype, a libertarian enclave disguised as innovation, where biohacking and neural-interface experiments had sidestepped international ethics boards. A city designed by Ryan Sowell to rewrite the future of governance, ruled by technocrats. He declared democracy dead and called empathy a "design flaw to be exploited" in one of his leaked investor calls.

As Zoe stands at the gates, Oneness University feels like Sympara's domestic twin, a tech eutopia that's polished, unregulated, and experimental.

A guard approaches her without a smile or sound. She knows what to do. She hands him the tarot card; he frowns, scanning the card and printing a pass with her name and a classification she doesn't understand.

ZOE S.
ACCESS TYPE: SENSORY PROXY
CLEARANCE: OBSERVATIONAL

He waves her through with military precision. The gates creak open.

Inside, everything is too quiet. A wind machine hums. The air smells of tropical perfume and something colder, synthetic. The walkway leads her toward a domed building that looks like a pastel town hall.

A woman in linen steps out, gripping a clipboard, hair slicked back, her lips glossy. "Orientation?" she asks.

"I was told I'd be meeting someone."

"You will." The woman smiles, tight and rehearsed. "Follow me."

Zoe follows her through a dark, soundless corridor. Her thoughts are loud. She remembers Maria's voice, trembling over tea in Salinas. Her nephew hadn't spoken since age three. Her niece had seizures. Her son twitched in his sleep. The brain scans from the pediatric clinic had disappeared without explanation.

Zoe grips her purse tighter, feeling the flash drive with the brain scans in the pocket. The last time anyone saw Alessandra, she was on a cliff at Salenan, looking out over the ocean, armed with the knowledge that Tex Chemical had been quietly poisoning entire communities of migrant workers. Zoe had traced the grants, the donations, the shell corporations. All of them pointed here.

To Oneness University.

The woman stops at a steel door, opens it, and vanishes without a word. Zoe steps into a cold white room. It's empty, save for two chairs and a mirrored panel in the corner.

She sits. Ten minutes pass. Then fifteen. Her fingers tighten around the flash drive in her purse. Then, the door opens.

For a beat, Zoe forgets how to breathe. Her breath snags in her throat. She had imagined bruises, restraints, and maybe a hospital gown. But Alessandra Wilder is flawless: her clothes are neatly pressed, her nails polished, she appears calm.

Zoe rises, her chair screeching behind her. Her body registers it before her mind does: a ripple of heat through her chest, then cold. A tightening behind her eyes. Her breath falters. She suddenly understands why everyone at Salenan mistook her for this woman. She can feel Alessandra's likeness pressing against her.

They are the same height. The same strawberry-blonde hair parted the same way. The same bone structure, as if their faces were mapped by the same set of coordinates. But Alessandra is... sharpened. Calibrated. Her skin looks poreless, impossibly smooth, like the texture of rendered marble in a 3D model. Her hair gleams unnaturally, every strand falling in elegant obedience. Her posture is perfect, shoulders relaxed but spine unyielding, as if she's been sculpted for balance. And her eyes, clear and unblinking, hold no shimmer of recognition, only assessment.

"Zoe," Alessandra says, smiling. "You made it."

Zoe blinks. "You're... alive?"

"Of course."

"I thought you were being held here. I thought—" Her voice catches. "I thought you were trying to expose your father. The pesticide coverup. The missing brain scans. The poisoned kids."

Alessandra's smile barely shifts. "That's sweet."

"Sweet?"

"Assuming I needed rescuing."

Zoe's confusion flashes to fury. "You vanished. You dropped off the map. The media thought you were dead."

"Which gave me the cover I needed to work without interruption." Alessandra steps closer. "It also gave *you* a reason to come here. You're very consistent, Zoe. Your morality makes you beautifully predictable."

Zoe clenches her fists. "You were going to go public. I thought you were being held here..." She cuts herself off. "I thought you were trying to expose your father and Tex Chemical for the chlorpyrifos scandal in Salinas Valley."

"No," Alessandra says simply. "I was never going to blow the whistle on Tex Chemical. Why would I destroy my father's company?"

Zoe feels a burn radiating in the back of her skull. Mirror neurons misfiring, trying to sync with a body shaped to match hers, but emptied of any real resonance. It feels like she is being studied by her own reflection.

Zoe's voice sharpens. "Maria told me about the kids in Salinas. The missing brain scans. You were going to speak out—"

"Oh, those," Alessandra says softly, stepping into the light. "No. I wasn't going to expose him: those brain scans are data."

Zoe blinks. "You knew what the pesticide was doing to those children. You knew it was damaging their brains."

Alessandra nods. "Yes. Chlorpyrifos disrupts the acetylcholine system, particularly in utero and early childhood. It impairs the prefrontal cortex and the amygdala. They can experience emotional regulation collapses. Their empathy? Gone. Sometimes even permanently."

Zoe's stomach flips. "You saw that—and didn't stop it?"

"I saw that," Alessandra says evenly, "and I understood it as a model, something to study."

Zoe holds her breath.

"They were blank slates," Alessandra continues. "Stripped of emotional connectivity. Their neurological deficits helped us isolate the circuits involved in empathy. That data became our framework."

"You used poisoned children," Zoe says, her voice breaking. "You mapped their deficits to build a product?"

"A solution," Alessandra corrects. "A neural interface capable of restoring what capitalism and evolution have erased."

Zoe backs up. "You mean what your father's company has destroyed. You're not solving a problem. You're profiting from one you helped create."

Alessandra shrugs. "That's how capitalism works, my dear. Create the problem, then sell the fix."

Zoe doesn't blink. "You recruited me, didn't you? Max was part of this from the start."

Alessandra's smile deepens. "You tell me. He complimented your article, didn't he? The exposé you wrote about Ryan Sowell."

Zoe goes still.

"I remember the headline," Alessandra continues. "'*The Charisma Trap: What Silicon Valley's Golden Boy Doesn't Want You to Know.*' It wasn't accurate, but it was provocative. You made Ryan look like a villain, portraying him as cold, manipulative, inhuman even."

"Because he is," Zoe says.

"And yet," Alessandra says softly, "your article was the reason we found you."

Zoe's stomach drops.

"I first read it during a late-night board review," Alessandra continues. "Ryan was furious, of course. But I... I was intrigued. You saw something others couldn't. You cared about the human cost. You were emotionally intelligent, possibly too emotionally intelligent. That's rare. That's... useful."

Zoe's voice is low. "So, you sent Max."

"We sent a version of him we knew you'd respond to. We needed proximity. Behavioral data. Mirror calibration."

Zoe stares at her. "He was never real."

"Oh, he was real," Alessandra says. "Just selectively constructed."

Zoe backs away. "You pulled me by using the very thing you're trying to simulate. You used my empathy to trap me."

Alessandra steps forward. "And it worked."

Zoe doesn't speak. A flicker of heat flares up her neck, then settles cold beneath her ribs. She remembers the scent at Salenan, the padded mats, the quiet suggestion to shed her identity. She thought it was a wellness retreat. Now, she knows it was a harvest site.

Her fingers twitch slightly against the seam of her coat. Her jaw pulses. Something inside her recoils, not from fear but from the horror of recognition. She'd been cataloged. Rendered. Studied like a nervous system in motion.

Zoe starts toward the door.

"You're not the hero here, Zoe," Alessandra says. "You're the proof of concept. You were easy to build around." Her voice is eerily calm. "Your hypersensitivity, the somatic knowing, the pattern of response in your mirror neurons. Your biometrics and facial structure had already been scanned at Salenan."

Zoe pauses. "You can replicate behavior possibly, but not what makes us human."

"You'd be amazed what code can hold," Alessandra replies. "We modeled entire affective simulations from your neural profile. You've been more useful than you know."

Something cold pulses behind Zoe's eyes. She looks at Alessandra for a long moment. "You want to fix the world? Start with the damage your father paid for. Start by telling the truth." Zoe's hands shake as she pulls documents from her bag, the brain scans, grant disclosures, shell companies, the connection between Tex Chemical and Oneness. She slaps them down on the table. Her proof.

Alessandra doesn't look surprised.

"I know everything," Zoe says.

"I already know what you know," Alessandra replies. "You think knowledge is a threat. But the truth holds no power if no one believes you."

"I'm going to publish an article," Zoe says. "Every name, every grant, every brain you've used."

Alessandra laughs. Not cruelly, but elegantly. Like someone who's heard this before. "You'll try. *The Daily Quest* won't touch it. Their lawyers will call my lawyers. And if you self-publish, our surveillance disclosure team will flag you for breach of NDA. You signed the waiver, Zoe, at Salenan."

"They were buried in the intake forms."

"And now they're buried in metadata and timestamps. Your consent has been captured in a dozen ways."

Zoe's hand is on the doorknob, but something inside her recoils. A cold pressure clamps beneath her ribs, a phantom ache in her throat as if she's swallowing back a scream that doesn't belong to her. It's Alessandra's fear, raw and residual, caught in the architecture of the room or maybe in the circuits of her own nerves. Zoe doesn't just think it, she feels it with her entire body. And for the first time, she stops trying to explain it away.

Zoe's voice is flat. "You're scared."

She opens the door.

Alessandra doesn't speak. But her eyes flicker with something raw and unguarded: it's a recognition of sorts.

CHAPTER THIRTY

Lionesses Hunt in Groups

Karolina is the first to arrive. She stands at the cliff's edge, wind pulling at her coat, dark hair rippling across her shoulders. Her face is calm, but there's something clenched in her jaw, a practiced stillness. Max once told her this place was sacred, a space meant for transformation. But she sees it clearly now. It wasn't sacred. It was a set. She watches the sea churn below, breathes in the salt and wind, and waits.

Zoe arrives next. She looks windblown and flushed from the climb, her expression unreadable. There's a journalistic intensity to the way she moves, eyes alert, scanning, as if recording something only she can see. Her hair is loose; her eyelashes tipped with mist. She stops beside Karolina, not quite touching but close.

"He brought me here, too," she says quietly.

Karolina doesn't respond. She just nods. They fall into silence as the wind gusts, cold and alive.

Then, Lillian appears at the top of the path: she's quiet, observant, with a stillness that reads more like attention than hesitation. There's something luminous about her, though she's dressed plainly. Her gaze takes everything in: the cliff's edge, the sea, the footprints, the angle of Karolina's stance.

"We all ended up back here," she says as she approaches. "There's something in that."

"A pattern," Zoe says.

"A memory that doesn't include him," Lillian replies. Her voice is soft, but it lands like a statement of fact.

The last to arrive is Sasha. She cuts through fog and sunlight, her platinum hair catching in the wind, her eyes focused as if she's walking into something she's already seen. She doesn't hesitate. She walks straight toward them and smiles, tight but real.

"We should go down soon," she says. "The tide's coming in."

No one argues. The tide pushes higher. The sea is whispering louder.

Zoe steps toward the path first. The others follow without needing to be asked. The wind moves around them like a breath held at the edge of something. And then, one by one, they begin to descend.

The path is steep, treacherous, but they move in sync. Karolina helps Lillian down a slope of loose rock. Sasha steadies Zoe as her boot slips. The beach stretches open at the bottom, raw and wide, the wind sweeping patterns in the sand like a signal.

The sand is coarse beneath their feet, strewn with bone-colored driftwood and salt-bleached stones. There are no signs left of the search teams, no caution tape fluttering from rocks, no footprints but their own. Just the sound of the ocean, patient and endless, and the false memory of a woman who had never disappeared.

They stand at the edge of the water, Zoe, Karolina, Sasha, and Lillian, the four of them barefoot, quiet, the wind lifting strands of hair across their faces. The sky above folds into deeper blues, the last light of day catching in the silver crests of waves. It's a place that had once held fear. Now it holds something else.

Zoe breaks the silence first. "It's strange," she says, her voice barely rising over the tide, "how empaths and psychopaths find their way to each other. Like magnets, opposing forces that should repel, but instead they attract."

Karolina turns her head slightly, listening.

"We are each other's opposites," Zoe continues. "And that's what creates the pull. Psychopaths are drawn to who we are and what we radiate, our vulnerability and emotional intelligence. They see that as leverage, filling in what they lack."

Karolina's gaze drops to the surf. "And we're drawn to the absence. To that blank space inside them. We mistake it for depth and try to fill it."

Zoe nods. "It's not love. It's a feedback loop, a circuit, where one emits and the other absorbs."

Lillian crouches by the shoreline, trailing her fingers through the foam. "We thought we were in a relationship with him," she says. "But we were in a case study."

Sasha's voice is quiet but steady. "He didn't want to understand us. He wanted to take what we had so he could be more like us."

Zoe's hand moves instinctively to the place just below her sternum. "Yes, he studied our empathy like it was code, something to embed, a trait he could extract and install." Her fingers curl into the fabric of her shirt. "But empathy isn't a system that can be implanted. It's a lived feeling, a genuine connection. That's how we know what's real."

They stand for a long moment in the hush that follows. It's not a hollow silence, rather a space filled with recognition and understanding.

Karolina's voice comes in an almost a whisper. "I loved him." She looks down at her hands. "Even now... some small, stupid part of me still does."

Zoe doesn't flinch. "I do, too," she says. "I won't lie about that anymore." She looks at the others, her eyes clear. "It doesn't make us foolish. It makes us human."

Lillian stands slowly, brushing sand from her palms. "He mirrored what we gave him. That's all he had. But what we felt? That was real. That was ours."

"No one can counterfeit that kind of love," Sasha steps closer, arms crossed against the wind. "They can try to mimic it, manipulate it. But they can't create it."

Zoe exhales, long and low. "It wasn't our empathy that broke us," she says. "It's what brought us here."

For a long moment, they all stand together, shoulder to shoulder. Not as versions of who they were when they first came to this place but as someone else refined by fire, tethered by empathy, sharp with knowing. The tide creeps higher, curling around their ankles. None of them move. Around them, the beach feels sacred and secretive, a place that's not just forbidden, but a place the world had forgotten. Or maybe a place where something could begin again.

Lillian's voice moves with the wind, barely above a whisper. "Did you know that lionesses hunt in groups?" she asks. "They don't chase what they can catch alone. They go after what's dangerous. What requires strategy."

The others remain still, listening.

"Each one knows her place in the circle. They trust each other, and move without a sound, like a single mind split across many bodies." She pauses, the silence between them deepening. "It's beautiful, really, the way they cooperate. But also ruthless. They don't shy away from their power."

"It's as if some part of their nervous system knows they share the same circuitry," Zoe says. She finally takes out the pendant, the one Max had worn, the one that had surveilled her heart rate, her breath, her empathy. "I don't want this in the world anymore," she says.

Karolina crouches to dig a shallow hole with her bare hands. Lillian finds a stone and presses it into the sand. Sasha brushes hair from her face and whispers something the wind carries away.

They bury the pendant.

Then their phones buzz, one by one.

Zoe looks down at her screen:

TEX CHEMICAL BRIBERY SCHEME EXPOSED:
HOW A MYSTERIOUS SILICON VALLEY UNIVERSITY
HELPED TO COVER UP A POISONOUS PESTICIDE'S
EFFECTS ON CHILDREN'S BRAIN DEVELOPMENT

No one speaks. They already know.

Karolina reaches for her hand. Lillian takes Sasha's.

They don't walk into the ocean. Not yet. They stand at the edge of it, bare feet in the cold sand, the water rising slow and steady. The tide tugs at the edge of the truth as if testing its weight. No one replies, but something has shifted. A kind of gravity pulling them inward and forward at once with a recognition of who they are. They are no longer four women with separate reasons for being here. They are a system now entangled in a powerful shared circuitry.

Zoe turns to look back up the cliff at the path that led them here. Behind them, the soft geometry of Salenan dissolves into shadow, the place where they were studied and watched.

Zoe turns to look ahead. Four sets of footprints make a jagged trail in the sand, fragile, impermeant, and real.

She has another story to write.

Epilogue

The TechX Film Festival is a spectacle of egos. It takes place inside Hangar One at Moffett Field, a structure Zoe first saw as skinless, a striped skull with its synapses exposed. From the outside, it still looks like something half-alive, its metallic bones humming faintly under a low, electric sky. No one says what it was rebuilt for. No one asks what happens there.

Tonight, it hosts the festival's most anticipated screening: *Architects of the Mind.*

Inside the dome, Silicon Valley's elite sip turmeric cocktails and pose beneath flickering logos. The air smells like ozone and over-polished concrete, cold despite the bodies packed inside. Light pulses from overhead in slow, neural rhythms too soft to register consciously, but just enough to disturb breathing patterns. Screens flicker. Drones hover somewhat discreetly, livestreaming the event for the public. Music with no discernible melody drips from the corners of the space like condensation.

The music lowers to a hum, and the audience is ushered to their seats. The theater fills, the dome darkens to mimic starlight, and the audience settles.

On-screen, the opening frame appears in simple black-and-white letters:

The trailer begins. A missing person poster flutters across the screen. The photo is softly lit, and the features are serene; it's Alessandra Wilder. Below it, one word:

LOST

The film cuts to a montage of blurred surveillance footage, wellness retreats, and synaptic maps. Glistening labs at Oneness University with rows of fMRI machines. Bodies sleeping under pastel blankets. A pendant glinting, women laughing in sunlit fields. A neural interface catching the light.

The trailer cuts to black. Then, one word in stark white:

FOUND

The lights rise. A murmur spreads through the audience as Alessandra Wilder steps onto the stage. The audience gasps and then erupts at the sight of her.

She's dressed in white linen, clean, almost ceremonial. But what draws every eye in the room is what rests atop her head: a shimmering mesh cap fitted snug to her scalp, webbed with silver threads and tiny nodes that pulse faintly with light. A neural empathy implant, she explains, is designed not to control the mind but to enhance it.

"Imagine if you could feel more," Alessandra begins, her voice rich and unhurried. "Imagine a world where our brains don't just process data but interpret feeling, where we can engineer emotional intelligence at the neurological level."

She places a gentle hand on the mesh cap. "This isn't science fiction. This is the foundation for a new kind of human being."

Applause swells.

"What we lost was never just a person," she says. "It was potential. The capacity for connection, for a conscience."

She gestures behind her. On the screen, brain scans flicker to life. Damage and restoration. Flatlines and bright signals.

"The empathy deficit isn't just a psychological gap," she continues. "It's about missing infrastructure, evident in our brain's wiring, and today

I'm here to tell you, that empathy is something we can rebuild and rewire."

She touches the mesh. "In fact, we already have."

She turns to the left as Max Furtherlore takes the stage. His dark, messy, curly hair is now polished, his face is clean-shaven, and he is smiling. Despite being on the stage, he appears humble. He knows how to perform, and he knows what the audience wants from him. Behind him is the logo for *Architects of the Mind*. He opens his arms, soaking in the moment.

"Our participants showed us what connection really looks like," he says. "They are not just subjects. They are the future of humanity."

Alessandra places a hand atop her neural implant and reaches her hand out. Another man walks out onto the stage. He is blonde and tall, and his face is waxen. Ryan Sowell.

"This isn't speculative or spiritual, this is infrastructure. We are building a world where empathy is no longer a trait, it's a feature that can be implanted." Sowell beams.

The audience rises to its feet. Applause crashes through the theater like a tide. The crowd begins to cheer again.

Then a scream, and another. The cheers fracture into panic as FBI agents flood the aisles. One agent leaps onto the stage.

"Ryan Sowell. Max Furtherlore. Alessandra Wilder. You are under arrest for conspiracy to commit unauthorized human experimentation, wire fraud, money laundering, and unlawful use of unapproved biomedical technology. You have the right to remain silent..."

Alessandra lifts her hands calmly, with a smirk. The mesh on her scalp still flickers like fire under glass. Max doesn't move. Ryan tries to speak, but the microphone has gone dead.

And from the very back of the theater, near the emergency exit, four women stand watching.

Zoe. Karolina. Lillian. Sasha.

No cameras catch them, and no spotlight turns their way. But they are there, whole and irreplicable. They turn in unison and disappear behind the curtain, their silhouettes briefly visible against the glow of the EXIT sign.

ACKNOWLEDGEMENTS

It is with deep gratitude that I thank my mother, who taught me how to dream, and my father, who has always been an anchor for so many in the ever-shifting tides of their lives. To Leslie Coutterand, Karola Sánchez and Sandra Pelikan, this work of fiction would never have become a reality if it weren't for you and the intersection of our lives. I remain forever grateful to your compassion, receptivity, support, and sisterhood. You have forever impacted how I understand my own energetic makeup and the connection we share.

A sincere thank you to all of those who have entered my life over the course of this novel, offering their support, encouragement, time and talent. To my editor Domenica Newell-Amato, dedicating her precise and intuitive eye to my novel during a big life swell of her own. To Joelle Hahn, the Brooklyn Book Doctor, who provided a loving container of support to help nurture this novel in its early stages. To Lissa Hunsicker Kenney, LCWS, the first person I trusted to share that I was writing a book, whose consistent grounding and encouragement provided a launchpad. Thank you to my early readers—Catherine Simone Gray, Avary Halliday, Angela (Dio) Kaufman, Taylor MacDougall, and Kate Marcin—for helping me cut and carve the final pathways of the plot. To Marcella Hammer for showing up week after week to stoke those witchy writing fires during the pandemical years. To Rachel Rogers whose design brought the cover to life, and to Siobhan Mullen for capturing my essence in a photo. Last, but certainly not least, to Jessika Hazelton at The Troy Book Makers, for her sharp eye, patience, and persistence in helping to bring this book into its physical form.

And a final, profound thank you to those who have appeared in my life to teach me lessons: may we all keep learning. It is my hope this book enlightens both the hyper-sensitive and the desensitized. We are in this together.